THE SIDEWAYS MAN

NIGEL WILLIAMS

To the two Gs - thanks for everything!
Love, Nigel

Chapter One

So, where do I start? Here, I guess, an introduction as I sip coffee and taste bile.

Meeting me on the train, down the pub or at the gym may give you the impression that I am an affable, reflective person who holds similar opinions to yourself. You might like me. I celebrate the same joys others celebrate, the evil in the world disappoints me, and I sometimes wish folks would be kinder.

I kill people. Not for vigilante justice, or for mercy, or war, or for any other mundane reason. My one need is deep connection, the kind that remains untarnished forever. My sincerest desire is that all those I have been with in my pursuit of this dream love me, even during our ultimate climax.

I usually strangle, relishing the tactile intimacy, and move my face close to theirs to show the love in my eyes and share their last breaths. During these moments, survival instincts may force their body to flee or fight, but their mind and soul accept the precious gift I am sharing. Before the end, even those base bodily instincts fade away. Pushing and shoving hands lock onto my shoulders to hold and reassure me. Their eyes change and look into mine with acceptance and even, dare I say it, *love*. Their lips part as though for a kiss, expelling a last sweet breath and releasing their souls to the blue heavens. I love, and will always love, every one of them.

I watched a film where the central protagonist talks about one-night stands and how only complete strangers could give you that extra tight hug. Over time, the magic fades; the champagne becomes flat. I don't let it. I don't let that intense connection fade, become shabby and forgettable. That is inconceivable. When I form that bond, when I know we are everything to each other, then I preserve it in perfection forever. I discard unimportant flesh and the distractions of the outside world and bring my love inside me.

I remember how they looked, and the looks they gave. Their smell, their movement, their shape. Within me, I store every aspect of them and our relationship, every conversation, every moment. But much more than a catalog of instances. Nothing is lost. The taste, texture, and essence of all we were is protected forever.

Few can give the depth, level of closeness, and sheer emotion that I crave. I have a type. Physical looks, ethnic background, or gender are unimportant. My type of person is one of the Sideways People. People who fit in ever so slightly sideways to everyone else but don't understand why. They deserve more and know it, but never seem to get their due.

They are easy to find when you know what you are looking for: the homely, shy girl who becomes friends with the confident, desired girl and lives in her shadow while hoping someone will notice her. The middle-aged woman in the bar supporting her friend through some soap opera drama, silently wondering why no one supports or hears her in return. The lonely older man who envies another's family and friends and wonders why he never had that, despite his willingness to center his entire life around others.

Sideways People take many forms but have one thing in common: they give more kindness and treat others better than they receive. They would never admit it, but the injustice of this rankles. Many take refuge in ideals of God and heaven where injustices become righted through divine miracles, where they receive what their goodness has earned.

For the rest, there is me.

I balance the scales; I make things square. I give these people what they deserve. My sole aim is to become whatever they need me to be. My roles have included the flirtatious young scamp whom they can mother while fantasizing about behaving scandalously with. The suave and eager boyfriend. The needy friend whom they can feel superior to and look after. I am not limited in any way—my sexuality, desires, and traits change to reflect what they want. Like everyone, I have many unknown sides to my personality, which surface and become dominant according to a Sideways Person's need. I am the mirror that reflects their needs.

What we shared, and what I gave them, was far more significant than the physical law I broke with them. We chose each other, the price of our bond remaining unspoiled and eternal, paid in more than a common coin. I hope you can understand that.

I wish we had met before all this happened. We could have shared something real.

There appears to be no manhunt for me. Few people know my behavior and patterns and would notice anything illegal. I have family—parents and a couple of brothers—but our interest in each other's lives is perfunctory and disinterested. My environment and approach changes frequently, and I always make some effort to tidy up afterwards. I am also gentle. The media can't slather over tall tales of rooms swimming in blood, of grotesquely mutilated bodies, of human flesh consumed raw, straight from a screaming victim. I've met that kind of person in another land and mutilated myself fighting him.

My experiences with the Sideways People mean I have lived a remarkable life, seen and understood things that are beyond most people's comprehension. I have experienced different lives and shared souls, witnessed the world through multiple eyes. Fantastic events have taught me that human beings are capable of perfection, but this achievement causes unforeseeable consequences. I met my soulmate, the ultimate Sideways Person, and through progressing this experience flawlessly, I opened a portal to another world.

My last and truest love was called Laura. Laura enabled me to open this portal, to become a hero and stop an evil monster. By paying a high price, I released those enslaved by him.

Can we take a step back? Can I try to explain how I became this manner of person? What built in me, how it happened? Why Laura fit me so wondrously and how everything became perfect? My understanding of my psyche is not perfect. No one fully understands themselves. Buried needs and half-understood emotions drive all of us. All I can do is recount moments that leap forward significantly.

We will get to Laura, though. That perfect moment. Crossing over and coming back. What happened over there and returning broken with my soul smashed.

Chapter Two

As a very young child, I was awkward and ugly. Bucktoothed, unwashed and unable to dress properly, with oversized shirts flapping loose from trousers. It looked like fate never intended for me to succeed in the cruel world of the schoolyard, and this proved true.

Even then, I played the part that other people needed for me. Other children could be the hero, schoolyard conqueror, sometimes even the sadist who didn't need to hold back. To all of them, I was the victim they could release their darker side on, to live out their glorious fantasies by vanquishing with little significant repercussions.

I wanted to be better than this. I wanted to be popular, capable. Not this weird outcast. To have someone understand me and see value in my viewpoint and self. I wanted to be the one in a large group, laughing and jeering at someone else, rather than always being the one sneered at. Achieving this was way beyond me, though, and I remained, at best, an object that could be used and discarded as needed. Fellow pupils rebuffed my attempts to become proper friends, regardless of how willing I was to accept condescending treatment and tell them what they wanted to hear, and my school peers firmly kept me in the role of scorned freak. Two older brothers, each content to inflict pain to make themselves feel bigger, did not help this matter much. I would describe my early childhood memories as being rather unhappy.

I adapted and improved my social skills with time. The rest of my pre-teen years became a predictable pattern of ingratiating myself with the popular children. The trusted second-in-command who made them unassailable within their gangs, the foil that helped emphasize whichever quality they wanted to portray.

Incidentally, please don't think to yourself like some tinpot psychiatrist, *"Ah, childhood trauma—feelings of isolation and inadequacy"*, as though that defines the reasons for my activities. That is tawdry. My behavior is not that of a typical serial killer; I may end physical life, but our relationship exalts my chosen, and they live on in me in a far grander manner.

There I was, though. Forever the second, never the lead. I enjoyed the role. Was very good at it, in fact. But the world changes, particularly during youth, and my role also had to change. *"The teenage years are always difficult."* Parents will nod in complete misunderstanding. Harder for the teenagers enduring it, many briefly fluttering with being a Sideways Person. The insecurities, the desire for popularity, to have friends, can lead to hard places and feelings of isolation.

For most, the passing of years takes them from previous school friends and provides an opportunity to re-invent themselves in fresh places with new people. It took me longer, although I got there in the end. I went to university. I made friends. Within our circle, I was the least important, but still included. Compared to my later intense relationships, these bonds were shallow, but still, I cared for these people. We visited nightclubs together, attended lectures in a group, cooked meals for each other and freely talked about all matters, whether big or small.

Once I left university, I rarely communicated with these friends, barring the odd Christmas card or drive-by meeting. They all moved to the same area and socialized with each other more than they did with me. This felt unfair but seemed unavoidable despite our attempts to catch up. New friendships, work, and family commitments ate into our available time and things were never the same again.

These friendships—and they *were* friendships—awakened the need and hunger within me for more. To have and to hold people who would forever see me as crucially important. I wanted to be the absolute center of someone's world, as important to them as humanly possible, with them incapable of casting me aside. Even as a callow youth, I was that romantic, although my incomplete vocabulary would have prevented me from articulating it.

My school days and university experiences polished the skills and desires that would eventually become the real me. I understood what others wanted and, later on, could intuitively play the required role. My personality, such as it was, was easily sublimated to enable others to feel good about themselves. I also learned how to form relationships and friendships, but with this came the sad knowledge that inevitably they would end.

Somewhere along the line, I also recognized others like me, learned to spot Sideways People. The kindest, most wondrous people in the world. Those who put others front and center, hoping eventually it would be their turn to be noticed and important. Only the most perceptive and refined people can reliably spot and understand them.

There was an element of stalking to my behavior whilst ensuring I understood a potential soulmate, but it was not sinister. Rather, it had an admirable aim. I found out everything I could and watched them closely to recognize their routines, who and what they really were, so I could provide the perfect offering. If all worked out, it created an equal relationship. I gave them what they wanted, and they gave me what I needed: the joy of knowing they were with me forever. I'm all about being fair.

Chapter Three

I landed a job at a hospital and earned two promotions in quick succession. Competence in my daily activities led to confidence, which helped to overcome some of my desperate need to please.

I'd gotten even better at socializing and mingling with others. Colleagues would have described me as a witty, social creature. Most workdays, I would ask who fancied going out. I drank most evenings, out of sociability rather than addiction. After hours would often find us in a bar, drinking until closing time. We would exchange stories about weird things that people had needed treatment for and future uses for the miscellaneous objects that patients inserted into different orifices. When the stories ran dry, we would complain about various managers and how they wrecked different departments.

On this specific occasion, I was sitting down in an outside area. Smoke blowing from my nose, surrounded by people that I identified as friends, having had a few drinks. I felt like a lord, the absolute head honcho. Every young person should have this feeling, even if it is undeserved.

"Excuse me, sorry—can I have a cigarette?" asked a soft-voiced young lady.

I glanced over. Pretty, shoulder-length blond hair, wide and generous lips, smooth and unblemished skin. Her eyes hid behind darkened glasses, but I got the impression she was staring at me. Although attractive and dressed in a way that highlighted it, she still gave an air of being folded in somehow. The tilt of her head to one side while drooping it forward to hide her eyes, with one arm crossed in front of her body, all suggested shyness. My usual approach would be to make a quip, be witty to draw her in. This time, I just let my gaze rest on her sunglasses a moment longer than was normal before nodding and waving my hand at the box. Bobbing her head in thanks, she smiled, took one, and went back to her seat.

I turned my attention back to my friends. I could be noisy and an attention hog, getting attention through being the jokester. On this occasion, it was different. Maybe it was fate trying to set me on my intended path, or just the excitement of being in a group and someone actually approaching me for my company. But the blood sang as it danced around my veins; adrenaline pumped through my system. Genuine wit issued forth from my mouth and there was an edge to my humor that stopped people from trying to turn it back on me. My friends revolved around and placed me in the center. Everyone looked on, rapturously enchanted by my charm. (This may not have been the actual reality—I'd drunk a fair bit. But it's how I like to remember it.)

When not speaking, I would turn to glance at the pretty girl's table. There were three in total. Two older men with graying hair. They were surprising company for her, being at least a decade older and incapable of bringing her fully into their discussion. The girl nodded at their comments and conversations but said little as she smoked her way nervously through her cigarette. Sometimes, she would notice me looking. I would keep her gaze for a second longer and then turn my attention back to the people I was with.

I tried to work out the dynamics of their situation. Why they were all together, what the bonds between them were. I guessed work colleagues, perhaps part of a larger work outing which had fallen through, leaving just this disparate three. That was the only explanation. She had dressed for a social night and gone out, despite the diminishing numbers. Perhaps she needed it more than most people. Certainly, she seemed to need my attention.

She soon returned to ask, "Sorry, could I have another one?" I made eye contact, smiled, and offered her the box.

"I feel bad though, taking another one off you, feels like I owe you something," said the girl. It seemed blatant that she was trying to get some kind of hook up going on, and had decided that I, rather than the people she was with, was the best target. Despite her obviousness, she looked awkward. Her body was still closed in on itself, so defensive you wouldn't have credited it with her open approach.

"No need. Sit down and join us," I half-requested, half-directed, while pointing at the empty chair opposite me. She sat down and told me her name—Becky.

On previous occasions when I talked to attractive girls who displayed even the slightest interest in me, I tried to attract them by being funny, by cracking endless jokes. Most people understood this as nervousness. This time was different. I was confident and didn't bother with small talk or light banter. I asked questions about herself and every aspect of her life.

My colleagues had noticed Becky and me being attentive toward each other.

"He's nice, you know," a work friend named Claire said to Becky, having leaned forward with a craned neck, her blue eyes intent. "Just much too cocky."

Becky seemed to respond to this, to enjoy the attention that she and her arrogant paramour were receiving, and asked me repeatedly if I worked in sales.

I demurred, told her minor details about my job, and returned the conversation back to her. Whilst questioning her, she told me about her recent split from her boyfriend.

I ran the usual gallant lines about how he was a fool for letting her go, but she kept on insisting that it was her fault and that she could be difficult. The conversation carried on along that track, and then she mentioned this ex-boyfriend had strangled her when angry. Without hesitation and with complete sincerity, I stated he had no right and only insisted more vigorously when she replied about deserving it.

The night continued and the pattern of our behavior grew more pronounced and noteworthy. I became dominant, almost arrogant, but still the attentive and chivalrous gentleman while she continued her compliant agreement with my suggestions and answered my questions.

After fetching another round of drinks, we moved to a separate table and later in the evening I bluntly asked her if she had gone out that evening to attract male attention, to help her get over the previous boyfriend. She blushed, looked down, and nodded. Little else remained except to ask how I was doing at giving her the desired attention before inviting her to spend the night in a hotel. Surprised at the directness of my offer, she accepted.

With as much discretion as possible, we left together, ignoring the inquiring eyes of those we had arrived with. We spent the night in each other's arms. I asked her to tell me what she liked and then did it. As I pressed inside her and felt her skin and body pressed against mine, I pulled back and pressed my right hand tightly to her throat. Her moans of pleasure continued, and she held me tighter.

It was the most intense night imaginable. Beyond anything I had experienced before. Becky told me everything she thought and wanted. To her, in those moments, I was the most important person and understood her needs better than anyone else. She had needed someone with whom to share her thoughts and to command her into bed, but also someone she could feel comfortable with and feel no shame. The strangling, something she had taken as a painful sign of her own unworthiness and guilt, I turned into an act that brought delight.

It was strange, though. We fell asleep, and upon waking, we knew something had passed, and an end was coming. Still, we joined our bodies together in determined need and talked about private thoughts, though now there was a desperation in it. Our moment was gone. In the morning, we discarded the social niceties of exchanging numbers or asking to meet again sometime.

As Becky left, she turned, looked at me and raised her right hand in a painful half-wave, half-salute farewell. I watched her with an expressionless face, tilting my head forward in a nod. She exited the room quietly.

I sat on the bed after she had left, noting the bedding rumpled from the night's activities, the room holding her smell. It was quiet and I could hear nothing. Despite our intense connection, the sheets held more than I did. Our meeting had passed from a fleeting present into the past.

That did not seem right. I should not have gone from being the center of her world to a barely recalled physical encounter. I resolved that next time things would be different.

Chapter Four

So, we move on from the potential of Becky to my real first. The first time someone gifted me their soul for eternity. I suppose there is something extra about Liz; she helped me become an actual person who understood relationships and feelings. Liz made me the man I dreamed of being.

I worked with Liz. She was the office social secretary and organized most of the official and unofficial nights out. Many such nights involved her getting drunk, noisily being the center of attention, and flirting with her work colleagues. She was quite famous for it. People would tease her about some of her antics, and in this teasing, I would sometimes hear an undertone of disparaging mockery.

Many considered Liz attractive—maybe a little short, thickset with the faintest trace of a hook nose. She was also buxom, with good, olive-tinged skin and a defined, shapely face. Many office guys flirted with her, and some tried to press it further. None of them appeared to take her seriously, though. No one tried to date or forge a permanent relationship with her. The joking comments that people called out reduced her to being the drunk office flirt. People never seemed to recognize the effort she was making to keep people entertained. Only Liz invited shyer or new people to the office parties and often talked to them throughout the evening.

People dismissed this effort as Liz being the social queen bee holding court. Or as an attention whore, addicted to being the center of the universe's attention. I recognized the inherent kindness there, the desire to include everyone. Her due modest reward was to be important to people.

After Becky, I was hunting for someone whose needs I could fulfill in a way that no one else could. Someone who other people misunderstood, but whom I could understand and give something unique and precious to. To be the only person who appreciated their inherent beauty and truly saw them.

I understood Liz differently than everyone else, saw her more clearly. I saw a witty lady who could define and describe humor in every situation. To me, she was intelligent, attractive, and considerate. I liked the way she walked, thought it was fun, the way she twisted her body from side-to-side in time to her steps, and only I noticed how well she enunciated her vowels. Other people had dulled perceptions and could not see what was really there; I *knew* Liz.

Making Liz mine (to use an archaic and sexist phrase) was a long but easy path. Office social events were frequent, and an established core was always at the bar. At one of these events, I found Liz at the bar, surrounded by everyone from the office. If asked to guess, I would say she positioned herself in the middle; it had not organically sprung up around her. As I watched, she was trying to talk to as many people at once, twisting herself backward and forward.

This movement had caused her skirt to ride up her leg. Not deliberate, and not too noticeable. Still, one young man mentioned it loudly to his friend before turning to Liz to inform her she had revealed herself to everyone. I was returning from the bar and walked near her stool as he made his comment. With a mock shocked expression, Liz pulled down her skirt so that it covered more of her flesh.

"What did you think of everyone looking at my leg?" she said, noticing me as she turned around.

"I think they lack enough manners to even notice your physical form." My half-smile showed I was not at all serious. "Instead, they should try to understand your inner beauty, rather than reducing you to a piece of meat."

"Exactly." Liz gave a stern look of reproval directed at those who had commented on her apparent immodesty. We publicly exchanged our thoughts on those who did not know how to address a lady before I excused myself. We spoke little for the rest of the evening, although we exchanged occasional nods and comments as we passed each other. Being obvious was unnecessary; I had already achieved many of the things I intended to. Liz had introduced herself, and I had let her know she could talk to me and proved that I saw her differently than everyone else.

Before leaving, I told her we would speak again soon.

I already knew where I intended the relationship to end. It wasn't spontaneous. Becky taught me that my need was for permanence and importance. Achieving such a goal would take time and effort. After all, nothing worthwhile is ever easy. Liz was worth it, and my intentions were honorable. This one was for the long haul. Most wanted Liz for one night. My approach took a whole new track with a very different end goal.

I waited to see how things developed after letting Liz notice me. It didn't take long. While having a smoke outside the office one morning, Liz arrived with another person and walked straight past with no acknowledgement. I admit, I was crushed and wondered if I had misjudged things.

"Hello," she called and with a slight deliberate elongation to the "l" sound. Liz had turned around, seen that she had walked past me and called out. I smiled, waved, and greeted her back. It was a simple exchange, with little content requiring interpretation, but it confirmed I was heading in the right direction. *No need to panic.*

It was at the next office outing when this love affair further developed. I had arrived with the usual crowd. Liz was talking to everyone from the office at the bar. Unconsciously, my personality changed at the start of the evening, and I was in a more reserved mode, shying away from the limelight.

Liz worked the room, talking to everyone, making them feel welcome, but always heading in my direction. I waited, talking quietly with a small group of colleagues, pretending to pay her no attention. With no warning, my drink-holding hand was abruptly knocked aside as Liz sat on my lap. With a broad smile directed at everyone else at the table, she remained seated there and moved her arm around my neck.

"That's a little forward," someone joked to Liz after she had sat down.

"No. She's welcome here," I said in return. Liz smiled at this comment and helped herself to a sip of my drink.

We spent the night talking and flirting with each other, my earlier reticence disappearing as our conversation progressed. I became coarser than usual, something Liz claimed she found refreshing. I asked her about the number of men she had slept with, then gave a disbelieving look at the answer before suggesting that women halved their tallies. When she asked mine, I told her a fictitious number (way higher than it was) and suggested that men doubled theirs.

I let Liz lead me outside at one stage. Her purpose was quite clear. I wanted to start things moving, so I let her lead me. I kissed her then. Outside in the quiet, under the moonlight. Stroked her hair and face and told her she had superb soft, silken skin. I did not take it further and returned inside after our first kiss and asked her what she wanted from life.

It was a long conversation, and she gave me details about her views and wants. There was nothing shocking there. Liz wanted what everyone else does: adventure and excitement and someone that loved her.

The evening ended. The relationship was already important, but for the moment, I was the chivalrous gentleman. I walked her to where she was getting on the train, our arms linked, my wrist lifted so that I could stroke my fingers on her wrist.

"You're seriously good company," Liz said with a contented sigh, leaning her head against my shoulder. I kept quiet as we walked the rest of the way, enjoying the warm companionship of the silence. At the station, I leaned in to kiss her mouth gently. Briefly breaking the tenderness, I told her that although I wished otherwise, for the moment it was better that she left. It was true on many levels.

After that, Liz made excuses to visit me in the office. She would talk to others, pretend they were the reason for visiting, but speak to me last and for the longest. We dated and did all the things that young people in love do: visited museums, went skating, watched movies after eating Italian food. Sometimes we stayed in and ordered pizza while watching classic films.

Liz changed. At the start, she remained the drunk office flirt, standing in the center of a group of men, enjoying the attention. That continued happening, but then she would see me standing to one side, stone-faced, and she would leave the group to talk to me. Maybe she wanted to make me jealous, but I didn't respond. She used to like the fact that even after trying to get a rise and allowing some office Lothario to buy her a drink, I wouldn't say a word of blame or argument but would accept her company with absolute enjoyment. And so, as the relationship progressed, she decided what she wanted, stopped talking to groups of men, getting drunk, and the skirts got longer.

As I knew she would, she told me she loved me one night, her arms locked around my neck in the dark, her eyes gazing into mine. My head moved so that my lips were brushing against her ear to whisper, "I love you," in return. She rested her head on my shoulder, sighing softly in contentment. I realized things could not improve. This was our apex, and I resolved to not let it change. To keep it like this forever.

Next morning, I repeated I loved her and asked to take her away for the weekend. Just the two of us. I wanted to spend some time alone. For a second, she looked so vulnerable and open that my stomach clenched with a wave of protectiveness. Then she smiled and nodded her head with vigor.

There wasn't much to it. I found a location, organized a time, packed a picnic meal, wine, car rug, shovel, and took a spare set of clothes in case things got messy. Liz lived on her own with little opportunity to share our weekend plans, so I didn't worry about people knowing where or when we were together. It was not just time constraints and opportunity that stopped our plans from being shared—I think Liz wanted to keep things special and secret between us and would not have revealed our intended weekend tryst to anyone, anyway.

Liz was looking forward to it—as I parked outside her house, she charged outside in that bouncing manner of hers, smiling from ear-to-ear. Tears gathered in my eyes and I turned the music on while checking the side mirror so she would not notice my emotions.

The ride was short and chatty. Liz provided humorous commentary on sights from the car window, and I responded with puns and jokes that made her laugh, a silver tinkling sound. It was a sunny day. Liz would periodically smile out the car window at the weather and scenery. After arriving at the picnic site, we carried the picnic and walked off the beaten path, holding hands.

I led us to a beautiful, secluded spot. A river ran down by the side of a grassy knoll, bedecked with moss-covered stones. The water made a welcoming and joyful gurgling noise, undisturbed by the sound of any other human. It was a quiet area, known only to a few locals. Many years prior, I had visited there on a school trip and remembered it while thinking of where to take Liz for our final, most important date. The previous week, I had checked the area again to ensure it was as perfect for our needs as I remembered it. Liz always appreciated my efforts, and she was worth the time.

I spread out the picnic blanket, smoothing out the wrinkles with my hands, and unpacked the food and drinks.

I carefully poured the wine into plastic cups and finished unwrapping the food before looking at Liz, taking in and savoring her happiness. She had dressed overly smartly for an outdoor date: a black dress that showed off her figure and clung to her legs as she sat down. My breath quickened with suppressed excitement. With a slight tremble to my hands, I passed her a plate loaded with sandwiches.

The date passed from one savored moment to the next. We enjoyed each other's company in comfortable silence, sharing glances for long seconds before admiring the scenery or tasting the food. After eating, Liz lay back and closed her eyes. I took off my jacket, folded it into quarters, and gently raised her head to slide this improvised pillow underneath. She opened her eyes to look at me and her lips parted in a wide, generous smile.

I shifted myself so I lay on top of her. My hands moved over her body before moving up to caress my palms against her cheek. We kissed with tenderness, both intending to move things to a more intimate conclusion. I drew back, taking in every aspect of her, the inhale of her breath causing her breasts to rise and press against my chest. The only sound was the river languidly laughing as it carried on its journey. I closed my eyes and drank in Liz's scent: a mixture of perfume and sun-dried earth. I brought my right hand to encircle her neck. Liz still had her eyes closed, but her hands massaged my shoulders. I waited until she relaxed and then pressed down hard.

Liz's eyes burst open wide, her hands and arms tightened on my shoulders. Her body tried to prevent her soul's true wants. Her legs jerked apart, and her knees tightened around me as she thrashed her midriff from side-to-side. Hands grasped, encircled me and clawed at my back before I shifted my body and moved my knees to pin her arms down. We stayed locked in the moment for minutes before realizing we were approaching our climax. I bought more of my weight to bear down on my hand and moved my face closer. Her breath choked in short, shallow, and forced gasps. Her eyes widened in shock, but only moved to look into mine. With a sudden jerk, and one last convulsion of our bodies, it was over.

A sudden rush of adrenaline jolted through me, joined by a sharp, intense feeling of joy. As I closed my eyes and collapsed forward, drawing in breath in quick explosive gasps, I felt Liz and all that she had ever been rushing into me, filling me, expanding in my mind. *Becoming part of my soul.* The closing of my eyes allowed me to see her sights and visions throughout the different stages of life. It was the most perfect form of absorption and merging. This journey of her soul into me was absolute. I had felt nothing like it.

I rolled onto my back and got my breathing under control, but kept my eyes shut so I could focus on the glut of memories, thoughts, and feelings that swelled up inside.

It was only much later that I opened them again and looked at Liz. She was there, lying next to me, her hair mussed by our struggle and eyes open wide, staring at horizons that had fast receded. Her lips were parted. I leaned over and lovingly kissed her, moving my hands as to straighten her hair, only breaking our kiss to look into her eyes one last time before gently pressing shut the lids. They would not close properly, being stiff and resistant, and after a few attempts, I realized they looked more restful open.

I walked to the edge of a knoll before kneeling. My body trembled, spent, and the world spun as I leaned back, light-headed. My knees were on the verge of collapsing.

I scanned the area, searching for somewhere suitable to lay her body. It took a while to decide. I selected a spot near the riverside; it was scenic, beautiful. The water had softened the soil, and it was predominantly moss on top of stones.

Though I hated to leave my love unattended and exposed to the elements, a quick attempt at digging a suitable resting place using hands and feet proved too unwieldy and time consuming. I returned to the car to retrieve the shovel from the boot.

I returned to the selected spot, and initially moved the larger stones away by hand, before using the shovel to dig a deep, wide groove.

I lifted my first love and carried her over to the shrine before laying her reverently within it. The river had permeated the shape, and the groove had filled with water. It lifted Liz's hair away from her head, appearing to crown her, and I smiled at the image. The rest of the arrangement involved moving her limbs so they rested naturally, and brushing mud from the front of her dress. Then I replaced some of the soil, moved the moss-covered stones to cover and maintain her in this serene repose, putting the smaller ones around her before placing the larger ones on top of them.

It took ages. The effort exhausted me before I even half-completed the task, but it was worth it. Liz had the monument she deserved. The rocks ensured she would remain undisturbed, and the arrangement of moss suggested that everything had been in its current position for years. A thin trickle of river seeped through the tomb's head, expanding before emerging in a greater rush. I imagined Liz's spirit tracing this line of water out down the length of the river from its originating source to its last destination, a part of everything that happened along the way.

After staying longer, picturing Liz and seeing the world through her eyes rather than my own, I staggered back to the car with everything I had taken there, leaving the scene picturesque and seemingly undisturbed. My arms and legs ached from the exertion of creating that beautiful resting place. Sweat and mud covered me. Opening the trunk to retrieve the spare set of clothes and deposit the shovel was a painful effort. I awkwardly dressed, mopping the sweat from my face using the dirty t-shirt I had worn previously and threw it onto the back seat. I took a second to enjoy putting on the fresh cloth before opening the driver's side door to head home.

It's difficult to explain the experience. When I returned home, I had a range of contradictory emotions. I felt physically renewed despite the pain, while still being aware of an incredible strain on my psyche. I had never been so aware of myself and surroundings, where I was, what I was feeling, what I needed, but the color and texture of Liz's thoughts and feelings kept resurfacing. Food tasted different, and even some smells awakened unexpected associations.

I didn't want the day to end, but it had taken a toll. The ache in my arms and legs intensified under the spray of a warm shower, baptizing me into a new life. My tendons cracked when I moved or reached. Only pausing to turn the shower off and dry myself, I walked over to the bed, slid between the sheets and fell into a deep, paralytic slumber as soon as my head hit the pillow.

I dreamed often that night. Strange half-remembered memories that were not mine would appear, be lived and experienced before disappearing. Liz's memories, with their highs and lows, re-appeared and were savored. Always her thoughts returned to me. I felt how much Liz had loved me, how much freedom from insecurity I had given her, and the confidence she had felt that my feelings for her were enduring.

I woke in the morning as though from a deep sleep with my throat hoarse. My lips had gummed together, and the insides had stuck to my teeth, forming a dry barrier. For a moment after opening my eyes, I could move only my pupils, my arms locked rigid against my body, legs pressed straight down against each other. With a sudden burst, everything released, limbs unclenched, and I bounded free on the first full day in the dawn of a new world.

Our relationship did not end there. It never *ended*. Liz was always part of me, and I a part of her. The strength of our love unending. Her soul did not slip or dissipate from mine, and our feelings remained the same while I still held her within me. At night I still dreamed of her and the world from her view, still lived her experiences as though I was inside her body. No matter how many Sideways People joined us, nothing changed between me and Liz, nor did it for any of those that joined us.

Not until much later, anyway.

Of course, people noticed when Liz failed to show up at work, and unimportant people asked questions about her whereabouts. Every time someone spoke about Liz, I wanted to spread my arms wide and ask them to just look, *can't you see she's here?* No one noticed the change in me, their senses so blunted by everyday life they could not notice the miracle of two souls joined eternally in one body.

Some uncomprehending busybody informed the police, and they derisively asked me a few questions. I answered in a fashion I knew they would find satisfactory. We had not dated seriously and only sporadically, I said, and Liz had often spoken about dropping everything to move somewhere exciting and new. Besides, I hadn't seen Liz since the previous week, but I was sure she was alright. She would re-appear soon to regale us with a new set of stories. Don't worry.

People accepted what I was saying, or at least didn't disbelieve me enough to pry. Liz had often spoken about traveling and wanting to see the world, so it was believable that she had just left one day. I changed in the office, became less noisy and noticeable. I cared little for the everyday mundanity of these others. Preferred, instead, to focus on the work in front of me with deliberateness.

A year later, I found another hospital, gave my notice and left with hardly anyone realizing. No gift or card, not even a word of goodbye. I didn't mind, notice, or care about this casual acceptance of my departure. To me, these others just weren't important enough to feel slighted by. They lacked the emotional depth required to make me notice them. They were but shadows and surface shapes that had passed in front of my vision for the briefest of encounters before disappearing.

The one who mattered, the one with the requisite depth and refinement of spirit?

That one I was taking with me.

Chapter Five

After Liz, I stepped into a new hospital and a more senior role. Few people seemed to notice me. I would arrive early and do my job, attend the relevant meetings, ask for further work and perfunctorily engage in office chatter. I did my job well, but I never attempted to become part of the fabric of this new work environment. There was no one there worth my time. No one I could connect with.

Something was missing. I was looking for someone special. Someone on the same level as Liz. No one in the office met my standards. That was obvious. I explored the town after work, visited bars looking around for the right person, and joined all the usual social clubs (which I left after one meeting—the activity itself never interested me). I never found what I wanted, and always returned alone to my empty flat late to eat a simple meal before sleeping, then waking after a shallow snooze to return to work. This depressing cycle continued, and I despaired.

Liz remained integrated, but I wanted that initial exhilaration of falling in love again. To voyage on an intoxicating journey, building an indescribable relationship that entwined every fiber of being with someone unknown.

Then suddenly there was Kevin. My second. There was nothing sexual between us, and we had little in common. Until that point, I'd only found vulgar, obvious people with vulgar, obvious needs. This blight did not last, though; sometimes I feel that fate exists, that we are pre-destined to meet our soulmates. Call it divine providence.

It was just another night. I had been to an amateur drama club. I had hoped people willing to absorb and become fictional characters would have the refinement I sought. They didn't.

After the club, the other actors and actresses invited me for a quick drink before I could take my leave. Having nothing else, and unable to face returning to the flat alone, I accepted.

We went to the bar and ordered our drinks. A quick glance around showed a group of men in their early twenties, composed of varying sizes and shapes, boasting loudly about how manly they were. Which seemed to include talking about their drinking habits and their many spectacular successes with women. Dismissible.

I noticed one of them, though. *Kevin.* Tall, thin, talking louder than the rest and trying to fit in. Why he wasted breath on that worthless trash was beyond me, then and now.

I saw the looks his worthless friends gave him. Scornful. Sometimes they would laugh at his jokes, but sometimes they would half-turn, angling their shoulders toward each other as though to cut him out of the group. Kevin had noticed this, of course. He was too smart and perceptive not to, yet still he persevered to squeeze into their circle. I wanted to spit my drink out in fury at the group's behavior, to snarl at them for not recognizing what they had in their midst.

Kevin pleased me. I recognized and valued him. He would be mine. I sensed I would be his truest friend, the best he could ever dream of. We required no one else. These other pointless buffoons should just leave.

I edged forward and tried to move the group I was with closer to them so I could listen and glean something from their conversation. Nobody noticed my interest in the one young man.

My newest dear friend went to the toilet. His companions exchanged looks and, in silence, achieved consensus by walking out together without a word of farewell. When my gentleman returned, he seemed to know immediately that his companions had ditched him. The drop of his gaze and slump of his shoulders brought tears to my eyes, which I hid before anyone noticed.

"Sorry," I said after knocking into him by accident. Kevin shrugged, waved the contact aside and moved closer to the bar, hunched over his drink. "Your friends thought you had gone and so they left themselves, I guess," I said. "It happens." He looked up sharply but relaxed when he saw no mockery or cruelty.

"Why don't you join us?" I motioned toward the group I had arrived with, showing the half-forgotten actors and actresses who were oblivious to the wonder that was forming before them. Some of them noticed my gesture and smiled, nodding in assent. I inclined my chin in their direction, showing Kevin that he should come and join our table.

If I had been alone, he likely would have declined, figuring me as a desperate social reject or trying to make some kind of unwanted pass. But I was with a group, and he wanted to fit in and belong somewhere. He did not know that the entire bar and its occupants were beneath him and undeserving of his presence.

Although the idea of many friends appealed to my fresh soulmate, we still spent the night talking almost exclusively to one another. We acknowledged the others at the table but spent the evening joking with each other. He told me his name and laughed with delight when I told a few childish jokes. I chortled as he returned the favor. Kevin smiled, feeling pleased to be surrounded by people and belonging somewhere.

The people I had arrived with left. I implied we were old acquaintances as I nodded my goodbyes with a solemn promise of seeing them next week.

Kevin also waved goodbye to these people that I had already forgotten and whom neither of us would ever meet again.

Come the end of the evening, Kevin suggested we move on to a nightclub. I agreed, getting an idea of what he needed.

We spent the rest of the evening in a small, dark nightclub drinking excessive amounts of alcohol, dancing vigorously in the middle of the dance floor to a variety of retro hits and trying to seduce attractive ladies with varying degrees of success. Kevin seemed to associate these things with having a good time, and I wanted to support him in this.

To his credit, though, he tried to ensure that I also enjoyed the evening. Before every drink, dance, or chat to a group of girls, he would cast a querying look in my direction. I responded with every sign of enjoyment to his suggestions.

I was the perfect wingman. Every time we spoke to a group of girls, I would emphasize Kevin as the perfect guy, laugh at his jokes, and be the butt of his gentle mockery. After each pointed quip, he glanced across to ensure he had caused no offense. I would provide reassurance with a delicate shake of my head, smile, and subtly point to one young lady I thought he should talk to.

The evening's activities stretched into early morning. Kevin left with the indicated woman that he had chatted with for a couple of hours. Before departing, he ensured I could get home okay. Then he beamed, a smile stretching his lips, with barely contained pride that he wasn't leaving alone. I grinned, lightly punched his shoulder, and told him to go for it. We exchanged phone numbers as he got into the taxi.

Once he was out of sight, I strolled down the nearest alley and stuck my fingers down my throat. I needed to be fresh for work.

The morning and its associated alarm call found me already awake. The excess of excitement and adrenaline bouncing around my system had prevented sleep. I did not have the faintest hint of fatigue or a hangover from the alcohol. An all-consuming, rejuvenating joy kept such minor physical constraints at bay. *I had found another!* I knew where our relationship would culminate. Felt confident, even, that we would get to our goal faster than I had with Liz. That's not to imply Kevin was more important than Liz or any of the other Sideways People. I just understood his needs better and could become his reward with minimal change. We could reach the apex of our relationship in double time.

We texted each other during the day, with him trying to be a gentleman about the previous night while also portraying it as an everyday occurrence, hardly worth commenting on. I texted back to express envy while suggesting that we do it again.

We met for drinks, and I complained about the horrific hangover he had given me while mock swearing that I would never consume alcohol again. He smiled, shared gory details from the night before, and bought me a drink.

We spent a lot of our time together drinking. Kevin seemed to feel the need to go out frequently, and drinking appeared to relax him and help strengthen our bond. It took the hard edge off long workdays and loosened his tongue enough that he would tell me his thoughts. He acknowledged his friends did not behave as friends and was uncertain why he tried with them.

We started meeting regularly, and I would often suggest going to his house. For obvious reasons, I would create excuses for why he should not come to mine. Kevin interpreted this as kindness, being spared the effort of traveling.

Sometimes, after a few drinks, he would say I was "the best" and I would wave a hand, as though dismissing it from consideration. Inside, of course,

I was pleased and knew our moment was rapidly approaching, that our relationship would soon freeze throughout eternity into perfection.

As it had with Liz, our relationship changed Kevin. He remained considerate of other people's needs (he always checked if I was enjoying a night and ensured I could get home safely) but also displayed a newfound confidence. Kevin drank less, and his humor strengthened from insecure mocking into short and witty anecdotes. Sometimes he even swaggered as he walked. I liked the direction he was headed and felt pride in being his friend and the transformation that I was supporting.

I knew our time was approaching and made initial plans for the event. Kevin would not be assumed through strangulation. I stored a long, slender knife in the back of my jeans, ready for the occasion.

A few weeks back, we'd discovered a local bar to meet up in. It was ancient, shabby, and worn down with few customers. The place had little obvious going for it. The carpet was threadbare and sticky, but we liked it. We were regulars, and they seemed to value our custom. It served as our jumping off point where we would meet for a couple of drinks before heading elsewhere.

Most nights, the bar was empty. During peak hours, a couple of older gentlemen would sit in the corner and glance over at our arrival.

This time was different. In the corner, obnoxiously loud, stood a group of rowdy men. They looked familiar. I stared, puzzling out where I recognized them from. It took a while before I placed them as the ones who had abandoned Kevin the night we met. The ones who ducked out, dismissing him as nothing. I had removed the sting of their cruelty then and was ready to support Kevin now.

They glanced across at us, their bland circular faces ripe with bemusement. I didn't feel any kind of threat from them, although they were trying to project an aura of belligerence. Contempt rose within me, and I stood at the bar between them and Kevin, arms straight, my hands spread wide across the wood, my hackles raised.

"Haven't seen you in a while. How have you been?" one of them called to Kevin.

"Fine," Kevin responded with a fleeting, nervous smile, not engaging any further. He turned his back to them so he could talk to me.

The group continued staring. It distracted us, stopped the conversation and prevented the evening from gelling. I couldn't help but wonder, did they feel Kevin belonged to them, that he should be at their beck and call, forever their convenient jester? That was no longer the case. He had bloomed into something far greater. *I*, not them, had enabled the change.

One man in particular, short and with close-cropped blonde hair, kept stealing glances.

"What are you looking at?" I snapped. My voice came out low and choked through a throat constricted with anger.

It seemed to shock him, this short man, the directness of the question. He looked around at the group, as though to reassure himself that his friends had his back.

Then he lunged, head down, right arm swinging around high in an arc. I dodged and dropped my arms down around his neck in a chokehold, swinging my knee up and into his chest. He bellowed and tried to pull back, but I kept my grip.

His friends jumped forward in a pack, like the yapping dogs they were. Kevin grabbed one of them and pushed him away from me. The two twisted and jerked backward and forward in a clumsy, awkward dance. A punch landed straight at my mouth and I tasted blood. My angry hold on the blonde man tightened, and I twisted him around before throwing him to the floor. Without pause, I forced my hand into another's mouth, turning my fingers to start painfully stretching lips before slamming my head into his nose.

It was short and violent. I bit, scratched, elbowed, punched, butted and kneed anything that came close and only took a few barely felt hits. Kevin had thrown his foe to the ground and was half-heartedly, foot turned sideways, kicking him with no real harmful intent in the ribs. His heart wasn't in it; he was far too soft for this world.

They broke first, scrambling to the exit, falling over themselves and the furniture in their undignified haste to flee. Kevin stepped back to let his opponent get up and run. There were no backward looks, they just fled.

Kevin turned to look at me. A thin trickle of blood leaked from one nostril, which deflected to the side of an enormous and savage grin. His eyes blazed with satisfaction. While outnumbered, he had defeated those who had snubbed and disregarded him. Kevin strode to me like an all-conquering titan, pausing only to check I was unhurt. His whole gait and bearing were of a far taller and broader man.

Looking at him, pride tightened my chest and made it hard to breathe. I motioned him toward the bar. The elderly landlord muttered a comment about asking us to leave if there was any further trouble. He accepted our protestation of just defending ourselves, though, and served our drinks with every sign of good cheer.

We stayed the rest of the evening rather than moving elsewhere. Kevin's final and greatest triumph had forged him into his best self. The man I could love and spend every moment with. He was ready. This was our time.

As Kevin spoke, I drank and listened and admired. Kevin recognized I had enabled this victory, supported this achievement, and we talked about plans for holidays and trips.

We drank until late, left together, and Kevin threw his arm around my shoulder as we swayed outside. For a second, I considered the possible futures that awaited us. It was dark and late on a Friday night. People would be asleep, and I would not be back at work for two days.

"Can I stay at yours? Don't fancy going somewhere, but not sure I want the night to end. Besides, just painted the bedroom, and it smells," I asked. Kevin smiled, pleased that he could do me a favor and spend more time together.

"Of course," my caring friend responded.

We called a cab and waited outside in the dark until it arrived.

It was a quick journey back to his place, and I paid the driver in cash. I knew the area well, having been there several times before. There were no cameras, and I had asked the driver to drop us a slight distance away so I could clear my head by walking. Kevin had been drinking and was still frothing with pride and excitement at the night's events, making him noisier than I wanted. I shushed him, whispering that we should be careful not to wake the neighbors. Kevin was always considerate, and this quickly quietened him down.

We walked the short distance together in amiable silence. Occasionally, we would turn to look and smile at each other. As we drew closer to Kevin's home, I took a second to drop back slightly and scan the windows and doors to make sure no one was watching before moving closer to him. We reached his place and Kevin fumbled in his pockets for the keys before opening the door and letting us in.

Kevin flicked the light switches on and we both kicked off our shoes to avoid treading in dirt. I shut the door behind us, turned and faced Kevin. The lights illuminated Kevin's face. It was just the two of us, and I cherished the moment and the anticipation of what was coming. His eyes still gleamed with possibilities; his mouth curved upward into a perpetual smile.

He started saying, "Do you want—" and then suddenly, futilely, dropped his palm down onto the wrist of my hand as I had decided we were past petty wants. I moved closer, the knife already in his chest, and placed my other hand on his shoulder. Kevin adjusted himself upright, as though to pick himself off the top of the knife, before slumping forward. All the while he kept his quizzical eyes on mine as though trying to understand my actions. I laid his head on my shoulder and turned my face toward his. After releasing the knife, I tilted him so I could see his eyes and moved my mouth close to his. Holding his gaze, I felt his last breath leave his body and enter mine through my opened mouth.

Everything of Kevin carried into me through the air expelled from his now empty lungs. His triumph. His success. *Everything.* It all flowed into me, granting me incredible strength, but also *so much more.* The feelings humbled me. The absolute knowledge and reassurance of the strength of his love for me was beyond denial. I was the staunch friend he had always wanted and felt he deserved, who had treated him with the same enabling support that he had given others. My eyes filled with the gift Kevin had given me.

I'm told some tribes practice the art of cannibalism on the elite warriors of their fallen foes, believing this will grant them the strength and wisdom of the consumed. I needed to perform no such action. Kevin's very essence was now within me. I explored the confidence he had felt in his last moments and knew he had defeated all his doubts and internal demons. His thoughts and memories were merging with mine, giving me the complex flavor of his existence.

This new strength was used to carry his physical remains. My arms tilted him before I crouched and picked up his legs to rest him horizontally across my forearms. Looking for a temporary resting place, I moved him to his bedroom and laid him down on the center of his bed. I pressed his arms to the side of his body, straightened his hair and clothes before kissing his forehead with tenderness.

Little blood had spilled. Online videos had given guidance on angles and the best approach, but there were still some tidying and related tasks to do. It was too late that night to transfer Kevin to his final resting place, and I was in no state to drive. Kevin had said I could stay the night and would want me to eat, so I did. I let Kevin have the bed; the couch was good enough for me.

The next morning was spent moving quietly around his apartment, cleaning any dishes and cutlery that I used. I smiled in amusement as I checked the cupboards and saw only convenience meals. Kevin should have eaten more healthily, but no matter now; I had saved him from ever getting ill. Sporadically, I would check on him to see if there was anything else I could do for him. Whilst there, I borrowed a clean shirt and a few other things.

Although I had never seen where Kevin kept his car keys or watched his neighbors to learn their routine, I now knew both. I had some cash on me, which, when combined with what Kevin had, meant I could get the required incidental objects I needed. I waited until I knew the neighbors would be unlikely to see me and used Kevin's car to drive to the relevant stores.

As I approached nighttime, I deep cleaned the apartment and tidied it with fanatical zeal. No one was going to think Kevin was a slob. They were only ever going to think the best of him. By the time I had finished, it could have passed as a show home—it looked that good.

I returned to Kevin's bedroom and started going through his wardrobe—picking out his finest and most trendy outfit, before dressing him in the carefully selected threads. All this work had eaten into time, and it was comfortably past midnight. Few people were going to be around.

Kevin's strength was still within me and, even though his body had turned stiff, it was still easy to transfer him to the back seat of his car. I had to collapse the back seats and angle him slightly to make sure he fit, but it was no bother. I opted to take the quieter and more scenic route to our intended destination to avoid any disturbances. We passed only a few cars en route in the darkness, and no one would have noticed anything.

There was a small area of wasteland near the pub where Kevin had emerged victorious against those who would have belittled him. I had noted it a few weeks before and had considered it as a possible appropriate resting location because of its proximity to the pub where we'd had a few fun nights. Now, it seemed like the only logical choice. I wanted him close to that place, to where he had shown his final, greatest self.

It was late enough that it was nearly early and there was no one around. I retrieved the shovel from the boot of his car and started. To ensure the area looked undisturbed and would remain free of gawkers, I carefully cut the turf before digging and placed it to one side. I angled the created grave slightly so he could look over the site of his defining triumph for eternity.

With all tenderness and care, I transferred him to his resting place. Before covering him with the soil, I placed a four pack of beer next to his chest in memory of all the times we had drunk together. Having attended to his needs, I moved the soil back on top and patted it firm before replacing the undamaged turf.

As I finished, the sun had just started its ascent, and the velvety, comforting darkness was illuminated with dark red, copper colors. I retrieved the last can of lager that I had purchased earlier and stored in the car. Cracking it open and taking a large sip, I sat next to the disturbed earth and enjoyed watching the sunrise, as it illuminated the world with promises of a new day in bright, fiery colors whilst savoring the feel of Kevin inside.

"I love you, Kevin," I said, and knew he felt the same. Joyful tears streamed down my face, triggered by the sheer beauty of the moment. One last time, I surveyed the scene before retrieving all the unimportant objects I had brought with me and drove and dumped Kevin's car a few miles away before getting public transport home.

Some people had seen me with Kevin, but they knew only a few identifying details. Maybe someone would eventually ask for my description, but there was no way of linking that information back to me or my address.

I was free to explore Kevin's thoughts, feelings, and sensations for a while longer. If I got caught after that...well, that's the price of genuine love, I guess, and I would pay it in full as fair recompense. No matter what happened from here on out, Liz, Kevin, and I would be forever inseparable. We were perfect and undivided.

Kevin didn't signal the end of things. Others joined us, a fair few, but only when we could achieve utter synchronicity. I changed the role I played and who I was with each of them. Sometimes I was the perfect partner, male or female, the willing confidante, the friend. It varied for each. I fought, fucked, was fucked, made love, was made love to, rebelled, and conformed according to the personality of the one I was with. The only consistent thing was the sudden permanent capture of the relationship when it reached its apex. Each of these people then became part of me and me part of them. Together, forever.

I wish I could tell you about them all, these Sideways People. Our time and language are insufficient, though. If I tried to describe each, their uniqueness, our sincere feelings, we would be here until the end of time. You don't have that luxury.

Besides, I want to tell you about Laura, the other world, my contest, and why I am howling inside.

Chapter Six

As they tend to, the years carried on passing. They touched lightly as they rushed past, but there was enough for the hairline to recede; the temples tinge with silver, the paunch grow enough to be noticeable. Only slightly, but even so, I was no longer a shallow youngster.

An unconscious pattern developed. I would meet a Sideways Person, we would fall in love with each other, they would become part of my very essence with everything kept perfect, before finding a new job and moving on. Every couple of years, I would move somewhere different and change jobs. Build a new life.

When I was younger, I enjoyed this. The challenge of it, meeting new people and adapting to new circumstances. I would take delight in mastering new environments—of knowing and seeing more of my new associates and their qualities than they understood of mine. I think I saw it as some kind of victory.

Age was catching up, though. Each change eroded something, causing the loss of more steel from my spine. When I moved cities and jobs, I would have to take a second to metaphorically gird my loins before gritting my teeth and embracing the change. My merged Sideways People gave me the strength, love, and memories necessary to get through the most wearing moments. Still, part of me wanted to stop moving and stay somewhere with that one special person, someone who understood every aspect of me.

We all get soppy in the end.

I had started a new job, one that was to prove my last. It was a senior position, and I oversaw a medium-sized team that ensured data quality on all hospital records. When not working, I would take every opportunity to wander throughout the hospital, hoping to spot something incredible. I talked to many people, socialized with some, but grew close to none. Still, I walked and talked and waited. There was no real hurry. Those that had gone before sustained me, and these dearests filled my dreams and waking hours with nourishment.

It was not long after I had started this last job that I noticed her. *The one.* I was walking around the various departments talking to nurses. It was all professional and legitimate; I wasn't wasting time. In fact, I was trying to identify ways to ensure my team was recording episodes of care correctly. Seems a mundane surrounding context compared to what happened next. As I was talking to the lead nurse, I saw another nurse, *her*, out of the corner of my eye.

She trailed a step behind two nurse colleagues. She was shorter; her gait was square and deliberate. They strode ahead, turning their heads to speak to each other, but only occasionally glancing behind them.

Her? Well, her hair was blond, her features were long and angular. Her posture tilted her face downwards, so that she had her eyes turned to the floor. She was thickset, but still so alluring. Like catnip. I cannot meaningfully describe anything about her beauty or the feelings that the very sight of her evoked. That eloquence will be forever beyond me now.

I had stared with too much gaping zeal. When she rounded the corner, I snapped back into myself and realized how obvious I had been. I should have been talking about the most accurate mechanisms for capturing data. The lead nurse was looking at me with eyebrows archly raised, having noticed my sudden interest in this wondrous nurse.

"Sorry, miles away," I said, with an awkward, self-deprecating smile. "Do you know who that nurse was? I just think I used to know her at university but can't quite place her."

The lead nurse looked blank for a second before her face pursed with thought. "Laura," she said after a few seconds' pause.

I finished the conversation as quickly as I could while remaining polite. Who wants to talk about data when they have glimpsed the divine? This incredible woman, toward whom I felt such immediate, compulsive need and love, filled all my thoughts and prevented me from performing my professional duties. I immediately knew she was significant, but only had the faintest inkling of just how important.

My head raged with wonder as I returned to my desk and switched my PC on to check the staff directory. It was the work of mere moments to discover her surname, the department she worked in, and other members of her team. She was a trauma nurse, and I realized I knew a couple of other nurses who worked with her. I treated myself. I spent the rest of the day online searching for more details about Laura, smiling every time I opened a page that even potentially referred to her.

There was such a powerful temptation to simply walk downstairs. Let her see me, be confident this impact was mutual. There could be no other way; we were meant to be. I didn't, despite the powerful instinct. That I resisted is testament to my desire to ensure everything was perfect from the very start. Before introducing myself, I would know everything about her to ensure no cracks would ever appear in the foundation of our love.

Initially, I went out drinking with some nurses she knew. I made sure I met none of them on their own—I did not want any misunderstandings or false news of my being in a relationship with someone else to reach Laura's ears. While out with these side players in Laura's life, I would probe about her, trying to understand her motivations and drivers. Everyone seemed to know Laura, but very few appeared to notice her properly. Mentioning other nurses would get immediate responses and a plethora of anecdotes, but Laura was different. After asking about her, there would be a few seconds' pause and then an answer with vague adjectives like "nice" or "good at her job" would be supplied.

I wandered the hospital and the different wards, focusing on those areas where I knew she worked, searching for some trace of her. A few times, I would walk past her, nervous and uncertain. On the rare occasions when she noticed me, I would tilt my head in greeting and smile awkwardly before increasing my pace and rushing by. The importance of making a good impression, ensuring everything went well, prevented me from actually starting our relationship. I enjoyed it when I saw her, and she seemed to welcome my nods and presence, but I never started a proper conversation. I remained stuck, waiting for a tomorrow that never came, while dreaming of what could be.

"You after something?" Laura asked. I had visited the department she worked in. Unnoticed and unbidden, she'd quietly walked to stand behind me. She had paused for a second, waiting for me to turn and see her before speaking. My usual responses and platitudes spluttered as they fell incoherently from my lips, my eyes widening in shock.

"I'm always seeing you around, and I'm told you are asking about me." Her body was squared to mine, her head tilted upward so she could stare straight into my eyes. Her eyes, I noticed, were dark green, appearing unfocussed and dream infused, but they still regarded me with intense curiosity.

I wanted to show how well I knew her. I wanted to convince her that I could be anything she wanted. Instead, nothing happened. No words came out. A solid minute passed while I tried to make my mouth work. Eventually, I muttered to a point above her head.

"I saw you; I liked you. I wanted to get to know you," I said, mumbling, and forced my eyes to meet hers.

She stood still, regarding me in complete silence before asking with gentleness, "Well, why didn't you?"

I shrugged and tried a half-smile before venturing with, "I didn't know how to start it."

Laura nodded as though expecting that answer and carried on looking at me. My returning stare was direct, but I kept dropping it, as I could not fully meet her gaze for long. She flashed a smile, and her eyes reflected it. Then she looked down from my face and started walking past me.

"Can I speak to you again?" I said, scared I'd missed my opportunity.

She stopped moving and turned to face me. Her smile flashed again, this time for longer. There was an assenting nod before she carried on walking without speaking another word. For a few moments, I stood shaking, reliving the brief conversation and committing her looks and expressions to memory. Her eyes were unparalleled. I wondered what spirituality and thoughts gave them their dreamy air.

The rest of the day buzzed with an ecstasy of frenzied energy. Just speaking to Laura had sent pure adrenaline through my system, leaving me unable to focus on normal work tasks. People noticed and commented as I shakingly spoke to random co-workers. I wanted to talk to someone about what had happened to me, to explain its significance and importance. There was no one in the office who could understand these feelings, so I released excess energy by burbling jokes and discussing trivial matters.

That night I relived the experience. Picturing her, her movements, the exact shape of her body, and conjuring up the image of that initial fleeting smile that crossed her face. I knew I had to move things forward. I would have to be direct.

The next day, I fabricated pretexts to visit different departments to find her. It did not take me long. Laura stood waiting in the same spot where we had spoken the previous day. As I turned the corner, it shocked me to see her there, staring straight at me. It seemed she knew right down to the second when I would arrive. Her eyes, dark green and so mysterious, regarded me with ferocious concentration. As I walked toward her, I tried to pretend at confidence by swinging my arms. It was the best I could do.

"I have been waiting for you," Laura said in her quiet voice when I drew near.

"I have been looking for you," I said after a moment of hesitation. She tilted her head to one side and again let a slow smile spread across her face and reached out to hold my arm just above the wrist. An unbidden smile spread slowly across my face and held her eyes.

"Fancy a coffee sometime?" I asked in a quiet tone that hid my nervousness. She looked at me gravely and nodded again, the smile remaining fixed in position. She picked up various folders and walked away again without further word or explanation. I reached out and cupped her wrist with my hand.

"I'll need your number," I reminded her. For a second, she looked surprised before writing her contact details on a scrap of paper and handing it over. That task done, she turned on her heel and walked away with her even and square stride.

That night, I drank coffee and procrastinated over how to proceed. Being this awkward and uncertain was unusual for me, but everything needed to be perfect. What if I called and said the wrong thing? After agonizing most of the evening away, I settled for texting her with a proposed date and time and suggested a venue for the crucial and much desired coffee. In agony of indecision, I also placed a small *x* after the text to symbolize a kiss. My phone beeped in response seconds afterwards. It was Laura responding with a simple yes and two kisses.

Sleep was impossible that night, and I couldn't wait until lunch to see her again. I am conscientious at my job; I swear I am, but again I made excuses to visit those departments where she worked. It took no time to find her. She stood waiting in exactly the same spot where we had met on the previous two occasions. Her eyes held mine as I approached her.

I walked toward her, more confident this time. Some nerves had disappeared, others were better controlled. I smiled and looked, with no awkwardness, into her eyes. They were still dreamlike and carried suggestions of new heavens and earths. Despite their dreaminess, they regarded me intently. I always got the impression Laura paid absolute attention to me whenever we were together, and I learned later that one thing she liked about me was she thought I did the same in return.

"Why didn't you call instead of texting last night?" she asked, keeping her eyes locked on mine. Laura always caught me off-guard, making it hard to put on any persona or new trait.

I struggled words through an uncertain mouth to say, "I was nervous and found it easier to text." The response caused Laura to smile and reach out to touch my arm just above the wrist again. We stayed like that, frozen like statues, for a while longer before she released my wrist and let her smile fade.

"I noticed you signed off with a kiss," Laura said in her serious voice.

Flirtatiously and with raised eyebrows, I responded with, "I noticed you signed off with two." She nodded before turning to walk away in absolute silence. This time, I slid myself round to her side and picked up some folders she had reached across to carry. She looked at me in surprise and then carried on walking. I followed.

We spent most of the day together. Walking side-by-side in silence. Whenever I glanced at her, she would already be staring at me. She looked pleased whenever she noticed me glancing at her, which was often. I could not help myself—she was so beautiful, and I was drawn to her.

We went for coffee that night and discussed her work while drinking caffeine. Co-workers referred to Laura as competent but had to trawl through their thoughts to recognize it. Although they noticed her, they did not appear to see her as central enough to commit to memory. When I commented on that, she nodded as though it was something she had realized and seemed pleased I knew she was an extremely competent nurse.

We talked about many things in Laura's life that evening. I asked her about friends. She asked me to define what I meant by friends before replying that she kept in touch with a few people from school. Sometimes she went drinking with the other nurses. She asked me the same question, and I pondered before saying I socialized with a few people, but only on rare occasions. Laura had a family—a sister and a mother who saw her at Christmas and would ask her questions about her personal life that she didn't care to answer. She didn't seem intimate with them. It felt clear that I was already the most important person in her life.

I walked her home that night. I would try to steal discrete glances at her, but she always noticed me doing it, rendering the need for subtlety unnecessary and allowing me to just stare. As we arrived at her flat, she turned to face me. I leaned forward and, with eager passion, kissed her directly on her soft lips. Her arms leaped up and encircled my shoulders, pulling me toward her with vigor as her tongue circled mine.

I tried breaking free to consider the right action, and she noticed this. She slipped her hands to grip my elbows and leaned back to look at me. Seeing my reticence, she tilted forward and whispered in my ear, "I am with you," before pulling me toward her again and into the flat.

I spent the night inside Laura, telling her, with utter honesty, that I loved her, and she sighed the same back as she pulled me ever deeper. Everything about her was perfect: her scent, her mannerisms, her sounds and movement. The night was indescribable. The temptation to escalate the relationship beyond mortal form immediately was incredible (faster than with any other Sideways Person). I held back, though, sensing something else was coming, something monumental. And so it would prove.

Chapter Seven

We spent plenty of time together. My professional reputation must have collapsed. It became a habit for me to arrive late because I couldn't tear myself away from Laura in the mornings. I conceived random excuses to visit her during work. Colleagues found it difficult to find or contact me.

Laura maintained her professionalism and did her job with the same quiet efficiency and competency she had always displayed. Sometimes she would distance herself from me as she performed her duties. I asked about this, and she said she did not yet "wish to lose herself in me." Despite this need for occasional solitude, my attentiveness seemed important and dear, so I continued visiting her whenever I could.

Other people noticed our relationship, but I didn't care. Everyone else had become insignificant. Their only use was to tell me further new bits of information and observations about Laura. Colleague's lips would twist in derision or concern when they spoke to me, and I guessed they perceived my behavior as weird.

This was unusual. On prior occasions, in all my earlier incarnations, work colleagues had regarded me as professional and capable. Few would notice my objects of interest, and none guessed my intentions. Laura made everything different. It was impossible to deny the strength of my attraction.

Laura and I spent entire evenings together talking in depth about every aspect of her personality and behavior. I would tell her other people's words and views, explaining why I thought they had that opinion. Then I would express my views about her, her motivations and my observations specific to that day.

Laura would listen and either nod or shrug in silence, depending on her thoughts about what I had heard. Sometimes she would smile and ask me to explain my observations, and I would elaborate further.

Laura pressed me to talk about myself, but there was little to say. Without mentioning the previous Sideways People who were now part of me, there was nothing to describe. I could not share these details, and without these relationships; I am an unimportant individual. My lack of significance and endearing traits embarrassed me sometimes in our conversations. Despite my nondescript nature, Laura still made me feel as though I was the only person in the world through her attentive ways and all-consuming looks.

This bubble of contentment continued. Nothing deviated or changed. I don't know how long it carried on. Honestly, I don't. It crossed my mind that we had achieved perfection, and things could not get better. That I should merge with Laura to preserve her feelings and memories within me. I couldn't, though. There was always another eagerly anticipated day... I was always waiting for another perfect occasion. Maybe part of love wants everything to remain unchanging, even though greater opportunities exist. Our relationship did eventually take the next step, but it was not me who initiated this change.

I was lying next to Laura one night in the dark and silence. Just enjoying being there, my mind calm, savoring the smell of the bed, and the texture of Laura's skin touching mine. The gentle rhythm of Laura's breathing was slow, and I thought she was sleeping. It was relaxing, hypnotic. I had drifted into a mental blank void surrounded by beautiful sounds and smells when Laura spoke into the darkness.

"I want to take you somewhere tomorrow to talk about some things." The words formed from her soft breathing. Concern made me roll onto my side to examine her face and eyes in depth.

"Everything okay?" I asked, hoping with every fiber of my being it was.

Laura noticed my worry and moved her hand so that her palm rested on the side of my face before nodding. "I am with you," she moved her hand to gently stroke my hair. "I just want everything known between the two of us."

Laura stared at me for a minute. My face must have softened with the reassurance provided by her words; and she inched forward to rest her head against my chest before falling asleep with a soft sigh. I lay awake a moment longer, enjoying her breath feathering across my torso before I plunged into a deep, dreamless sleep.

I woke with a start, feeling the bed shift. Laura was standing by the bedside, still naked, looking at me with those eyes.

"We should get going soon," she said. I nodded, feeling slightly apprehensive, and swung my feet out of the bed. With quiet efficiency, we got dressed. While nervously pulling on a shirt and other clothes, I would turn and look at Laura with questioning eyes. She returned my glances and gave me a reassuring smile.

Laura drove us to our last destination. We were silent all the way there. Laura kept her eyes fixed on the road and refused to return the questioning looks I shot at her. She did not indicate what we were doing or where we were going. This carried on throughout the entire journey, maybe an hour, and I sighed in relief when the car finally slowed down and pulled to the side of a large thicket of wooded trees and shrubs.

We exited the car in silence. I knew something important was coming, but did not know what it was. I'll be honest, I feared the worst. Laura strode off in front, her face and eyes resolute as they pointed ahead, and

I trailed along behind. We walked past a thin sliver of a stream through to an open area where our walk ended. It was isolated, empty, and the place was silent. No animals were visible, no insects. Just us. Even the stream appeared to stop running to wait for us to do whatever it was we needed to do.

One tree appeared to have collapsed and rested at a steep angle against another. Covered in ivy and other comely looking parasitic plants that raced up and down its sides. Laura rested her back against this fallen tree and, with a slowness that suggested doubt, moved each of her arms along its surface so that they rested horizontally away from her body. She extended her arms, gripped her hands down onto the tree as though to keep herself in position, and turned her eyes on me.

I had been waiting in uncertain silence. Then beheld her eyes as they raised to meet mine. Rather than being unfocussed and dreamful, these orbs contained hints of whole new emotions that I could only dream of. Hard decisions cleanly made. They focused on me, made me the absolute center, taking in every aspect of my countenance and reaction but seeing deeper than that. Going past form and tearing through my soul.

"Tell me the thing about yourself that no one else knows." The quiet command appeared to issue through the air itself. My face became blank and frozen with shock. Although my mind was racing, trying to understand what she was asking, my slack round mouth could issue no words.

The moment hung. Everything was silent, locked in place. The only movement in the world was my head making slight shaking movements to protest innocence against some unspecified crime. I remember everything about what happened next. Never averting her gaze, with no possibility of mistake, she articulated the full names of three of my Sideways People in an even and determined tone. I looked into her face, straight into her eyes, and knew she knew.

"You know," I said unnecessarily. The adrenaline and emotional demands of the situation spread throughout my body. My legs appeared unable to support my weight, and I sank to my haunches to support my weight with my hands. Turning my head upward toward her and making myself meet that terrible gaze again, I forced further words through a tightly constricted throat. "You know, and you are the only person who could understand."

Laura carried on looking at me. Tears laced the side of her face and glittered diamonds when they trailed through the sunlight. She appeared to brace herself before taking a deep breath, nodding to herself and then said, "I am with you."

It took me a moment to understand what was happening. Laura knew my entirety, every aspect, even the sides normal society would disapprove of, and had chosen me. Her feelings remained unchanged, confirming in undeniable action that she was mine now and through eternity. When realization hit, I rose upward as though confronting the world's most necessary task and surged toward her, no impediments accepted, my arms outstretched and hands eager.

Those needy hands reached Laura first. They bound themselves to her throat, overlapping with each other in their attempts to cover as much flesh as possible, pressing in and around as hard as they could. Then reaching arms accepted her weight as they lifted her body off the ground and brought her face level to mine, her eyes to look straight across into my soul. Her sight looked into me and never wavered, giving me the secrets of the dreams that she and no one else saw.

The rest of my body wanted to join this communion and pushed forward into her. Her back arched across the tree, and my hands pushed her shoulders and neck further backward. Laura tilted her head so that her eyes locked onto mine. Our gaze never broke. Her hands still resolutely pressed down onto the supporting tree, never releasing once in the eternity of seconds that we were locked there. There was a sudden shuddering, choking sound and Laura was surging and rushing into me.

It was intense. In all ways. Painful beyond belief. Sharp pains stabbed into my left side, as though a spear had pierced there. Red blossomed across my eyesight and my head jerked forward to bang into hard wood. Confused feet stumbled backward, and I fell, again hitting my head on a root as I slammed to the hard ground. My eyes filled with strips of white light that grew blocks of gray, covering my vision. I had to concentrate hard to remember to turn my head to the side as yellow bile spewed from my mouth.

Throughout all this, Laura was with me, our locked gazes being the conduit through which she traveled into my being. I felt her and the intensity of her feelings toward me, the color and need I had brought into her world and the all-encompassing satisfaction she had felt at being seen at long last. Laura moved inside of me, spreading herself through every tendon and muscle, clinging to my lungs and invading and spreading throughout my thoughts and feelings. It was only her fortifying love and presence that gave me the strength to withstand the pain that coursed within.

I do not know how long I lay there. My eyes screwed shut tight to block out the pain. But I kept them closed after the pain subsided so I could concentrate and savor Laura's feelings and memories. I moved through her experiences and life, noting how she always tried to do the right thing for people, but felt they never noticed or appreciated her actions. This perception had been reinforced continually by people expecting her to do things well and then never noticing when she exceeded their expectations.

All that changed when she noticed me looking at her as she walked past with two other nurses.

Throughout the time Laura and I had spent together in our physical bodies, she was always certain that it was just her I had noticed, her and no one else. The feelings this caused encompassed and enwrapped her like a warm blanket. She had checked on me as I had checked on her. She had discovered my secret, but the strength of her feelings dwarfed the shock and concern this caused. Laura had resolved to make me hers and herself mine. And she succeeded beyond all comprehension in her resolution.

I lay there a long time, letting the pain subside and remembering Laura's thoughts. Even when the initial pain had subsided, my body ached and could only move slowly and painfully. The mere act of opening my eyes took effort. Returning my senses to the everyday world around me was almost more than I could bear.

I lay on my back. My arms had landed on top of me and had folded across my chest. My legs pressed straight down. One hit to my head had split the skin of my scalp; I had a vague patina of blood over the top of my vision and could see red trickling down the side of my nose. My palm came away bloody when pressed to the unseen wound.

It was like waking on a wintry morning after a deep sleep. I did not want to move or change my current position. I hesitated to look at Laura's remains but eventually did so when it became unavoidable. She was still upright, her body slumped against the tree with her arms outstretched, her legs collapsed, sagging underneath her. The force of our joining had tilted her face downwards, and it hung to one side.

Something caught my attention, but in the sunlight, I could not tell exactly what it was. A light smear appeared to be covering part of her face. At first, I thought it was the sunlight reflecting off something, but then I realized it was no reflection. It took me a while to get to my feet. My limbs still felt so weak, but I hobbled closer. This nearness gave greater clarity. I saw there was a white cloud suspended over Laura's nose and mouth.

I was near crippled at this stage, exhausted by the entire experience, but I still revolved my head around this shining vapor, scrutinizing it from all angles to better understand. It appeared to be composed of thousands of particles, which looked like perfect white raindrops. They could not have been—they were static, each suspended in the air as though gravity and time had forgotten them. The motes appeared to contain glimmering light, which leaked out through the surface in flashes of white.

I stopped looking at the fascinating droplets to spend a moment tidying up Laura. I reached round the white cloud in tender love to press shut those wondrous eyes and stroke her hair. Then I examined the cloud again to understand it better. Some droplets remained partially attached to Laura's nose and the side of her mouth. It was as though they had left her as part of her final breath. Maybe a scrap of her expelled soul could not make its way into me.

This final thought gave me pause. Every part of Laura that was not her physical body was now part of me. I did not want any of it to be wasted, any bit to be left outside. This was not a usual physical phenomenon, but something divine created through Laura's perfect actions. Without further delay, I swung my face into the center of the white cloud, inhaling as deeply as I could. The glimmering cloud disappeared into my nostrils as though looking for an excuse to resume its journey.

Explosive pain returned. This time was even worse, ripping outward from the left side to cover my entire body. Utter and absolute. Like a broken puppet with savagely cut strings, my legs collapsed from underneath me, and I dropped uncontrolled to the floor. My body jerked and convulsed in agony. That heart of mine felt like it stopped but then beat in a sudden wild frenzy. I tasted copper at the back of my throat and saw red spray forced from between grimaced lips.

The pain and damage left no room for awareness or consciousness. Red blackness rushed and locked me rigid in an iron, cruel embrace. My muscles spasmed, and warm liquid released from my bladder and spilled down my legs.

That was the last sensation before everything dropped and I went somewhere very different.

Chapter Eight

I don't know what happened after I collapsed unconscious in front of Laura's body. I have suspicions. Nothing definite, though. Gray blossoming as I lost consciousness. Then regaining consciousness but not being able to open my eyes. Pushing my other senses outward to understand what had happened, to identify what was different.

Something had changed, that much was clear. I was now lying sideways on a slope of some sort. The ground was damp and tacky; it clung to my soiled and ruined clothes. The greasy air trailed across my exposed face.

More than anything, I sensed displacement—a terrible wrongness. The entire essence of my physical form and spirit felt different. My skin was paper thin, as though my body was borderless and incapable of holding a distinct shape. My emotions and feelings had changed from the ecstasy I had experienced in my final physical moments with Laura to a dull throb of dread.

Something bad had happened.

It must be difficult for you to understand how terrible this was, but try. One moment I was experiencing the apex of human intimacy with someone who I loved and who loved me in return. We had merged and unified in our intimacy, but now something had changed, and I couldn't feel or experience her the way I should.

I was nauseous. The air looped and trailed like physical fingers within my lungs. I wondered if I was being poisoned somehow, whether I had wandered into a radioactive wasteland without realizing, and was having my life leached away. In the absence of any other options, I forced my eyes open.

I had moved, or been moved, somewhere else. Laura's previous physical form was nowhere to be seen. The wooded area where we had expressed our extreme emotions had disappeared. There were trees running downwards to one side of me, but they were skeletal, spiky things with damaged white bark that looked like petrified, diseased flesh. The slope I lay on appeared smooth and ran at a sharp gradient downwards; it surprised me that my body hadn't rolled while I was unconscious. The sight as I stared up the hill hurt my eyes, a smeared white light that both blinded and terrified.

Nauseous, I turned my eyes away. Above me, the sky was a blank sheet of pale color without sun or clouds. Looking down the slope was difficult, but less painful and unsettling. There was a thick fog that covered everything and made the world seem bleached. Within this fog, large, pestilential, green winged insects several inches long flew backward and forward in whining complaint. In an unknowable distance, the ground and sky merged.

I swung round and staggered to my feet. Surprised at how unsteady I was on them; I slid downward and tried to walk straight across to the trees. They looked like weeping willows that had long ago given up the ghost with the white leaching light, removing all memory of sap and spring.

I slipped when near them and grabbed onto a drooping branch to steady myself. It splintered lifelessly and a jagged edge tore through my skin. The wound seemed worse than it should have been. The splintered branch had pushed my skin up and sideways for a length of six inches. Despite this, the blood did not flow or leak but appeared and clung wetly along the length of the wound without dripping. I touched my head where it had split. It caused pain and a strange sensation of blood, but my hand came away dry with no new red on it.

I sat down in distress and tried to understand what was happening. My feet felt strange. There was a compulsion contained within them that I should—

Go down. Go deeper in.

And they twisted against my will, demanding to be set onto the ground to follow a downward path. They ached and felt unnatural, like someone had taken a stranger's feet and stitched them to my ankles. I tried to vomit and purge myself of this sickening air and distressing compulsion. Nothing came out, no food, no liquid. Just the sound of forlorn retching.

The nausea and distress forced a few moments of re-orientation. I closed my eyes and thought of my Sideways People, reassuring myself they were still within and part of me. I still felt them—their strength combined with mine—and took momentary solace. But the fog seemed to be stealing my essence and individuality. My skin and shell thinned, insufficient to contain these worthies, and I worried some form of disintegration would part us forever.

I stood and looked downwards to get an idea of the direction I should follow or see if there was some path that may be useful. I could see nothing past a few feet in front of my eyes, with everything obscured by fog. The only senses that appeared useful were my sense of smell, which detected a pervasive faint of rot, and my hearing, which heard the insects as they whined their way backward and forward. There appeared little choice but to continue down.

Chapter Nine

Turns out there were others. I had not noticed them when I first arrived. They formed in silence from the mist. I had not been walking long before I met some of them. They traveled in an indeterminately sized pack. Sometimes one would look startled before turning to walk to the side or bizarrely head upward toward that destructive light. The fog consumed them. Replacements appeared as though they were ejected unseen from the ground.

They were shorter than usual, with bland but angular features and colorless eyes. They wore drab robes draped over broad shoulders. Everything spoke of defeat and diminishment. Their eyes pulled downwards, mustaches and lips grimaced toward the floor. When they spoke, their lips didn't move, but the fog described the suggested words.

I tried speaking to them, grabbing hold of those closest, making eye contact while demanding where I was and where I needed to go. I heard indistinct mutterings about *"going down, go further in"* before they twisted out of grasp.

They spoke amongst themselves, though, and sometimes lamented deeds or complaints about charitable acts could be overheard. Their voices keened as they described how they should have helped their brother or done more for some invisible lover. I felt little but contempt. I gave time and money. For a chosen few, no restrictions existed.

The green insects hiding within the fog plagued these denizens, causing them to complain further and more heavily. Although the insects did not fly near me, they would be far bolder with the others. They would land on robes before laying eggs in the folds or flying into faces. The herd issued moans of complaint. Sometimes these insects would get crushed between hands and cloth and smear into green and yellow. This gave no peace from their irritation. The yellow and green streaks merged in unnatural ways and formed new, smaller insects that annoyed their creators with renewed vigor.

I traveled with the first pack I encountered. I felt no pleasure in the company or journey. These others were too engrossed in their own woes to pay me any attention. The air was thick with the irritating noise of the insects as my travel companions continued with their endless regrets and ruminations. The sounds dug into my skull and were a constant source of irritation.

Time flowed through an interminable now moment. I did not heal—the cut on my arm and the split skin on my forehead remained. My body was continually hurting and aching, the blood forever threatening but never spilling from the wounds. We traveled onwards and forever downwards. Sometimes, most of the pack would pause and rest together in response to some communal instinct. Others would continue while the majority rested, and in heartbeats we would lose these scouts to view.

When the pack stopped for this rest, they would sometimes mate with each other in full view; their bodies mechanically and drily joining before they completed, readjusted their clothes, and separately left. I would sleep during these intermissions. When I woke, it sometimes looked like the entire pack had moved on and a new pack had formed around me. I can't say for sure this occurred—the notes and types of complaint and whine varied to a small degree, but otherwise everything and everyone felt indistinguishable.

How long this repetitious process continued is unknown. I got nowhere for all I kept moving. I reached nowhere new—no landmarks went past us. There were still trees on one side, but these were the same ones that were there as I started my journey. The air was damp, and my clothes clung to my flesh before growing coarse and abrasive. Slight cuts and red marks appeared on my torso as this rubbing continued. I would have given up on the journey but didn't know how to—my feet still demanded the downward route and would compel obedience if I left it too long. What else could I do?

Forced by some unknown law or caused by divine providence, something happened that changed and developed my journey. I was moving downwards with one pack when I noticed one member stood static and had turned around to look in my direction. The other pack creatures just carried on in their own direction, unaware and uncaring about their unusual fellow. They moved downwards in their ambling gait with their heads low and their eyes downcast. Or they rested. No one else looked upward or had shown any interest in me.

I changed route downwards to move toward this anomaly, hoping for some kind of answer and resolution to my plight. I reached the watcher in just a few quick strides and, for a quick moment, we stood regarding each other with open curiosity.

It was a woman who waited. Maybe young, but in these conditions, with the obscuring fog and pale damaging light, it was difficult to be sure. Her eyes were pale blue, and she had the typical angular cheekbones of everyone else there, but there was nothing distinctive that explained her unusual behavior. She stared back and motioned for me to move on with her, turning and walking downwards as she did so.

I walked beside her, looking across, asking questions about her name and where she was from. She ignored me but would check if I was still next to her with slow, open looks. With surprise, I realized that when I was with her, there was a sense of progression; that my journey continued in some fashion. Little externally had changed, but now I felt I had crossed physical distance.

The next rest she lay down next to me, her face hidden by shadows and the ground; I tried to sleep on my side so I could carry on watching her. Her hands reached for my belt and undid the clasp. I looked into her eyes and could read no emotion there. I dropped my hand to brush hers away while shaking my head and making shushing noises. She stopped and tilted to look at me; I leaned forward to kiss her forehead before encircling her shoulders with my free arm. Comforted by the closeness of another person and the possibility of intimacy, I fell asleep.

I dreamed that night, the first dream since arriving in that unknown world. It was not pleasant. I dreamed in black.

My Sideways People stood around me in a circle. Their faces were accusatory, their eyes flinty and sharp. I mumbled in the middle of them; sincere promises that I would not let them go, that they would be safe in me for eternity. This just made their looks angrier, and some snarled.

I raised my hand in confusion to placate them and quell their fury when I noticed the dreaded omission. Laura was not present. All the others were there, but not Laura. She was the most recent and eclipsed even these treasured companions in terms of importance. I searched amongst them, calling out her name. That was too much for them and they crowded around, pulling and slapping at me; their hands sinking into my flesh and pulling it away, so it stretched like rubber. I screamed for Laura, but she never appeared, even as the others threw me to the ground with their hands ripping and pulling at my skin.

I woke with a start, jerking upward, my body cold with sweat. It took my eyes a while to remind me of my location. Even when my waking thoughts became less confused and I remembered and rationalized this land, I still couldn't shake how uncomfortable I was. Everything felt sore. I looked at my body and arms and saw angry red welts that were raised in semicircles from the rest of the skin. I cried in misery; remembering just the few brief moments ago (days, weeks, months, years?) when I had been with Laura, and everything was perfect. Now everything was disintegrating, all I could feel was pain and loss.

My tears must have woken the woman sleeping by my side. Her eyes opened and stare into me. I turned to her, the one person who appeared to notice me in this place. With patience snapping into fury, I asked through tears, "Who are you? What is your name?"

For a second, there was no reply, and her face looked thoughtful. Then her lips moved, and the word "Bea" was said through the fog. The answer felt oddly reassuring, as though it fit. Comforted, I lay down and slept a dreamless sleep.

Chapter Ten

Elsewhere in that place, in that entire separate world, someone else slept. Different to me as night is to day. I mentioned him before. The inhuman monster who took delight in pain and evil.

He lay, this monster, in the only place in this realm he did not belong. As he slumbered, fetid, cold, diseased wind brushed backward and forward over his body. The air sometimes changed his flesh into unrecognizable, horrifying forms which suited an unguessable purpose. He did not mind these transformations and slept, hoping for the opportunity to prove ownership of the small room he was slumbering in. He dreamed sweet, pleasant dreams, of—

Capture, trapped, screaming. But no one to hear. Smiling at her, to let her know it would not end. Chains, hooks, skin and flesh peeled back. Fingers twisted backward and bitten sharply through. Pausing only at nail. Blood, spray, flesh globules on floor. Rape. Insertion. Laughing at screams, enjoying humiliation. Pain. Pain. Pain... Pain.

Image after image, memory after memory, played through his head. Everything about his body was short and round, with stubble covering his cheeks, and he looked like he belonged in a jolly clown costume. Inside, though, everything was hooks and spikes and the color red.

As this short man remembered pain and torture and degradations of the most appalling kind, his face twisted into a smile and his erection grew as the shadows took form around him.

These shadows could not be explained by something as natural as blocked light. Too dark, too black. There, within the shadows could be seen an ever-changing parade of faces, injuries, flesh broken in forms that nature would never achieve. If, after looking at the shadows, you could bring yourself to view the slumbering man and check his face and the twitches that ran through his body and hand, you might guess at some link between his thoughts and the apparitions that formed around him.

One memory must have stuck in his mind for longer than others. Perhaps it was of a particularly excessive, cruel or inventive murder he wanted to savor for a while longer. Whatever the cause, one shadow grew ever more distinct and became recognizable as a young girl in excruciating agony. A powerful gust of that ill, sickening wind blew this dense shadow further away from the slumbering man. With a final twitch, it appeared to break free and headed outward.

***

A change in the sounds awakened me from my second attempt at sleep. The insects had gone quiet but the members of whatever pack I was traveling with were complaining much louder about their woes. They weren't screaming in fear, but there was an urgency and volume to their keening that had been missing before. It was as though they were desperate to complete their regrets before anything happened to them.

I looked around, awake and alert within seconds. I saw the cause of urgency. The pack travelers were kneeling around it in supplication, their hands raised in pleading as they expressed their sorrows in bursting shouts. I looked at this unknown visitor in shock and concern. It was black and small. Gaping at it, I noticed it bore the form of a shimmering, black caricature of a tortured young girl. Eyelids pinned open with rusty iron staples, lips rearranged into a grotesque smile with steel wire, one eyeball dribbled down a scarred cheek with the partially severed optic nerve visible. Its flesh had suffered many other injuries—one arm ended in a stump; torn clothes revealed horrific burns and scars. The thing was so terrifying that even the all-pervasive fog pulled back from it in fear, and the insects fell silent.

Whatever it was, its fury and intense pain were obvious. It lifted two of the kneeling pack members, tearing them into pieces that disappeared into the fog. Only a lingering faint red mist marking the visceral violence remained. My attention was so fixated on this grotesque apparition I did not notice Bea rushing to stand before it in concerned confrontation. It was only when the grim black shade reacted in anger to her presence that I realized Bea was in danger.

I moved with urgency. Bea was the one person I had met whom I had any type of connection and understanding. The only person who might add to me and ease my distress. As I moved toward the damaged monster, pressure built in the wounds in my forehead and arm as though something was pushing its way out.

I reached Bea's side and screamed at the beast in determined bravery to attract its attention or drive it away in fear. The force of the scream and resultant release of emotion tore me open. My skin, or the essence of my being, was no longer potent enough to contain the Sideways People. Something pushed out, either in response to the monster or my own emotional release, and I felt it leave with a sharp pain and giddy shock. The most sudden and appalling birth imaginable.

Gray mist coalesced in front of me, seeping from the non-bleeding splits in my skin. Then it took form and moved forward to confront the beast with a familiar bouncing step and swinging upper body. It was Liz. I recognized her. Even after all this time. My first love was separate and facing danger.

I would have moved to protect her or tried to call her back into me. I swear it, but it was impossible. Liz's departure caused severe damage, and my body would not respond. Liz stood unperturbed in front of the beast, which released its fury and anger upon her with devastating attacks. Teeth and hand turned into razor blades and broken wine-bottle shapes, raining down and tearing into Liz. Liz did nothing apart from taking the force of anger, only giving a tremble of fear and pain when something brutal beyond comprehension was slung and ripped into her flesh.

Even as Liz endured this attack and shuddered as it performed brutal abuses upon her, the beast faded away as though the fury that drove it dissipated in the violent release. Liz remained as discrete and defined as she was when first released, and it soon became clear that the contest would end. The anvil that came from me could take the hammer beating upon it.

With a last gasp, the tortured child fell to its knees and started to shake and fold in upon itself. After this process started, it took little time to complete. With one last petulant strike of a small fading child hand, it disappeared.

I shook myself and moved in horror to the side of the gray revenant, in hope that I had made a mistake, that it was not Liz. I knew, though, that it was; a fragment of my soul had torn from me, leaving damage I could not yet define. Tears fell from my eyes. My hope abandoned me.

With trepidation, I moved to her side. "Liz," I said, voice breaking, "I am sorry, I am so sorry. I did not mean for you to have to come out here. It is wrong, you can come back in."

Liz turned her head to look at me with indifference and contempt. She made no move to re-enter, and I could not force her. Given I had allowed the environment to take her from me and place her in the path of such pain and harm, I could make no moral argument for her return. Not that I knew how to enable this reunion, even had I wished to.

Liz looked past me up the hill toward the sunlight (if that is what it was) and walked upward against the gradient. I tried to look after her, but the white light hurt my eyes. When she passed from my pleading sight, I tried to walk after her, fighting my feet and some base instinct. It was no use; the light frightened me too much, and my feet slid ever downwards on this foul earth, carrying me with them.

I gave up. It was pointless. Liz had gone. I looked down at my midriff, expecting to see a torn hole with both halves only attached through thin strips of flesh, with maybe a small section of spine remaining. My body should have shown the extent of psychic damage, the scar remained on my arm and the other wounds were unhealed but nothing new had been added. Nothing physically had changed.

I knew I was different and would never be the same. I could remember everything about Liz. Every word, every action, every memory, but it different. The departure had sundered our souls, snapping the synergy and linkage. Every memory remained, but I had no sense of her emotions or the feelings we had for each other. No sense she was still with me. Perfection had been flawed; the joy and closeness vanished. All gone.

The battle had destroyed my memory and containment of Liz, and I kept thinking of the moment after our last moment when she lay underneath me and did not move. One of the large green insects came unbidden out of the fog and flew into my mouth, spewing eggs and maggots into the protesting orifice. I spat the revolting mess onto the slimy ground and no more insects disturbed me.

I looked around for Bea and saw her standing, unmoving just a few feet away. She gazed at me with a sad, almost disappointed look in her eyes. I stumbled forward and threw my arms around her shoulders. With a last gulp, I collapsed against this supporting tower and broke into bitter sobs, burying my eyes into her shoulder. I was trying to block the world around me and cry my pain out, like a small child discovering the utter finality of death for the first time.

Which, in many ways, I was.

Chapter Eleven

He woke then, this other. The one who bore the most superficial similarity to me. He groaned as he shifted his body on the cold stone floor. His feet urged him toward a moldering door behind him, the invading fetid wind seemed to want to blow him outside. Still, he obstinately remained in this place, the one place in this land that he did not belong. All other places were open to him, wanted him urgently. No barriers or gates existed for him or stopped him from going anywhere else he desired. He yearned to be trapped here, felt he deserved it, and could not understand why the land had not chained him to the walls.

Again and again, he reviewed his memories to understand what else he could have done to earn this throne. He could think of nothing. Except... Maybe some fucker, some utter fucking cunt, had thought of something he hadn't, had fucking done something he couldn't. When he found this fucker, he was going to fuck his brains out of his fucking skull through his cunt eyeballs.

And now something had been fucking taken. Something had reduced one of his hard-edged proud fucking deeds and made him *less*. He did not know which. Fuck, there were so fucking many, but something had gone.

He tried to review his memories to understand what had happened and got lost in a temporary reverie as he pictured one young woman who he had lied to, coerced and kidnapped, before letting himself go to town on her. Man, he had shown his skill and dark savagery with that one. Hard-bitten cops had cried and vomited when they discovered her stripped flesh and realized what her last weeks had involved. How he had laughed and savored his victory when he heard that. They probably still had nightmares about that discovery whilst on their death beds.

Not that he could remember when he had done this, or even whether those cops were still alive. He had been somewhere else. He couldn't remember much about that place except those many times when he captured someone or a group and had his fun with them. No one forgot him. He was the absolute worst there was, the biggest bad ever. Except, of course, the other who *actually* belonged where he now lay. What the fuck had that person done? Surely nothing remained?

Most of his memories had faded. He dimly recalled he was once called Michael, although the press had given him a variety of flattering lurid sobriquets. The papers believed multiple people must be responsible for such a wide range of victims and tortures. Michael had always felt disappointed by this lack of perception. He felt he had always been consistent in his skill and approach, and the press should have realized one supreme artist unified all kills.

Michael had many unparalleled gifts. He could sense people capable of feeling true agony and was a master at trapping these unlucky ones. Once he had captured them, he was a genius at discovering what they feared most and the best route to inflict maximum suffering and horror. Then he did it again and again, until their flesh and spirit collapsed, and they left. He never released them himself. He loved their pain too much for that, but with enough damage, everyone went through the dark door to escape.

Except they hadn't escaped him, not really. When he had first got here, he had realized they could never leave him. They belonged to him. He had arrived with a vague sense of his name, the sweetest of memories, and apparently the trapped souls of those whom he had destroyed. He could summon them whenever he wanted to. Remembering a victim, their pain and how he had beaten them would cause darkness to form around him, which would eventually take the outline of that remembered person.

These specters still feared him and trembled at their memories. Obviously, he had tried to continue their torture and destruction in this new place, but found their bodies could not suffer additional damage. However, it brought him pleasure to summon them and laugh in their faces. He would look into their eyes and savor the memories, knowing they also remembered. The looks on their faces as they relived the pain and torment, was a sweet release. He relished this power. When he had finished laughing at them, he would force them back inside with a promise that he would call them out again soon, just to finish reminiscing on the good ol' days. They always shrieked in protest and tried to break free, but he never allowed them freedom and trapped them again within his flesh prison.

That was it. That was what was different. One of his specters had somehow broken free. He had fucking lost somehow. He concentrated and felt within himself who it was. It was one young child, a girl of about six years.

She had been shopping with her mother for some new clothes and other bits and bobs. He had watched her, noting her skippy step and the absolute trust she had in her mother and the whole environment around her. She had soft, wide eyes and a fluting curious voice that asked questions about everything. He made her regret that trust, to regret that curiosity about the world around her. Her mother had released her hand for the briefest of seconds to turn over and admire some cloth, and he had swooped. He had grabbed the girl's hand and moved his finger to his lips in conspiratorial silence while winking in fellowship at this stupid bitch. She had trusted and followed him to where he took her. Which was a place where he could express his unsurpassed skill.

Afterwards, he had been unsure who he was punishing. The worthless girl or her negligent mother. The mother would know all her life she was to blame for everything that happened to her daughter. It would make every waking moment, every exhalation, one of complete torment. Michael had resolved to ensure the mother had full, in-depth understanding of what had been done. He had repeatedly asked the young girl where she lived during his fun time and laughed and cut her, regardless of the answers.

After discovering her parents' address, he had dumped her mutilated corpse outside their house in the middle of the night. They would discover this masterful artwork and would never be free of the image. It would make their pain so much worse. Everyone would see it. Everyone would know his sheer, savage dark might.

He had called her out sometimes, this young girl. Told her she was bad, that she had deserved what he had done and then explain that because of her carelessness, her Mummy and Daddy had lived in pain every day for the rest of their lives. Was she happy now? The specter would always scream in anguish and try to strike him with the one hand he hadn't sawed off. He would let her futilely flap to show that she did not have any power and could change nothing. Then he would send her back into the dark within, where the others waited and wailed.

Now she had gone. She was free. It was all over for her. He urgently willed her back inside, the surrounding darkness sped off in different directions to hook and retrieve her, nothing happened. He was furious. This was a debt he would collect. Someone, somewhere, would suffer for this. People did not know what suffering was until Michael taught them the meaning of the word.

He concentrated again and sent the darkness out from him in expanding circles and felt something. It was at the outer edge of this land. That fog seemed to have dissipated in one small area and the air had become cleaner. The girl had achieved freedom there somehow.

There were some of those whining pack animals nearby, but also a man who was different somehow. He was sobbing bitterly onto the shoulder of a woman that also didn't belong there. Michael's darkness probed the pair more. It could not read or understand the woman. Could not interpret her form or presence. But the man had others inside him. Others who were seeping outward through his wounds and skin.

This monster, this Michael, concentrated hard on the darkness, which was clear as day to him but invisible to everyone else. He concentrated on the presence and feel of the black until he felt it solidify near these two. Grunting with effort, he imagined himself spreading along this line of darkness and then being solid at the other end, near where he wanted to be.

With a last burst of ferocious concentration, he traveled and moved.

Chapter Twelve

I was crying. There was no way I could prevent tears or accept the trauma of separation. Bea stood opposite me as my arms clutched her shoulders. After a pause, her hands lifted and gently patted my back in a soothing manner.

I felt old. *Torn.* Nothing good was ever going to happen again. The future stretched out and all it contained was torment. I had been traveling for an indeterminate period and had not reached anywhere. My forehead and arm had painful wounds but did not release blood or heal. Dreams caused red welts to cover my flesh, which ached and tore at me.

Worst still was the sensation that I was losing the Sideways People. One second, I had been with Laura and transcended every definition of love. The next, transported to a land where the memories and sensations of the Sideways People could be lost. Where I could take no solace in or even feel their love. Something had already ejected one out of my body and soul, with no hope of remedy.

If a kindly god had offered me the opportunity to lie down and die, I would have accepted. I wanted everything over and done with. Suffering such frustration and pain was pointless, and I would not betray my Sideways People by losing the prize of what we shared.

I ignored my feet, which were urging me on with my journey—
Further down. Deeper in.

And lay on the ground willing death upon me. Nothing happened. I opened my eyes and saw Bea standing over me. Her face was unreadable. Her stance, unmoving. She just stood there, statuesque, with clear expectation that I would continue my journey to my unknown destination.

Then she moved to one side, revealing someone new and distinct. He was short, dressed casually in old, faded jeans and a worn t-shirt covered a large paunch. He had a round face and dark eyes. The air smelled of copper and I immediately knew him for what he was. A monster in human form. In this place, it was obvious, there could be no doubt.

"Who are you?" he demanded. The words an accusation and declaration of war. He had no accent. Unlike everyone else in this land who seemed to communicate through the fog with words appearing directly in the ears, I saw his lips move and felt the words come from him. I ignored him, hoping to express disgust through silence.

He stepped forward then, moving toward me. I looked at him in idle interest rather than any fear. His shape seemed indistinct. The color of his sallow, rotund flesh appeared to leak into an aura of darkness that bled around him. This darkness, this inky black that surrounded him like armor, appeared to be growing in size, making his skin appear darker and more metallic.

My form responded to him. Pressure built up around the wounds in my arm and forehead. I could feel gray-silver clouds appearing at these wound edges. The red shapes covering the rest of my body stretched outward as though inside things were trying to push free. Kevin was being forced toward the edges of these doors. Once pushed out, I knew he could never return, and I stood to prevent this expulsion.

I moved toward the grotesque man with sudden fury in my being. My intent to incapacitate him triggered something in the land, as though it responded to our mood. Everything went silent and then suddenly there was a ferocious roar as the vast multitude of insects burst fearfully away in hordes. A great plague went in every direction, blocking out all light, and the only noise was the sound of their determined flight.

We stood and looked at each other, surprised. Then his face twisted with pure rage, his hands hooked into claws that reached out for me, legs crouched to enable him to pounce forward. The armoring darkness solidified around him while tendrils spread outward and took forms that suggested mutilated flesh. I moved backward, raising protecting hands and felt my resolve and barriers weaken. Kevin, or one of my other Sideways People, started to push through my edges and open wounds to defend me. I shook my head in denial, but knew conflict was inevitable.

The land itself stopped us. I knew then that it always meant for Myself and The Other to destroy each other. But first we had to know the truth about each other's lives.

As our defenses and aggressions rose, the fog solidified around our bodies, holding us in check and rooted to the ground. Shapes and forms shifted in the mist behind us, infused with colors and took presence. The movements played out our lives for all to see.

The mist surrounding me played out the Sideways People, those that I have loved and chosen to keep with me forever. My relationships with the Sideways People, how I became what each wanted, every one of them, and the final perfect moments in our relationship were mist displayed in silvery-gray colors. Michael looked at them with a surprised air whilst stealing appraising glances in my direction. I looked at the mist around Michael to understand exactly what he was—

Jesus fucking wept!

It was impossible to understand half the things there, but I knew I was witnessing willful degradation and pain on a scale beyond comprehension.

These horrific acts being repeated and performed on legions of men, women, and children across a depraved lifetime. The why of it I could not understand, nor would I ever want to. My body reacted to my distress by trying to vomit violently.

"That's it? That's all? Nothing else?" The Other asked in clipped and startled tones. He jabbed his forehead toward me with every word, as though to emphasize his anger. I knew him now, had seen what he wanted more than anything, but did not see how it involved me. It was the most perverse and intimate introduction imaginable. I knew his name was Michael, also knew he would never understand what I had done or why.

The Sideways People, our feelings and beautiful integration, were not things that existed in his world. He must have interpreted me and my actions as though of a common garden, inadequate, serial killer. One who could not apply the imagination and skill he possessed.

With each of us having a greater understanding of the other, the fog released its grip. I sagged and slipped to my knees. Traumatized by the visions. The Sideways People no longer threatened to escape my body. That pleased me but also caused fear, as I knew I would need their protection. Michael observed my distress for a moment longer, as though ensuring it wasn't a trap, before striding forward confidently, a wide smile spreading from cheek to cheek. When close enough, he swung his foot backward before arching it forward, so his shin smashed across my mouth. I flipped over and tried to run down the slope, scrabbling to my feet as I did so.

Michael caught me easily and reached around to grab my throat. With my neck held, he punched the back of my head. I saw the soil rise to my face, to my nostrils and smelled blood and the faint taint of rot that clung to the spoiled grass and frigid ground. I grew afraid and tried to reach inside to release one of the Sideways People, hoping to gain cover or protection from the summoned angel.

The assault stopped suddenly. I spent a moment assuring myself I was okay, before looking over my shoulder to see what had saved me. Bea was striding toward Michael, who reacted as though she was holy fire and burned. He would make sudden jerks in my direction as though he wanted to break free and then twitch away when Bea moved to intercept him.

"Alright." The words shot from thinned lips that had pulled back to reveal feral teeth. "For now. I'll go. But I will be back. I always come back. Then I'll teach you. You can't be the one that is better than me. You won't even get through the fucking barriers." He stepped back and slowly shrouded himself in black armor. With a blink, he disappeared as though he had never been.

Chapter Thirteen

That Other. I knew everything about him now. His name, what drove him, what he wanted to be. The fog had told me everything about him. I knew I was lucky. Things would have been unpleasant if Bea wasn't there. The adrenaline still flowed through my body, making me nauseous with its demands. I was glad I was alive. I had even been willing to call forth and abandon a Sideways Person to have them defend me.

I turned toward Bea, hoping she would see the gratitude in my eyes. The mist and robe shrouded her face. Her eyes and expression could not be seen or understood. It occurred that she might have seen the details of my life in the fog and misunderstood the display. I stopped and looked closely, trying to understand whether anything was wrong.

She stood in silence for a second before I heard the words sighed, "We are there. Time to move to the next place."

Her expression was rigid and unreadable. It was impossible to feel confident until I understood her intentions. She was trying to guide and help me, so I looked around to understand her meaning.

Then, I noticed it. Looking upward, the fog was still thick and illuminated by that awful burning light. The view downwards, however, was different. On prior occasions, when scanning downwards, the sky, ground and fog had merged into a sea of dull colors. Now it had changed. I could see the ground for a few inches forward, but then nothing. The fog suspended in the air like a thick curtain from the ground upward, rendering everything hidden. Swirls moved upward and downwards, but sight through was impossible.

I tried to move my hands through the fog. Each time, my hands were pushed back when they tried to penetrate the thick curtain of smoke. I looked around at Bea, an unspoken question on my lips.

Bea's features were not visible, but the tilt of her head showed uncertainty. She would step forward before stopping, as though expecting me to lead through the thick fog. At each pause, she would nod her head at me and then the barrier to demand I move forward. Each time I would flap my hand at the white curtain, only for it to be thrust back toward my body. When this happened, Bea would start forward for a couple of steps before demanding I try again with silent gestures and looks.

After several attempts, Bea appeared to accept I could not move through this line of thick white fog and returned to my side. She turned her head toward me, and I got a brief glimpse of her face. Her eyes looked at me but appeared to be thinking of something else, musing about other things, dreaming of different times. For a second, her face looked regretful and filled with sorrow. Then her eyes focused on me again and her stance became more determined.

Bea spat on her right palm and smeared this watery substance over her entire hand before reaching out to the curtain of white fog. Her hand passed into this barrier. The unseen force did not push it back, and the hand remained in sight, with the fog around it becoming translucent. The skin and flesh appeared to peel away as it passed into the mist and became skeletal. Bea reached out for me with her left hand and, taking one last gulping sigh, pulled us both into the barrier.

My flesh was no longer rejected, but pulled in. The sensation was of being buffeted backward and forward, as though by violent waves. My clothes stuck to my doughy flesh as though wet, and for alarming seconds

I could not breathe and struggled for air in desperation. Throughout all of this, I was aware of Bea holding my hand and dragging me on. I ignored my empty lungs as they burned in desperation for oxygen and concentrated on the hand gripping mine. To diffuse the panic, my thoughts remembered the Sideways People and our moments of intimacy. When this proved insufficient to calm my desperation, my thoughts returned to Laura and our ultimate moment of perfection together.

With a last surge and with lungs that were sore and cramped, the fog expelled me. The release took me somewhere new, and things had already turned very different.

Chapter Fourteen

The barrier pushed me out, and my feet slid forward, dragging me downwards. The sudden jerking motion caused me to lose my balance, and I fell hard onto my back. I noticed something as I fell. My shirt had combined with my flesh all the way round my middle. I thought it had got wet and stuck to me all the way round, but when I tried to pull it free, I realized it had somehow fused with my skin. It was irritating; the shirt rubbed against me in many places, causing soreness and red patches.

Injuries sustained before this transmutation of my form remained. My forehead and arm had the non-bleeding wounds and red welts covered my body.

Passing through the barriers into a new place had only added to my list of woes, resolving nothing. Healing felt unlikely here. Time's passage was a mystery. Sleep was different and unnatural. I had laid down with shut eyes but not slept. Proper night did not exist.

I looked at Bea to reassure myself she was still there. She stood behind me, unchanging and unchanged since I had first met her. A squinted look up the hill revealed no hint of the barrier, just that painful white light smeared across the horizon. This light silhouetted Bea and cast dark shadows across her face and robe. She moved forward, making gentle shushing noises as she helped me stand. After I regained my feet, she tugged at my shirt as though to check whether she could separate it from my form, but seemed to accept its fusion when she saw my skin pull outward.

I looked around. It did not surprise me to realize that my environment had changed. In fact, it surprised me it had not changed more. Something had happened, and the normal rules and judgments of my original world no longer applied.

Around us the grass was darker than it had been, and sparser. The soil itself was dark and had a yellow tinge to it. The fog had cleared and the air smelled different. Less rot, more organic, as though vast quantities of bodily secretions and shameful emissions had spilled and been sown into the soil. Upon detecting this new stench, my stomach again turned and threatened to release its contents. I ignored this; I had gotten used to the nausea and knew my stomach had nothing it could release. The gradient downwards was steeper and more demanding. It required effort to stand still without sliding downwards, so I walked on with Bea by my side.

Other things had changed. There were no insects or trees. The only vegetative matter I could see was the grass underfoot. The noises that filled the air were different. Now there was a faint sound of sighs, gasps, and moans. Sudden bursts of violent wind carried this noise to me in quick snatches that disappeared without warning.

This new place had its own inhabitants, which was more disturbing than the pack-people I had traveled with before. These denizens sprang out of the air behind me or to the side, making noises of excessive need and desire while twisting their heads from side to side. Desperately seeking something or someone. Sometimes they would stop and examine me as though they wanted to approach, but they always realized I was different and moved on with no backward glance.

I examined the first who stopped to look me over. She was an exaggerated female and unashamedly nude. Enlarged breasts and voluptuous features, genitalia uncovered and displayed. An altered face made her look less human, though. She had angular and undefined features somehow, and nothing, except for the most basic comprehension of face color, was distinguishable apart from her eyes and mouth. Some unseen designer had enlarged her eyes, but made them robotic. They looked like large representations of normal eyes but made of brilliant glass. There were no pupils at the center, just wide circles of dark green. Her mouth was a jagged edged "o" of brilliant white perfect teeth. The face was expressionless, with no understandable emotion or humanity displayed; indeed, it would have been difficult to identify this one from others of its kind.

These people, if they were people, appeared to roam without constraint or purpose. Sometimes they would move uphill toward the light. Sometimes, they would individually appear running and scanning around in desperation. Other times, however, multiples could be seen, and things would then get bizarre.

If one, or higher numbers, of this group of people or creatures saw another of their kind, they would run and seize each other, forcing sexual acts and genitalia upon each other. Throughout this, they would shake and shudder, rolling their heads and shoulders in a grim and sordid simulation of ecstasy, while issuing theatrical fake moans of pleasure. Sometimes a third or more of their kind would join in this unpleasant frenzy and they would continue their abuse of each other.

Their presence, and the ability to see them, seemed to be linked to the gusts of wind. When the wind blew hard, they would appear and if they saw each other, they would seize upon each other. Consent appeared to be a given or unnecessary. Sometimes they would try to speak, to encourage each other to ever greater peaks of ecstasy. Their lips would appear to close over the perfect white teeth in a weak copy of speech, but there was no link between their lips moving and the scraps of grunting, orgasm degrading conversation. When the wind stopped blowing; they would vanish.

I saw nothing worthy or even titillating about these people. No need to interact with or try to understand their pointless activities. Their actions appeared emotionless and answered no need. It goes without saying; they aroused nothing in me. I preferred it when the wind did not blow, so I did not have to see them. Plus it was easier to make progress.

When the gusts tore in violence across the land, I found it hard to keep on my feet and almost fell several times. Inexorably, I tried to continue downwards and when left to my own devices, I would travel in a straight line, figuring this was likely the quickest route to my unknown destination.

I would have carried on walking in this straight line until I found some kind of end point, but Bea appeared to know where I should go. With gentle gestures, she would point me in new directions or head toward an area of ground that was indistinguishable from others. I would head where she showed and when we reached one area, I would look at her and then either head straight downwards or go where she pointed to next.

I wanted to talk to Bea. To further build the intimacy and closeness I had felt earlier, when I had rested my sorrowful head on her shoulder. Maybe she needed to care for someone. I don't think the history or stories that the fog displayed had changed her feelings. She spoke with little sighs about helping me—

Go down. Go further in,

Or—

Getting me to where I needed to go.

Other than that, she said little and was unresponsive to probing looks or direct questions. It was hard to read her. She always walked close by and frequently looked across. Her expression seemed tender, concerned, and sad. It was only much later that I realized I had only the vaguest idea of what she looked like. That is not unusual; as I said earlier, I am not motivated by physical looks or presence but more about the richness of the interior tapestry of a person's life.

I think Bea intended for me to meet other people within that place, so I could understand the nature of the land I traversed. It cannot be coincidence we happened upon the one person/creature capable of communicating or telling their story. We were heading downwards, occasionally weaving from side-to-side with no apparent destination. In sudden bursts the wind would start blowing and gusting around and we would see the bizarre denizens of this unnatural place appear, notice each other and intimately grapple in forced, dispassionate fashion before disappearing with the wind.

My feet continued their ordered journey onwards and downwards, feeling a compulsion that they could not settle on the ground here. Occasionally, I would fight their determined urging.

It was on one of these times that we met someone different. I had stopped to cling onto Bea. To take strength and determination from her. For reassurance that I was important to her, and she would be with me forever. As I held her in desperate need, the wind blew around us and another person appeared—someone I felt I was meant to speak to.

It was a middle-aged man with a round face and kind looking gray eyes that twinkled with unshed tears. He faced us, standing on bowed legs, dressed in a smart black suit and crisp red tie. The man looked indistinguishable from those you see commuting to work every morning, except smarter dressed than most. Now and then, his right hand would dart toward his crotch and start stroking the swelling area.

We approached, Bea trailing behind me. I stood opposite him for a moment before kneeling down. I felt little fear, but his sudden appearance and clear expectation of our presence was slightly unnerving.

"Who are you?" The wind seemed to strip the words out of my mouth and carry them toward him.

"What does that matter?" was the response. The voice was even and masculine. The sounds appeared in deep, measured tones. It was disconcerting to hear the words and a few seconds later, see the lips close and open as though forming them. The eyes carried on staring at me, glimmering brightly with unshed tears while his right hand got bolder and started fumbling at his fly to reach inside.

"How did you get here?" I asked again. I was trying to understand my journey into this land, maybe even identify some way out. But the question appeared to flummox him. His expression may not have changed, but his stance drooped and became dismayed and disorientated. The shoulders sagged and his neck dropped. His eyes remained fixed on me, though. The lips opened and closed, unconnected to the words I heard.

"I belong here." Again spoken in the same clear, even tones, but with an undertone that suggested sorrow and sadness.

"I don't," I blurted in urgent interruption. "Even my feet insist I leave. There is nothing here for me." This unknown man fell silent at the interruption and carried on holding his current stance with his hands fumbling inside his suit fly. Then his head appeared to change direction and for a second his eyes appeared to pass over me and look at Bea. Then his attention centered itself upon me again.

"I had a wonderful wife," the forlorn man said in a wistful voice. "I loved her so much. Swore every oath of faithfulness to her, and she was faithful to me, no matter what temptations life put in her way. I loved her and the children she gave me. Then a new girl started in my office. Young. Blond hair, and a tight butt. A bit stupid. Thought I was the big cheese and important. Thought that screwing me would be the key to advancement. So, I fucked her. Felt so much adrenaline. Started fucking her friends. Then

I fucked every other available woman in the office. Got a disease, a serious one. Gave it to my wife. She left me. Took my children. Carried on giving it to others. I never saw them again. I betrayed her for the sake of momentary pleasure." After a long pause, he said, "I belong here. You can only stay here if you belong here. The only way to leave is through the barrier. To cross, you will need to belong to where you are traveling to or to be helped through." As he spoke, his hands started rhythmically moving backward and forward within his trousers.

It baffled me. I shook my head to show how puzzled I was.

"Is it your lust that brought you here or makes you belong here? That's not me. I was never that banal. I gave my body to others to bring them pleasure or give something that they needed. They mattered to me, and I wanted them to have something from me." I paused and looked at him again. "Not sure I understand how you came here or what this means."

"I stopped thinking about people as people. They were just objects I could try to satiate myself with. I didn't even care if I was infecting them. Only the sensation of possessing them mattered. Did not even care about myself. From there, it's a straight route to here." Again, these words formed an unbroken monotone of even notes. There was something about him. The way he accepted what was due to him, that he belonged here, moved me.

"Can I help you?" I asked in response. This place seemed empty and pointless. The people (or whatever they were) appeared to gain no pleasure in their existence or activities. Maybe I could take him with me. Show him other things and explain different types of relationships. I doubted he could become a Sideways Person or that I could build a significant level of relationship with him, but we might share something. Maybe if I had another new friend besides Bea, I would forget my misery a little. Not feel the pain from my wounds so much. We could look after each other until we found a way out. Maybe we could alter his future at the same time as healing me. Those hopes were dashed by his response.

"You can't leave where you belong," he said, shaking his head. "You can go somewhere you belong to more or you can remove the things that make you belong where you are. Maybe someone could take you onwards. I don't know. But I can't just leave. That makes no sense."

I carried on kneeling there opposite him. I don't know why or for how long.

The wind blew in a new direction. The unnamed man first lost his clothes, becoming young with a massive erection. His teary eyes turned glassy and reflective, mouth opened in a wide fake smile. As every denizen of this part of this land was, he became, shedding all humanity. Other creatures of this part of the land appeared, and they jumped upon each other in an orgy of impersonal penetration and groping. Then the wind stopped, and they disappeared.

I looked around in unease, hoping that somehow, I had just lost sight of him. That was not what had happened; he had faded away with the wind, as though he had never been there. I sat there trying to understand his words and how they might apply to me. There was a mistake. There had been no route to here for me. I was as different to that man as chalk was to cheese. That much was clear.

Chapter Fifteen

I was not the only one who felt there had been a mistake. Someone crueler than I could possibly imagine being was having a rare moment of reflection.

What on earth had that been? What had happened there? Michael paced backward and forward in fury, his fat, round face grimacing and tightening in anger. It should have been easy. No mess, no fooling. *That little man should be screaming my name in horror rather than freely walking around. He didn't even realize how fucking lucky he was. Maybe that prick thought he was my equal. Fuck that! That would not continue.*

But he could not be! He could not own the center! He belonged somewhere here. That was clear, maybe near the center. But not in this room. Not above me. Who the fuck was with him? She did not belong here. Was that how he crossed the first barrier? Maybe they did not block beings like her. Maybe they were inconsequential to her kind. That might enable his progress, but why make the effort?

He stood by the fireplace in the room he wanted to call his own. Feeling the icy wind coming down from the fireplace and blow through his form. The wind changed him as he mused. It blew through him and elongated and changed his body, so it resembled a gigantic dark serpent that stretched and coiled around the room. Michael considered where that Other belonged, his temporary snake scales glimmering dark in the guttering light. Wherever it was, he would only get there if Michael allowed him. Michael would let the Other get to the right destination and chain him to the ground there. After, of course, a little educational play.

Oh, but he wanted to teach that cunt a lesson. That boy, that weak pussy, had stood against him as his equal and dared to look down his nose at him. He wanted to re-confront that fucking cunt in the flesh and teach him who the boss was. He knew he could make that Other scream in fear. Had felt the panic when he had looped his fist around that weakling's neck. He enjoyed that. Knew things were possible here that biology would not allow in the regular world. The land and atmosphere would join in his fun.

But she frightened him. He could barely look at her—she had blazed with the brightness of the sun and burned him. He knew he feared her. That galled him. That fucking galled him. Something in fucking female form driving him, *him*, away. Women feared him. That was the natural order; the way things should be.

Also, what happened to that aspect of his soul that had broken free? That young girl he had tortured and trapped without the possibility of release. Gone now. No longer contained. Even the air where she had escaped smelled sweet and clean. That could not happen again. Things had to change. Something had to be different.

He moved to the corner of the room and stood there in silent thought. The wind blew again through his form, shifting and shaping his cells into new positions, new purposes. He sent his thoughts out to that Other and his guide and realized they were closer to the middle.

Michael felt the fury building inside, twisting around his insides before bursting out in white light through his skull into an incoherent scream. He turned to the stone wall and punched his knuckles again and again into it. The walls themselves responded to the violence of his intent. They grew spikes and daggers, things that cut flesh wherever his fist landed. They stabbed him, causing sharp bursts of pain, bleeding and damage to his hands. After one punch, a severed finger slithered unnoticed down the wall before being swallowed by the shadows near the cold floor. Michael did not mind the loss. Was pleased, saw the transmutations and cruel growths in the walls as proof he belonged in this room, that secretly it was his.

Of course, Michael knew where those two were now. He knew everything about this land and everyone in it. He could go there straightaway if wanted. Nowhere was closed to him. But this needed examination. This needed to be thought about. He wanted the Other, and the lady with him, dead and tortured, and within him and tortured some more. Still, his thoughts contained a note of concern.

Sometimes in the past he had needed to be patient. If he had wanted a particular person, or if there was powerful protection around a target, he patiently stalked them first. Followed them around, inserting himself into their lives. Sometimes becoming a close friend and confidante, other times being an unnoticed shape in the background. He had enjoyed both approaches.

When he had become a friend, he had asked them to go where he needed and enjoyed their shock as they realized he had betrayed them. When he had remained a hidden shadow, he had gathered all the required information unnoticed and reveled in the mastery as he constructed plans that made the victim his.

Things needed to be different here. The land and atmosphere would not allow him to pretend to be anything else. He could not blindside them and approach them as some kind of friend. He was not sure he could gather useful information about them, nor that he would be unnoticed if he tried to follow them. In fact, he doubted that would be possible. After all, Michael was as different to the other residents as the Sun was to the Moon. Maybe a test of their strength would be suitable? Maybe he should just understand their capabilities from a distance and decide what to do? Sounded sensible. Sounded tactical.

He slid backward through his memories and the thoughts and feelings of those he had trapped inside. Some felt more appropriate to face the Other in that part of the world. They were the ones he had dehumanized and raped, or the ones where he had lured them with false promises of satisfaction. He relived their pain and concentrated on the methods he had used to break and defeat them. As he did so, a black cloud surrounded his arms. Without flinching, Michael slammed his right hand into a wall, knowing it would grow mutilating hooks and cutting edges. It did so, and his red blood spurted outward against the dank stone surface. The black cloud disappeared into his wrist above the gushing wound and sprayed outward, contained within his blood.

The liquid clung to and glimmered on the wall like an obscene black mirror. Michael viewed it with satisfaction, any pain controlled and hidden by the cold, cruel sneer his lips twisted into. Thinking of those selected victims, he concentrated and pushed them outward from his form, through the damaged hand and spurting blood into the suspended black, reflective shape. The surface appeared to move, with the victims forming within, their surfaces tinged red and black. Once passed a certain point of completion, they would drop onto the floor and carry on their unnatural creation, their mouths moving in agonized cries of pain and horror.

These were the ones it felt most appropriate to send there. Michael liked to think he always did what was suitable and proper. They were a multitude, far more than this Other could handle, and he felt confident the released revenants would be victorious.

That Other and Michael had seen each other's magical number of victims. Michael knew he could summon more revenants than anyone, far more than the Other. Even the obvious number advantage excluded the fact Michael had done more to those he had absorbed. Incessant and ongoing cruelty had made them madder and more furious. The beaten child that had broken free without permission was still just the remnants of a child. These carefully selected ones would be very different.

If these summoned beings were insufficient, Michael would know he had underestimated the other two. The only possible way Michael could see them surviving was if that woman interceded more directly than he thought possible or somehow appealed to other powers to intervene. The Other might release a few specters for defense, but not enough to stand against Michael's legion. Either way, Michael would know more and be in a stronger position.

Michael took a second to survey those beings he had expelled from his form, nodding in satisfaction as he noticed the mutilations and tortures he had inflicted. Michael strutted up and down in front of them, like a General inspecting his troops, reminding them of his control and how he had gained them in first place. When he passed by, they would stop moving and try to hide from his sight. Occasionally, in silence and utter futility, they would plead for freedom. Michael laughed at this.

After a few sweeps, he grew satisfied with the control and impact he had on them. Erect and proud in front of his damned cadre, he willed them to destroy that Other and his companion. In silence, the shades waited around him until a powerful gust of wind blew them on their way. Michael stood in smug satisfaction, waiting for the outcome. He was certain they would win and certain they would return to his body after victory. This place, this room, was his and no one would ever take it from him.

Chapter Sixteen

I had finished with the transforming sex creature and puzzled through his words. This place was a prison, and people transformed according to their weaknesses and sins. Beyond that, I knew nothing. How people got transformed, how I got here, and why I wasn't healing, were still mysteries.

The shirt, now fused to my flesh, was another impossible event. I had tried tugging it harder, hoping it was damp and stuck, rather than merged with my flesh. The sharp sensation of pain and the sight of my body distending with the cloth convinced me we had somehow become one.

Bea had moved closer after I finished speaking to that punished man. She seemed to seek my contact and, at one stage, placed her arms around me in a fervent embrace. I think the change in her perception had occurred after she had heard me talking about sex and love-making.

During the embrace, she seemed to want to draw me to the floor, to the damp, stenchful ground. I complied, but the draw on my feet got too strong. When I relayed this to Bea, she made noises of whimpering distress before applying gentle force to keep me from moving onwards. I reached toward her and kissed the side of her face gently, breathing in her scent and pressing my cheek against hers. She felt so familiar. I closed my eyes and remembered all the people I loved and held within me.

I opened my eyes and looked at her, noticing the tears that traced down her face. Clearly saw features that looked familiar for some reason. The compulsion in my feet was undeniable. It forced me to move again. She looked so hurt and worried that sympathetic tears rose in my eyes in answer. Bea stood in solidarity next to me, keeping her right hand gripped in mine. When I marched downwards, she kept hold of this bond to prevent further progress, even jerking on my arm and motioning upward toward that painful bleak light. It was only when she saw I had no choice that she agreed with a small nod to proceed further downwards.

I kept my hand in hers while considering how to show I appreciated her. My thoughts turned to bringing her joy in this bleak and forsaken place. She seemed to carry a weight and could not let her true self show. I considered what she wanted, how I could be what she needed, and while I mused on this matter, I smelled and felt the stench of wrongness in the air.

Bea also felt it, and we looked down the hill. There were no creatures around, the wind was still. It was still obvious that someone or something was heading toward us. We could not see them, could hear nothing apart from the usual distant cries and moans, but something was different. The air felt tight around our skin, making it difficult to breathe.

Without warning, they burst into being around us. They filled the air with screams of anguish and pain. They were similar in form to the child revenant that we had seen earlier–their forms dark and showing torture. I knew Michael was responsible and had murdered, assumed and controlled them somehow. Too many to count quickly, but they must have been more than a dozen. Some of them walked, some of them crawled, some of them hopped on only one leg because the other was missing, or they had other cruel mutilations. All had suffered beyond normal human inventiveness.

The manner of their death had imprinted upon these vengeful and forlorn souls. Broken forms were twisted and bound with chains, many had sliced and torn genitalia, some had hooks passed through wrists and hands. Many had all this done and more. None could have deserved it.

On some faces, I saw the remnants of trust and innocence overwritten by intense pain and anguish.

One lady had her arms bound behind her back and crawled forward with ungainly balance on her knees. Her mouth drooled blood and saliva where violence had smashed her teeth. Some of these white shards were driven through the side of her cheek with the roots protruding in obscene v shapes. The others also oozed violence and the need to do unto others as they had received. Their arms raised, reaching whilst the air thickened with the intent of blood.

I barely had time to raise my hand or gasp in concern when I felt one of my angels rush outward in my defense, seeping through the cuts in my body and expelled from my lungs. I had expected Kevin to burst free to defend me. In hindsight, I am not sure why. Liz had been my first genuine love, and the first dragged outside. Kevin had been my second. But my Sideways People were too mystical to follow such mundane logic.

The angel who coalesced in gray form was Nancy. When we first met, she had been married to a cruel and ungrateful man. Nancy was attractive, with brunette hair framing a heart-shaped face. She had shapely angles. Her husband had not recognized her beauty or appreciated his prize. She gave no impression of joy when we first met, appearing instead to view the world through a thick, unemotional mask.

I had sensed she kept so much inside and wanted to release everything. One night I had walked into her office, told her she was the most beautiful woman in the world and that I wanted her. I trembled with desire while speaking. She had moved to me, kissed me with violence and lust, and then stripped our clothes and had me on the office floor.

All Nancy needed from me was pure want and desire. She had ridden and taken me with undenied passion and naked hunger. After a while, after being convinced she was beautiful and wanted, she had confronted her husband and said she was leaving for someone else who made her happy. After ending her marriage, she came to my flat to start our new life together. She had looked so strong and satisfied, I realized this was the apex of our relationship and strangled her to bring her within. We'd been together ever since.

Now she stood separately, in front of me. She had her back to me, and I longed to turn her around and see the message contained within her eyes. Instead, she faced those ghoulish and damaged specters that threatened me with harm and spread her arms wide as though to embrace them all.

Those beings that could see her stepped forward and ripped her with either their hands or the chains enmeshed into their forms. When they got close enough to my released angel, they shone with yellow light and gradually broke down into small fragments. Nancy still had to bear their assaults. Like children, they struck at the one trying to heal them. All the specters focused their attention to Nancy, drawn like moths to the yellow light that consumed them. As they broke down into fading chunks, they traversed through the light that now linked their crumbling forms to Nancy, where they merged into her.

Even though they numbered a legion and despite the apparent slowness of their disintegration, the confrontation did not last long. Michael's released victims became frenzied in their intentions and needs. Scrambled toward release with intense urgency. After mere moments, all had gone.

Nancy remained after defeating and freeing all the enemies but dropped to her knees and crossed gray arms across her midriff as though embracing all those inside. At no point did she try to turn her head or eyes toward me, nor attempt any form of communication.

I moved with speed this time. I had no intention of abandoning Nancy like I had Liz and kneeled behind her and moved my chest forward and downwards, so it rested on her back.

"Come home," I said into her ear. "Come back home. You will never be alone when you are with me, and I will treasure you forever." I stopped speaking and wrapped gentle arms around her waist while pulling her toward me. It hurt beyond belief when I heard the sobs that came from her as my arms passed through her insubstantial form without touching; I couldn't bring her back home.

Nancy became less and less corporeal, the thickness and depth of the gray that composed her form became lighter and less noticeable. Some of this gray seemed to flow down her arms into the soil, whereas some of it leeched sideways into the surrounding air. Gradually, she passed into utter translucence, and I knew she had gone.

The land we were on appeared to appreciate the sacrifice I had made. Where Nancy had kneeled, the grass grew green and healthy in seconds. The air lost its greasy, diseased organic smell. I stood and breathed deeply. It was as bad as Liz had been. The separation had reduced and maimed me in ways to a depth that no one else could ever understand.

I had expelled someone I loved, rendering our previous relationship unimportant. I had betrayed something sacred and holy. The price I paid for doing so was correspondingly and justifiably huge. No longer could I feel her closeness, share her emotions and triumphs. If I closed my eyes and concentrated, I could still feel the bare mechanics of our relationship. Never again would I be able to close my eyes and understand the world through her or experience the savage intensity of her emotions when she had arrived at my flat that night, intending to start a new life in my arms.

I stood and looked round for Bea. She stood a few feet down the slope from me. Her face had turned stony again and her eyes were distant and determined. With a sharp jerk of her head, she showed we should carry on our downward journey. My face crumpled with disappointment and rejection, but I followed her anyway. What else could I do? Who else was there?

Chapter Seventeen

Bea headed downwards, striding toward a pre-determined destination. Before this, she walked to the area where Nancy had disappeared and clutched a handful of the sweeter air as though to capture it. She snatched at me with her spare hand, grabbing my forearm just above the wrist before forcing me downwards after her.

Bea's force dragged me along like an errant and naughty schoolboy. While stumbling in her wake, I looked around at the desolate land. On random occasions, the wind would blow hard, and the strange, barely human, glass-eyed creatures would appear, indulging in their impersonal mechanical rutting rituals before disappearing when the gusts stopped.

As we moved downwards, their interruptions on our journey became less frequent and when we saw them, they appeared insubstantial and distant. Still, I pondered them and their form again and remembered the conversation I had had with one of their numbers.

They appeared to be, or at least *had* been, people who had given themselves over to sex and the pursuit thereof. Now this hunger consumed them, forcing a repeat of pointless acts which brought no pleasure with random, non-connected individuals they would never see again. As they dehumanized those they had fucked, something had dehumanized them. Their eyes, the supposed portal to the soul, replaced with glassy orbs that contained no emotion; their voices and lips becoming methods of communicating theatrical and false groans of pleasure rather than intimate thoughts and feelings.

I knew why this land hadn't affected me, but still didn't know why I had been brought there. I had only ever used my body to bring people pleasure and answer their needs. I would not undergo the same transfiguration as I had never committed their crime.

That might explain how I had sweetened the air and atmosphere with the release of Nancy. What Nancy and I had shared was the antithesis of this place. She was very important to me; I had understood her as a person and used my flesh and love-making to answer her needs and set her free. I had never dehumanized or treated her as less than she was. The refinement and superiority of my spirit over all those that were captured here would explain my compulsion to carry downwards. That my feet seemed determined to carry on stepping in a set direction, regardless of my will or volition, was determined proof I should be elsewhere.

What happened to Nancy caused me concern, though. She could not return to me and instead had crumbled into the earth and air around her. Did that mean she belonged here? That, for her, lust had been the center of our relationship? Our physical relationship had been of extreme importance to her. Sometimes we had not even spoken during our gasping rendezvous—we were so intent on bodily union. Had she dehumanized me or treated me as an object?

The idea hurt deeply.

The thought flashed across my mind before fading away, leaving me ashamed of it. As with all the others that I had contained, Nancy and I had merged our souls. I knew, without doubt, what I meant to her. She had loved me; I had made her feel alive and wanted; she had believed she brought me complete pleasure and wanted to see what a life together would bring. No one else had mattered at the end. As with all the important ones, she had become part of my being. It had only been me.

I was focused on these thoughts and did not notice Bea stop. Turning and looking at me in confusion, she flung the clenched hand that held the sweeter freedom air at an indistinguishable point in our downward path. The released air sprang forth with great vigor, tearing upward and downwards with such violence that it left white trails in its wake.

It resembled the wind that sporadically blew across this land, but its appearance did not presage the appearance of any punished people. Instead, an invisible circle appeared to trap the rushing wind. The circle stopped the violent swirling tornado escaping. Outside of the circle, the wind was impotent and could not be felt.

My treacherous feet suddenly surged downwards in a slipping motion toward this cyclone of furious wind. I tried to turn sideways or to backpedal, but whatever I tried, my feet would continue carrying onwards. It was seconds before I was in the circle being buffeted by winds.

It was a strange sensation. The winds blew around me either way or the other; all the while alternating between clean, fresh smelling air and a revolting attar of rot and corruption. The wind appeared to be trying to blow me outward and away from the circle, and yet my feet compelled me ever onward into the center.

With appalling suddenness, my feet won, with the wind letting me right into its very center. It felt like grasping hands were pulling me left and right, different parts of my body being shifted in different directions. The wind left trails that crisscrossed in front of my eyes, rendering me partially blind. Through grimaced features I saw Bea step forward into the cycle and be borne onwards and passed me with floating grace and carelessness. I grasped at her with desperate need, but she evaded me.

Then all the light disappeared, and my sight went dark. There was the frightening sense of being pushed and shoved backward and forward by throttling hands. As one, the hands reached a consensus decision and threw me in the same direction with almighty force.

I burst free of the tornado into a new place.

Chapter Eighteen

It would have given me some satisfaction to know that my earlier, costly victory had hurt my destined opponent almost as much as me.

Cunts! Cunts! Cunts! What the fuck? Michael paced backward and forward in utter fury, his thoughts incoherent with rage and desperation. He would walk toward the walls and strike them with different parts of his body. His knees, elbows, fists, and forehead pounded into the cruel stone surfaces. Seconds before his flesh touched a wall, it would sprout hooks, knives, and barbs that would dig into him and release globs of flesh and rivulets of blood.

He shoved his face into the wall and a suddenly protruding spike punched through the skin just between his nose and lips, coming out the back of his throat, its width forcing his front upper teeth downwards from the gum and into his throat in a gushing torrent of blood. The foreign objects almost choked him, and he stopped for a second to spit them free. The pause forced him to think and collect his thoughts, and he examined himself and the damage his violence had caused.

Michael took deep, shuddering gasps of air, drawing them deep into his lungs as he tried to calm himself. With a look downwards, he saw splatters of blood present on every square inch of his body. Those fuckers were responsible for this and for stealing his captured souls. They were probably walking around laughing about how they had beaten him. For a second, the rage built again, but he forced it away and made himself consider the situation.

Undoing the damage was possible. In fact, it might even give him an advantage. Those cunts would not beat him again. So, they had beaten a mere fraction of those specters within him. Big fucking deal! He had so many he did not notice them individually. Plenty more where they came from. They could try their pathetic fucking tricks on him instead then. They would see a real man. That fucking Other and the woman who guided him.

He walked to the fireplace and felt the wind that flowed back and forth from it move across his body. He took deep breaths and drew the foul stench within himself. The diseased air moved throughout him, changing and shifting his cells into new shapes, one that would better suit his purpose. He felt himself twist and pop upward and outward, growing bigger. Around him, a black aura encircled. With closed eyes, he concentrated more intensely and felt his jaws twist and distend with new rotten teeth. Keeping his concentration, he felt a sudden burst across his shoulders and new cancerous growths swelled to completion. Then he was closing more than one set of eyes.

With this last set of mutations, he felt ready and prepared to confront them again. This time, there would be no mistake. He settled and reached out around himself with his thoughts, discovering where they were. He felt a moment's panic when he realized they were closer again to the center, but he crushed that feeling downwards. This time, he would stop them. Their journey would end now.

Knowing Michael's plan was beyond me. I had not yet mastered or learned much about that land through which I traveled. I knew passing through that wind barrier had hurt and transformed me further. The throwing hands had ejected me some distance away, and I had landed badly on my back.

My eyes were closed. The pain in my side made it hard for me to concentrate. The force of ejection had torn part of my shirt free from my flesh. Most of the t-shirt remained fused to me. But on one side, flesh and cloth had ripped asunder, with the cloth leaking blood down my legs. I looked closer to understand what had happened. There, joined into the shirt, was a great lump of living flesh that had somehow become part of my clothes. Unlike the rest of my wounds, which could not naturally release my blood to fall to the floor, this pound of meat still lived and quivered in pain while dripping blood in a continuous trickling flow.

The rest of my face felt battered and different. In sudden distress, I touched my face and noticed a severe change that hinted at obscene surgery. My nose pointed sideways. I don't mean that a severe break had caused it to veer to one side sharply. Rather that the whole organ had snapped free from my face, twisted by forty-five degrees, and then returned to settle at this new angle.

Instead of it starting and originating between my eyes, it had moved, so it started underneath my left eye and originated from the tip of my left cheekbone, with the nostrils flaring and breathing underneath the right. I had to touch it several times to prove to myself that this had occurred. It still feels like a nightmare now. I could almost smell my eyeball, and the rain now channeled down my face and deflected sideways under my eye, where it would funnel downwards and merge with the blood leaking from my side.

This part of the land was now sleeting heavy, cold, slimy rain that blinded the eyes and forced the head to turn downwards toward the ground. The ground itself was dark gray, mixed with streaks of brown and black and greens. Stretching off in every direction were plum shaped, organic, soft looking, dingy boulders on the ground. Slimy rain and age-old moss covered them. Some of them lay on top of the wretched ground, whereas the soil and moss had partially submerged others.

I looked around, squinting my eyes against the rain, and saw Bea waiting downslope for me expectantly. She seemed unaffected by the rain and stood with straight back and raised head arching above the land. I moved down the ever-present gradient toward her; carefully stepping over the boulders that littered the ground, my feet sinking a few inches into the earth every time they landed.

I had not wanted to tread on the boulders, and it was only when I heard a sigh after a clumsy foot crunched through the side of one with a crushed rotten fruit feeling that I understood why. There was noise and movement. Crouching down, I looked at the boulder with interest.

Only when I looked closer did I realize it was a person, as were all the boulders that dotted around. Their entire body was a mix of gray and purple, as though the dank atmosphere had poisoned them. Arms and legs had shrunk down to the size of baby limbs. On rare occasions they ineffectually flapped to the side of their extended, rounded belly. All the boulder people had their faces pressed down close to the ground so they could bury their lips into the soil.

I manipulated one's face to more closely examine them. For each, the neck had disappeared, leaving an infantile bulbous face attached to a swollen torso. Their faces were expressionless, their eyes closed to allow the development of other senses, with gray dirt scabbing over their lids.

The only part of these boulder people that continually moved were their mouths. They turned these to the soil, sucking and chewing everything close without pause for breath. Their mouths were much larger and more elastic than normal, but lacked any defined shape. Inside were stumpy rows of yellow diseased teeth worn down to stubs. Sometimes the inner cheeks would display a shocking red ruby color as they masticated, the vivid color even more startling when compared with the drab hues covering their bodies.

I found them, and their single-minded determination, fascinating. They made me think of discolored tortoises burying their faces in lettuce. When I lifted a face further from the ground, the thing made a pathetically weak attempt to regain this source of nourishment. I played with this one some more, trying to understand them and finding their child like abilities and earth eating amusing. A gentle pull at a nearby arm caused it to come free from the body with a soft plop. The separation caused no blood but rank rainwater and chewed soil leaked from the wounded arm.

I held it in front of me, turning it this way and that. It was as pliable as a boneless and sodden sponge. A squeeze caused brown water to shoot from the torn edge, followed by dank earth when I twisted the sodden flesh harder. In amusement, I turned around and carried it to another of the boulder people. Lifting its head, I placed the torn arm under the moving lips. Immediately, the mouth moved and consumed the arm, wolfing it down as though it was the tastiest and most nutritious food. The sight brought a burst of surprised chortling from me, and for the first time in ages, a smile crossed my lips.

I had forgotten I had company, that I was not on my own. Suddenly I remembered and started to my feet in embarrassment, feeling like a teenager caught masturbating by prying parents. Bea stood waiting for me, having not moved at all from the spot where she stood. The boulder people had distracted me, and I had moved away from her, lost in my investigations. The hood still hid her face, and her expression was not visible, but her straight and unbending posture now had the strictness of judgment. With more than a twinge of embarrassment, I headed downwards toward her.

Stepping over one boulder, an explosive force lifted me from the floor and flung me into an air saturated with visceral violence. I landed heavily and looked around to understand what had happened. A sudden alarmed shock drowned out any pain. Michael was only a few meters away, but it was difficult to recognize him.

Michael had become physically inhuman, and he bore only a vague resemblance to his previous self. He noticed me looking and stopped moving forward, so he could mockingly twirl around and around to show what had changed. His entire body was wider and seemed designed for violence, with twisted muscles and twitching tendons. Clothes could not contain him and none would fit. He had spouted an extra pair of long-jointed muscular legs from the base of his spine that pushed him forward from behind. His previous legs were longer and thicker, as were his arms, while his hands ended with fingers that closed into sharp nails. Most surprising was the fact he now had three heads.

These heads grew on broad, twisted shoulders. The upper middle teeth in each head were yellow, rotten and grossly distended past the neck. The heads themselves had elongated, had dark hair all over, and looked canine, an impression only reinforced by a pair of feral, narrow animal eyes. Michael fixed all six eyes on me and with uneven steps ambled toward me, his hind legs pushing him into the air and forward. His gait was awkward and jerky but gave an impression of incredible power.

I turned and ran, screaming for Bea as I moved. A force smashed into me, knocking me face down onto the floor. Michael's hot breath fell across my back. With an explosive burst, his arms grabbed hold of my elbows and flipped me over so I could look at him and understand his dominance. Saliva and drool dripped down from elongated central teeth onto my chest. I saw his lips move in a grotesque caricature of a smile.

Michael moved his nail ended hands over mine, forcing them open from clenched fists to supplicant hands. With deliberate slowness, he pushed his sharp taloned fingers through the palm of my right hand into the sodden earth beneath. I screamed in agony, and pleading words shot from my mouth into his sneering visage. His answer was to move his other sharpened thumb into the center of my left hand and to gently press it so that it slowly penetrated all the way through my soft flesh and into the ground underneath.

I screamed anew, trying to reach within myself for a Sideways Person I could release. None answered. None would hear the call and push their way through my skin. I pleaded in soft urgent tones with Michael, offering him anything, *anything at all*, if he would just let me go. He smiled in triumph when I promised to be his compliant slave and pushed his nails deeper through my palms.

This intrusion forced soil into the punctured skin. My hands fused with the ground and sank beneath the surface. Color and rational thought appeared to leak out through the gashes in my palms and the cold, diseased earth seeped through me in exchange. It awoke hunger, such terrific hunger, and I turned my head to the side and chewed through the cold wet soil and grass that was closest to my lips. The first bite caused my body to heave and reject the cud, but I took a second and then a third bite, feeling hunger grow and my body swell to accommodate these new all-encompassing needs.

A blaze of light distracted me. Bea ran with furious determination into Michael's side. She was utterly different, not even human. A blazing warrior angel encased in armor forged from that same smeared, painful white light that burned forever behind me. All sharp angles, metal, and righteous determination. Michael had his nails through the center of my palms, holding them in contact with the ground. The force of Bea's assault lifted my hands free from the ground and the hunger disappeared.

Michael had punctured my palms clean through and I could see through the holes. I turned my head to Michael as he fought with Bea and screamed at him, hoping my desperate fury would release a Sideways Person to destroy that bastard. Again, none formed. I hobbled toward the two of them, hoping to help Bea.

Michael was a force of vicious nature. He was huge, standing on his new hind legs trying to bring his elongated and heavy form downwards to smash Bea, who only just saved herself from destruction by reflexively forcing him upward, using blasts of cursed white light. In response to her armored form, he had encapsulated himself in a black cloud that allowed the horror of his form to be sensed but not viewed. His three heads swung around Bea trying to bite, devour and cause harm. Bea covered herself in the white light and so the two pushed against each other.

I could not see the blows exchanged, or the weapons used. I saw nothing penetrate either the white light or the black cloud, but the contest caused both agony and anguish. Where the white touched the black, a wavering was visible and fire sprung forth, spreading along the parts where their essences touched. Soon the golden consuming flames covered both of them, leaving their flesh untouched, but causing both to screech in agony.

Michael's focus was on crushing Bea, on bringing all his weight down and smashing her into the ground. His mouths drew back across his teeth in cruel snarls and wolflike howls echoed from him. Bea stood there, her back arched under his weight, face set in determined concentration, her mouth open, letting out gasps and cries of pain.

Michael was winning. His fury and sheer weight appeared too much for Bea. Even as I watched, one of Bea's legs collapsed under her and she slid gracelessly to her knees. She raised her hands above her head in defense to hold his weight further away. Her back arched backward in pathetic weakness.

I would not let Michael win. My feelings toward Bea were complex. I was unsure if she was even my friend, but she was the only one who paid attention to me and had stayed by my side. There had been moments of closeness and even the odd spark of true intimacy. Regardless, if she died, there was no one who could save me from Michael, so I had to protect both of us.

I ran toward them screaming in determined anger and reached down in an instinctive habit to pick up a rock or stone that I could use as a weapon against the demonic Michael. My run placed me beside a boulder person and when I reached down, my hand went straight through its back with minimal resistance. My fingers came back out, holding various loops of graying pink and shreds of diseased flesh. The stench of it was awful. Pus and shit rolled into rotten flesh. Without thinking, I pulled my hand back and threw the foul mix at Michael.

His new form seemed to have altered his instincts. Made him more animalistic. As the putrid flesh passed near a side head, it swung round and opened its mouth to consume it in a snapping motion. The movement appeared to distract him from Bea, and she used the opportunity to move her legs underneath her to better support her standing.

I understood how I could help her now. With a spurt of speed, I ran between the boulder people, and twisted, pulled and punched at flesh to dismember and break free arms, legs, heads, or other unknown parts. I threw these dismembered body objects at Michael's mouths. Soon, the digested earth and rank water that formed the lifeblood of the boulder people covered every inch of my body. It was worth it, though. Michael could not help himself and his jaws would snap at the flying putridity. Every morsel of vomit inducing food distracted his attention from Bea. She looked stronger and was back on her feet, pushing at his black cloud with questing hands, trying to find a way through.

I twisted the head off one of the boulder people and threw it at Michael's central maw. This distracted all three heads, and he turned to snap at it hungrily. The distraction was all Bea needed. With sudden ease, her hands punched through his black cloud and tore into his midriff.

Almost surgically, Bea moved her thumbs up and down through his midriff, tearing at the seams of his skin and unpinning him from central neck to navel. Michael arched his body and head backward in pain and howled at the gray sky. Out of the wound spilled dark shadows and curled shapes. These dark forms weren't the expected entrails but were instead some of the souls Michael had imprisoned.

They spilled onto the ground in front of him like unloved, birthed abortions. For a few seconds after their shocking ejection, they did not move and left Bea to fend against Michael's rage and might. Then, almost understanding the world they were in, they stirred and, with uncertain movements, started forward; like children learning to walk. Upward they reached and stretched with their tortures and mutilations, revenge their clear and deserved goal.

Around Michael they snaked, covering him from every angle like flesh chains. Their force pulled him down to the floor. He struggled with all his might, but then more freed themselves from his cut belly and joined the fray. They lifted all four legs off the floor, leaving him flying in mid-air in surprised dismay, before they slammed him to the ground. They swarmed around him, first forcing his three heads into the soil before pushing the rest of his bulky body into the ground. Others grabbed his limbs and pulled them in every direction as though he was a spider whose legs they intended to tear free.

I watched in hopeful delight as Michael lost to his assailants, his body taking on the gray and purple hues of the other boulder people. The ground hid his faces and heads, but I knew that beneath the surface his lips would consume the rank earth in desperate need. I rejoiced and started dancing near his struggling body.

I will never understand what happened next or the reasoning behind it. Michael deserved everything that was happening to him. That this pound of flesh and pint of blood was being torn free and consumed by his own murdered souls made this divine justice. Bea, though, flared into a conflagration of glimmering yellow light and ran toward those grim, unforgiving dark shades. Bea spoke sharp commanding words, and although she spoke in an unknown language, I still somehow understood the gist. It was something about another's will. The shades that touched her burst into flames and disappeared into the flaring light.

Without his assailants pulling him down, Michael had the strength to free himself from the ground. His heads re-appeared in a shower of crud. Then he pulled upward on his arms and legs and yanked his torso free. I backed away in panic and looked around for a hiding place when, with a last effort, Michael surged upright, free of the beckoning ground.

For a second, I feared our uneven contest would continue. That there was little chance I would survive it. But the confrontation had damaged Michael. Even as I watched, another dark shade slithered itself from the broad wound in his abdomen.

With a dazed and uncertain look, Michael ran lolloping down the hill further away from me and Bea. His heads bunched together in the center of his broad shoulders and the faces showed a look of extreme concentration as the darkness re-enfolded him.

In the next instant, we were free of his presence.

The small area of ground where the shades had escaped Michael appeared free from the curse of this part of the land. Wind and icy rain no longer drove through it. The air was sweet, and the pervasive moaning seemed quieter.

My feet wanted me to move toward this oasis, they twitched with the desire to carry me into its center. Bea had already moved toward it, turning her back on me with clear confidence I would follow. I didn't. Spent, I sat down with little care on one of the boulder people. Its flesh gave way, making it shape itself around me. I looked down and saw it had continued to chew and suck on the ground; unaware I was there.

I shaded my eyes against the white light and looked upward at the boulder people whose bodies I had used to win the battle against Michael. They had been fragmented but as far as I could tell, seemed unaffected by me ripping out body parts. I could not see those I tore the head off, but all lay where they always had. They filled the air with the gentle sighs of masticating and swallowing. The rain pelted into my eyes and ran down my face, blinding me, the water greasy and unpleasant to touch.

I noticed Bea looking. She motioned to the calmer oasis where Michael had lost his trapped souls. My feet twitched in response, but I lifted them off the ground to control their drive. Bea motioned onwards again, and I shook my head. She carried on looking at me in silence. In response, and with great theatricality, I raised my gore covered hands and wiped them on the side of the boulder person I was sitting on, hoping for some kind of emotional response from her.

She gave none. A failed attempt to wipe the flesh ruin from my hands onto the supine boulder person just smeared it into thick whorls. I looked in interest, noting the stained blood was grayish mixed with purple, with clumps of flesh and other substances stuck to my forearms. I closed my eyes and held my arms up to the rain. Then I opened them again and saw the rain had mixed with the polluted body parts and streaked it downwards in lines. The body waste had not been cleared but instead had pooled near my elbows.

The rain and my accepting its touch awakened something anew in me. Hunger. My eyes turned to the soil, and I longed to place it in my mouth. To chew it, to satisfy the need to consume. Other needs and hungers awakened. I wanted to drink and opened my mouth to swallow the foul rain. This made the hunger and thirst worse; I licked at my arms to get more water and swallowed the blood and mess that had accumulated there. Irritation rose as the desire of this impossible to scratch itch built up. The only possible solution was to lower my head to the floor and eat the ground.

My other desires awakened and saved me. I wanted to smoke and drink. Most importantly, I wanted to be with someone. To hold them close and share their breath while their eyes widened. I wanted to float within the thoughts and soul of another. My eyes closed, and I remembered being held close in the folds of someone's arms, feeling the press of their flesh, drinking in the scent of their skin. I shifted my thoughts and remembered my last night with Laura. The thought of looking down at her as she lay beneath me, her skin pressed along the length of my body, her eyes searching mine, revealing the thoughts and needs of her soul. Her scent drawn into my lungs and becoming a part of my essence.

The memories of these moments with the Sideways People gave me strength. They were in and part of me; if I gave into these cursed hungers and thirsts, they would be trapped here with me. Trapped in this cursed ground. They deserved better. Shuddering with the effort of ignoring my desires, I reluctantly opened my eyes and searched for Bea. I was getting some answers before leaving.

The rain bothered me less than it had. I could see through it and ignore its unpleasant tactile sensations and the desire it awakened. Bea stood still and had not moved from her previous spot. She seemed concerned when she saw me open my eyes and motioned me downwards toward the glen of calm where she had torn free some of Michael's victims. With deliberate emphasis, I shook my head, crossed my arms across my chest, and fighting the need to continue downwards, I planted my feet on the ground to ensure she knew I would not be moving until she answered my questions.

In silence, she walked upward toward me. I realized things were different for Bea than they were for me. She moved upward with no sign her feet wanted to move in any other direction. The light to my back, which cast me in shadow and was so painful to my eyes, did not bother her. I motioned her to sit down on a boulder person nearby. She declined, choosing instead to crouch opposite and close by.

"We need to go down. Go further in," she said in a soft, sad voice that carried to me through the splatter of rain.

I looked at her and asked in sorrowful tones, "Why?"

She continued to stare at me silently. I was not angry, I was practical, resigned to my fate. There was no way out; I just didn't want to be some obedient puppy following orders. I wanted Bea to accept and understand me as a man who faced full on what was heading toward him.

"This place," and I motioned around me to the boulder people, "seems to alter people. Their obsessions become part of their lives."

There was a pause. I waited for a response, but none was forthcoming. I stayed there longer, hoping that silence and expectation would force her into words. Bea said nothing. I motioned to my face and side, to the fused shirt and torn flesh, at the wounds that did not bleed but would not heal.

"I am being altered," I said. "Why or to what, I don't know. These people differ from me. I don't have their obsessions. I am different from everyone we have met here." Again, I motioned, but this time to the oasis caused by Michael's downfall. "I am different from him. As different as night is to day. I never caused pain, or certainly I didn't cause more than anyone else in everyday life."

I waited for a response or for her to at least acknowledge my defense. It was unclear why, but I got the impression I should explain myself to her. It felt like I was being punished for some unknown reason. She needed to know I was in pain.

"I am losing people I promised would be part of me forever," I said in a voice which hinted at tears. "It would be wrong for me to lose any more." This prompted a response, but not one I was expecting.

"The people we love never leave us." Her words did not appear to be spoken conventionally but were delivered directly into my ears. The tone of voice was ambiguous. It lacked factual clarity; and she seemed to be implying two different things. I should have thought about that, but I became angry.

"That's just a platitude. A fucking sop told to children to make them feel better when they lose their first fucking pet. It does not apply here." I felt she was belittling my suffering and the sacrifices I had made to get here. That she was just giving the expected fake emotional responses instead of trying to answer my true deep anguish. I deserved better than that. My lips hitched back over my canines in a snarl.

Bea saw my anger. She did not move. The robes still hid her face and form. It crossed my mind that I was still uncertain what she looked like, that everything had hidden her face for so long that I could not describe her features. Then her voice returned through and part of the rain.

"It is true. Losing a parent reminds us of our own mortality and makes us better placed to understand what is coming. We carry their genes within us. Their teachings shape and are part of us and determine what we are and what we do. They remain with us forever, never to be separated."

I shook my head in angry denial. This was still a standard hallmark sentimentality that did not concern me. It was also untrue.

"Losing a child is the worst pain that one can suffer. When you lose a child, you lose not only the source of pure and unquestioning love that flows in a conduit both ways between you, but you also lose the possibility and claim of immortality. The pain and need for them never leaves you. The love you feel, that two-way connection never leaves, no matter where you are or where you go."

Bea saw I was still not moving before saying, "Losing a friend is no different. What they feel for you remains a part of you to be remembered at will. Even if the memory goes, then its sensation stays as long as you live. Love separates us from unthinking animals and makes us more than them."

"I was more than a friend or parent to the people I loved," I responded to her softly. What she was saying still felt unfocussed and not directed at me. I wanted her to understand, "I was their soul mate, and I gave them everything that they wanted and needed. Maybe you don't understand. I don't deserve this; I only want to be with the people I love."

Bea paused for a brief second and swept her hands around in a circular motion that took in all the boulder people and the surrounding land. "Betraying love is the most heinous of crimes. Everyone looks down at those that abandon their friends and family. Those who break cherished oaths have the least satisfying and settled lives."

"I have never betrayed someone I care about," I said. "I have never let things change. My feelings have and always will remain the same. As it should be, my love is eternal and unchanging. Greater than a parent's love for a child, a friend's love for a friend, greater than any other."

This was the most I had explained myself to anyone in a long time, and I wondered what had prompted this rash of unguarded openness. I looked at her, hoping she appreciated the depth of feelings that I had and the deep bonds I shared. Maybe if she could understand me, I could build a similar all-encompassing relationship with her.

Bea stayed silent for a while before asking in mild curiosity, "Do you feel you belong here?"

My feet answered that. I had to raise them off the floor as they tried to drag me downwards and onwards. I looked at the boulder people. They were all isolated and trapped in their own worlds, with no concern or thought for anyone else. Only their own hunger and need drove them. I was different. My desires and wants were greater and grander by far.

I shook my head in answer and kept on looking at her. Bea seemed part of this land and understanding of its logic. She had referred to people that love us never leaving us. It was possible she understood something I did not. Maybe she saw a way where I could re-integrate my loved ones, drawing Liz and Nancy back within me somehow while protecting the others against expulsion. Maybe if I went where Bea was guiding me, then everything would be right again.

"I will get you to where you belong," Bea said. "Carry on, because I will help you get to where you need to be. Come, because it is me asking you." She stood and carried on standing. Within moments, she appeared to have grown. The light that was on my back hit her face and illuminated her features.

Bea pulled back the hood of her robe and looked straight at me. For a second, I was speechless. She looked so similar to Laura that tears rushed to my eyes and threatened to spill over my sideways nose.

There were differences between Bea and Laura. Bea was taller. Her eyes had none of Laura's dreaminess but seemed more suited to prophecy than the otherworldliness that Laura's dream-filled orbs had expressed. They both had the same square face, though, with the same straight gait and determined manner of walking.

Bea nodded at me and without waiting to see my reaction, headed for the calm area that the rain appeared to avoid. I lowered my feet onto the ground and slid downwards as they compelled me with increased urgency onwards. While moving, I raised my hands toward my eyes and brushed away tears. This saltwater appeared to clean my hands and remove the worst of the gore and dirt that had accumulated on them.

I guessed the area of calm was another of the barriers that allowed passage from one place to another within this land. Bea stepped unafraid into that area and continued on. If only because she reminded me so much of my beloved Laura, I would have to follow. Also, she appeared to know more about this land and had answers I needed.

My feet demanded that I step into the barrier, and this time I willingly followed their prompting. The air smelled sweet, tasting of perfumed scents and cut grass. I think when Bea or I opened these mystical doors, this exertion made entering the portals (or "barriers" as Michael had called them) painful for me. This time was different. As I stepped into them, I felt like I was being bathed in light and drawn upward.

I do not know whether Bea said anything. I could not see or hear anything, but the light soothed me. It felt like warm hands running over my body. I had no sensation of physical presence, as though earthy precepts did not constrain me anymore. I enjoyed this sensation for a moment but then felt concerned. If I had no body, where would my Sideways People live? I had always assumed that they had been entwined into my skin and the fiber of my being. If I had lost my corporeal presence, then where would be safe for them—would the lack of a physical home push them out and into the ether? No sooner had this concern moved across my mind than the white light and sensation of floating disappeared.

Instead, the world turned black. My flesh re-imprisoned my spirit, and I plunged downwards. This drop did not last long and with a final forceful, jarring sensation, I landed on trembling feet in a new place.

Chapter Nineteen

Maybe you think I am too accepting of strange things? That transformations, translocations, and new types of people would cause rejection, rather than acceptance? Maybe you think you would have understood where you were by now and acted differently?

That might be true for you. These unfamiliar sights and places may have overloaded your mind and caused you to scream. Please remember, I have lived an unusual life. I shared uncommon bonds and chartered different existences through my Sideways People. No one else has experienced reality in the same way. No one else has seen the world through different people. I have accepted and held souls within my core. This unknown land I was in and the difficulties it was causing seemed like a natural progression to my unique life.

I had landed somewhere new, but I was trying to block it out by concentrating on my Sideways People. I could reconnect with a memory or person by visualizing them. The world outside was hot and humid, but by focusing on better things, I could partially block this unwelcome sensation. I tried to relive other times, and the sensations afforded by loved people who had loved me in return with such passion.

It was difficult. In my proper and prior world, I could immerse myself in a Sideways Person and relive their feelings, remember their histories and see the world through their eyes. Here it was harder. I could still see their sights, but everything was shrouded as though seen through a veil. Their feelings were still accessible but felt muted and distant compared to my usual clarity.

My thoughts kept on returning to one of my failures. A man who I had tried to freeze too early in our relationship. Someone who did not understand the significance and importance of my offering. Maybe he was just incapable of loving someone to the required depth.

His name was John. I had met him while trawling through dating sites on a whimsical Saturday afternoon. His profile suggested a lonely man who was trying to appear bigger and more glamorous than he was. He used almost hyperbolic terms to describe himself, boasting about his humor and successes. His profile picture showed a timid-looking man, hair receding, who had dyed what remained raven black, despite being too old for that to be credible.

Piqued, I had emailed him, pretending to be impressed with his gifts and attributes. We had met a few times. Always we would meet at the pre-agreed location and when the date finished, he would ask to stay at mine. He was trying to hide the fact his car and house were not impressive and did not equate to his projected successful image.

I will not describe what happened between us in great detail. It was a mistake, and his feelings were insincere, based on lies or some shallow flesh instinct. I feel none of the pleasure I get from talking about my other sincere Sideways People. Long story short, I had shown John how impressed I was with him as a person and praised him for his wit and wisdom. Any appearances presented to the outside world were unnecessary with me. I understood his intrinsic worth and considered myself lucky to have met him.

I had planned the perfect evening together, cooked dinner and spent the evening pleasuring him slowly in bed. Then I asked to spend the next evening with him at his place rather than mine. With the realization his pretense of material success was unnecessary, he had agreed and sighed as though the release of evasions and lies unburdened him. Shifting myself up his body from his crotch, I stroked his hair and asked if he loved me. With a broad, genuine smile, and his arms wrapped around my shoulders, he told me he did without limits or reservation.

That was my cue. I moved my face in front of his until our eyes were mere centimeters apart. One hand stroked his face while the other sneaked around to the side of his neck. I reared up, brought my hand down on his larynx.

John's reaction was swift and immediate. His face twisted with anger and betrayal and his fists swung round to punch the side of my face, his knees raised and tried to drive into my groin. We wrestled for a while, falling off the bed with him landing on top. He carried on punching me, but he could not get my hand off his throat. He weakened, and I rolled myself on top of him while ignoring his flailing arms, determined to end his pain and grant him the sweet heaven of permanent union.

Then something terrible happened. His eyes filled with fear and tears, and his lips moved to utter words of pleading. Not the usual instinctive responses of an unneeded body but soul deep rejection of me and my love offering. I carried on pressing downwards, hoping this blip would pass and he would understand and accept what we were sharing.

He didn't. Even at the very end, when my loving eyes held his, he struggled and sobbed. When he died—and I was unprepared for the suddenness and quietness with which he did it—I felt nothing. There was no movement of him to me, no exchange and merging of feelings. There was nothing. Nothing at all except the memory of his desperate rejection.

Of course, I swiftly realized I had been lied to and led on. It was the only possible explanation. That John had used me and pretended feelings he simply was incapable of. I was both hurt and furious. I had dragged his naked body into the shower with me and washed all the residue of each other away. By the end of it he didn't even the faintest hint of my scent on his skin, and I was similarly free of any trace of him.

I had dressed angrily, and decided I didn't even want to touch John again, so had retrieved kitchen gloves before wrapping his body in unused, impersonal bed sheets. Rather than the usual ceremony I perform to honor my loves, I had dragged his body to the car and dumped him in a nearby forest, before driving off to leave the rats and other animals to eat him.

I have always avoided that memory because of the way it made me feel. Now, however, my thoughts kept returning to that failure and the look in his eyes as they shut and he drew one last determined breath. My throat felt ashen, swollen. A weak adrenaline boost shot through my body in response to the remembered fight, leaving me wasted and nauseous.

Although I never felt him transcend to share my body in the outside world, it was possible that maybe a smaller fraction of soul had entered and was causing me to remember him. I tried to concentrate and push him out of one of my wounds or through my thinning skin. Nothing occurred; he was not there. My exertions released no gray ghost. I experimented with other Sideways People. When I thought of them and pictured their ejection, I felt them crowding at edges, eager to be released.

I wanted to think of Laura. Everything had happened so fast since we had been together, and I had not yet experienced her emotions and feelings. She was the one, the absolute pinnacle of everything I had ever achieved, but I had not yet understood or savored what she had given me. I swam within myself and looked for her. For her worldview, and our shared feelings.

Laura was not there. I caught different aspects of her; the memory of her perfume would cross my nose, or the way she looked at me when I was talking. I could not, however, merge with her, nor feel the full significance of our relationship. Panicked, I ran within myself from one Sideways Person to the next, ignoring them and the opportunities they offered. I caught glimpses of her, but never enough.

My eyes filled with tears, and my mouth dropped open and trembled while wet snuffling noises escaped. My nose dripped snot down the side of my cheekbone. I let my head sag forward, and for a moment, everything swam around me in swirls of confusion and misery.

It did not help. This indulgence in misery. It never does. I gave into it for a short period. Then I realized she must be within me somewhere. I had felt her migrate inside and could still get a faint sense of her. This land must somehow have blocked full integration. When I returned home, I would make amends. I would make Laura's bravery and purity count for something.

I opened my tear-blurred eyes. Bea stood near me, staring in my direction. With arms outstretched, I staggered toward her. Embraced her with intense need, burying my face in the cloth covering her shoulder, remembering once again the smell and feel of Laura.

This gave me the strength I needed, allowing me to pull back to look at the world, knowing before I did so it would be different from the last time I had surveyed my environment.

It was hot. The heat hit hard, making my skin tight and crowded. The air was thin and muggy. It was difficult to draw enough into the lungs, and I started sucking at the atmosphere through my mouth to get what I needed. The earth beneath my feet showed no grass or living foliage, the searing heat rendered the ground barren, gray and dusty.

As expected, the ground sloped toward an unseen and unknown destination. My feet urged me downwards, but for the moment I could ignore them. I looked behind me up the hill, not in hope but to confirm the blinding white light still stood behind me. Although the light was at my back, the heat assaulted me from all directions. There must have been multiple light sources, but I could neither see nor sense any sun.

Movement through the last barrier had brought no further transformation or mutilation upon me. The previous changes remained: the cut on my arm, the fused shirt, the sideways nose, red welts and torn flesh that seemed to live on after being separated from me, were all still there. My movement to this unknown part of the land had been gentler, and I was grateful. Nothing had healed, but I had suffered nothing new.

Bea motioned downwards, as though to show we should continue our unending journey. I nodded and reached out to hold her hand, hoping we would carry on our journey so comforted. For a second, Bea allowed the physical contact, then shook her head and twisted her hand free.

She carried on downwards, and I trailed after her.

There were different people in this area. The heat caused the ground to shimmer as though invisible lines wavered upward, changing the display of the land. Within the air currents, these new people appeared.

They appeared to be metallic. When they moved, it was clunkier than it should be, and their feet hitting the floor caused a ringing bell like sound. They had silver and gold looking skin and lacked mouths. Their eyes were clockwork cogs, and their hands raked around into sharp claws. They wore no clothes and did not appear to have genitalia. For all they were naked, they appeared to wear vast quantities of glittering chains and decorative ornaments that covered their bodies in sparkling lines that dripped from their necks and wrists. The heat should have made these ornaments unbearable, but it didn't seem to be an issue.

These people separated into two interchangeable groups. One group appeared to be carrying a large metal rucksack fused to their backs, the weight of this load slowing them down. The other group did not have this metal backpack attached but appeared determined to gain it.

Those without backpacks would run after those with them, unimpeded, and without the additional weight, they would overtake and capture their prey with ease. This capture would then turn into gory theft. They would cut the fused metal backpacks free from their victim's back, the tearing of metal causing a high-pitched screaming noise. This severance caused immense pain, and the back of the robbed would run red with blood that flowed in great rivers to the absorbing ground. They would fall over onto their backs and tremble and roll on the floor as the natural red dulled and healed by slowly turning back to metal under the baking heat. They made no noise (other than the sound made during the metal tearing) but gave the powerful impression they would have been screaming.

Those who liberated the backpacks would swing them onto their backs. Once positioned there, the metal would melt and fuse to its new owner. The host would stand still, looking around them in stupefied wonder while this merging occurred. When the backpack had fully fused, they would take on a wary stance and their visages would twist in concern. Slowly, and impeded by the additional weight, they would try to run off before another of their kind liberated them from their burden in such cruel and painful fashion.

Around and around, these two interchangeable and fluid groups would chase after each other in a vicious circle of forced surgery, followed by desperate and unsuccessful flight. Sometimes one of them would accost me as they ran by in search of one of their kind whom they could rob. Generally, they would ignore me and run past when they realized I had no backpack, nor was I interested in acquiring one. Sometimes, however, they would run their baked-hot, claw-like hands under my shirt as though searching for something of value. Their heated metallic hands would burn me, and I would cry and jump back.

This would often cause them to understand that I had nothing of any use to them. They would turn and carry on running downward without a second look in my direction. However, one seemed determined to retrieve something of value from me. His claw hands ran over my body, causing me to cry out as my flesh burned because of the heat. In slow motion, one claw tapped on one button on my shirt as though to determine whether it had value. Then it twisted its claw and punched the sharp edge of it through my midriff and pulled it downwards toward my nape.

The sudden pain was too sharp to comprehend. I think he cut through my windpipe because when I opened my mouth to scream, I just felt muscles tighten around this hot, hard hook as though to vomit it out. I couldn't. It's one claw cut into my abdomen, and I dropped my hand on top to stop it moving any more.

The wound did not bleed natural blood. No healthy red surged forth and fountained free. Something much worse, much more damaging, happened. I felt two Sideways People drop out through the gap and onto the baked floor. They were gray and folded in on themselves. My eyes filled with tears at this psychic loss, and I concentrated on holding the claw steady and keeping the rest of my cherished inside me.

I knew who dropped out, of course. I didn't need to look at the gray forms at my feet. One was Claire, who had rebelled against pretty much everything and wanted a lover she could hate the world with. The other was Lisa, someone who wanted a stable life with a husband and children. I had given these two opposite women what they wanted and called them both home to me at the perfect moment.

Now they lie entwined with each other at my feet in this barren world of blasted soil, like discarded entrails. As the claw man and I stayed locked in a statutory tableau, these two gray sister angels of my nature shook themselves from each other and moved upward, their arms reaching out toward me.

Their hands caressed across my body before, without warning, they yanked and pulled me in different directions. I howled and, ignoring the metal appendage buried in my gut, tried to tell them it was not my fault, that the creature had forced them from their safe home.

I don't know what would have happened if Bea hadn't intervened. She again burst into white light that flamed gold and red and ran next to me. Almost without thinking, she grabbed the claw that was buried within me and tore it free, both from my gut and its owner's socket. It came forth with a metallic screaming noise, and Bea tossed it disdainfully to one side. The monster leaked red and looked at the orphaned shoulder in surprise before running after the disregarded limb in silence.

My beloved Claire and Lisa kept pulling at me. Their hands seemed to tear open the fresh wound in my middle, and the other Sideways People rose, clambering in response to their intentions. I screamed in fear before Bea saved me in the only possible way. She reached out and touched the two gray forms, causing both to disappear in a burst of yellow flame.

Their expulsion caused a breath of fresh air to appear and blow over us. Not that I noticed. The loss traumatized me, preventing full awareness. I hadn't even had the chance to apologize or explain their expulsion before the flames had consumed them. I didn't understand the yellow flame and whether it annihilated or cleansed. The thought Bea might have destroyed them; it tormented me.

I stood there reeling at the enormity of what had just happened. In the space of seconds, I lost two parts of my soul. I tried not to think about them, not to remember the times and moments I had shared with both. A useless attempt—I was like a child probing at a rotten tooth with a clumsy tongue. My thoughts kept twisting back to them and I no longer shared or could feel the love they had felt for me.

Bizarrely, my thoughts kept on returning to our last moments together and the sound they made as they gasped their last. It caused a frustrating repulsion, similar to nails scratching down a blackboard. My fingers bent and then twisted into fists before pressing at my temples to block out the unwanted noise.

Chapter Twenty

It is unclear how long I stayed like that. At one point, I turned to Bea, demanding to know Claire and Lisa's fate. Emotions got the better of me. My throat constricted, reducing my voice to a series of sobbing gasps.

I remembered the platitudes trotted out at funerals about being reunited with those that you love. It felt like it applied here. I guessed that Lisa and Claire, and indeed Nancy and Liz, forced out of their loving corporeal host by a cruel claw or unfortunate incidents, were even now ascending to heaven where they would wait for me. My eventual death would lead to a joyful reunion, and we would be together forever. The thought comforted me and gave me reassurance.

Bea stood in front of me the whole time. I could not see her eyes or her face, but I accepted she had performed those actions to save me. I could not allow myself to feel anger or hatred toward her. For the moment, my feet were free of their usual compulsion to carry me downwards.

The tear in my stomach was something else, though, and demanded attention. I could feel the Sideways People gathering at the edge of the wound, threatening to spill outward. With urgent looks, I scoured the floor and horizon for something I could use to stick myself together and keep the wound closed. I needed to keep myself whole and maintain the integrity of the union between myself and my remaining Sideways People.

I found it quickly. Bea had thrown the claw she had torn free near us. It lay on the ground in the baking heat, unclaimed by its former owner.

I picked it up before dropping it again as it was so hot that touching it burned.

I believe in fate. You can't "just happen" to meet so many giving people as I have without crediting some kind of guiding destiny. I doubt anyone has met as many spiritually and emotionally advanced people as me. Some encounters resulted from the most fantastic and improbable coincidences that were clearly fated to happen. It was obvious some unknown force had left the claw to aid me.

Considering the best way of doing what needed to be done. I pulled my right hand up into the sleeve so that my shirt insulated it. Without pausing or reflecting on what I was doing, I grabbed and pressed the scorching object against the wound in the center of my body, seeking to cauterize it shut.

The pain was immediate. Streams of continual heat crossed my wound, and the claw burned, searing the wound. The flesh and skin bubbled and dripped like melting plastic. Even the areas surrounding the seared flesh turned a bruised birthmark purple. It was successful, though. The melting flesh sealed closed, and although it did not feel as tightly sealed as skin should; the threat of seepage and loss still loomed large, it felt better. I reckoned if I was careful and concentrated hard, I could keep everyone safe inside.

I pulled the claw away, and it came free with a wet pop. Globules of black flesh still clung in crumbs to the edge. I flung it as hard as I could in front of us and watched as it sank down into the ground.

The movement seemed to create a ripple in the air. I saw something new rise from the ground where the claw landed. It gleamed brightly enough to be painful to watch in the reflective heat, but I was still curious about my unintended creation. My feet regained their compulsion to travel in a predetermined direction, and Bea motioned me onwards. It seemed like the intended path was toward this new object. As I moved closer to the sudden eruption, frenzied, glittering movement shimmered around what looked like a huge golden statue. This idol appeared to have sprung forth at the exact point where the claw landed.

It reminded me of the poem *Ozymandias*. This statue displayed a bearded and cruel visage, looking like an old Greek representation of Zeus. The lips were parted, and the mouth leered with lasciviousness. The whole thing was made from expensive looking, glittering substances. Several of the precious metal creatures speedily tore around it, performing the same ceaseless painful surgery on each other in a never-ending cycle of cruelty and desperation. Droplets of blood and metal sprayed in the surrounding air, but none of it touched me or stained my clothes. The creatures ignored us. They would run past and around without even acknowledging our existence, but also without ever touching us.

Occasionally, a creature would touch against or brush into the metal statue that stood towering in their midst. As if soldered together, the merest contact appeared to bind the two together in an instant. The creature would look around in distress and make screeching noises before becoming smaller and smaller. The area that touched the statue would become discolored like weathered copper, and through this, the substance of the creature appeared to pass. Within seconds, the creature would disappear out of existence. The discolored area of metal on the statue would gradually fade and revert to its previous burnished, precious metal gleam.

I stayed static for a while, watching this spectacle, trying to understand what I was seeing. I enjoyed the drama of it and didn't find it disturbing. After a while, though, I grew tired of the scene and tried to continue my journey downwards. I stepped around to the right and took a few steps onwards.

In front of me was the golden statue, as though I had never moved around it. The creatures still milled back and forth around us, ripping metal rucksacks off each other before having it ripped off them. Puzzled, I took a few steps around the other side, only to realize the statue was again in front.

At first, I found it amusing. I tried to capture and see when I was twisted around and placed in front of it. I would smile at the statue when I returned to the starting point and saw it looming in front of me as though I hadn't moved. Soon though, it got frustrating, the continual noise and clanging movement of the creatures, the ongoing spray and droplets of blood, the noises of amputation and removal.

Give me an offering.

I heard these words then. They appeared to originate from the statue. Although the lips remained static in their cruel leer, still I heard the words issued in an unemotional voice.

Give me an offering.
Give me an offering.
Give me an offering.
Give me an offering.

The voice kept repeating, again and again. Pressing my hands over my ears did not block the insistent demand. It was horrible. I would look at the mouth, the unmoving lips, press urgent hands against my ears and still, the voice would continue its clear demand.

In desperation, I fought the compulsion in my feet and walked backward away from the statue, keeping my eyes on the statue and back to the horrifying white light that remained behind me. The further away I stepped from the statue, the quieter the voice became. After taking several large steps away, it droned down to an indistinct murmur I could ignore. I sat and looked at Bea.

"What should I do?" I asked her, "We both know I need to continue going down, but I am incapable of further progress. This isn't where I am needed, and I don't want to remain here longer than necessary." The heat kept on hitting down on the top of my head, shoulders, and neck. For a moment, I wondered why I was not sweating and whether I would get sunburned. Then I remembered that nothing natural happened here, and there was no sun, just light and sickening heat.

Bea moved closer and sat on her haunches opposite. "Give him an offering," she said.

"Of what? What can I offer it, whatever it is?" Bea looked at the statue but clearly already had the answer, "The statue seems to absorb those people that belong here, and those people are obsessed with stealing those objects from each other's backs. Maybe you could give him one of those packs or one of these people?" She phrased it as a question, but it still had a feel of command.

I found my mouth turning upward in a sad smile, as though my defeated and disappearing masculinity was something that I was being forced to acknowledge. "I can't do that. One of those things just ripped into my guts without even thinking about it. If you hadn't stopped it, it may well have torn me in half." Then I paused and looked at her before saying. "You could do it, though. You seem to have power. Both Michael and one creature have been driven off by you. It's possible you could do it."

Bea just stayed opposite me, shaking her head. My temper flared. "Why not?!"

Bea responded with the surprising and soft riposte of, "Because this is your journey."

I wanted Bea to clarify what she meant, but I did not know how to start that conversation. There was also a certain obvious truth to it. My feet demanded I go downwards. I had unwitting surgery performed on me. Wounds had appeared and not healed, and I had undergone startling transformations. I was at the center of whatever was happening here.

"How do I do it then? They won't let me take one of them, and I don't have the strength to overpower them." I turned and asked.

Bea seemed to have all the answers, and I was confident she would tell me. Although the journey was mine, she was my guide. No one else in this place had personality, foibles, or the ability to convey information on anything but the most limited topic or needs. Bea was different in every way. She was quiet and did not volunteer information but was always present.

There had been both moments of intimacy and annoyance between us. Shades of authentic emotion. If it hadn't been too soon after the raw, supreme beauty of Laura, which I still had not explored or relished, then I might have considered making her one of the Sideways People. Maybe after I left this place and had savored the full Laura experience, I could become what Bea wanted and lighten her load.

"After being released, those you have within you have proven useful before," Bea said in response to my question.

I shook my head. "They have defended me when I was being attacked. But I am not being physically assaulted. They are not my slaves. They do not obey my orders." The hint of anger in my voice seemed to surprise her.

"You hold them deep within you. If you didn't have an intense bond, they wouldn't be there. They may respond to your will. Let one free and see what happens." Bea's counterargument was persuasive. I looked at Bea sharply, trying to understand what she knew about my Sideways People and their link to my nature. Her flat features revealed no hint of knowledge, but I resolved to have an in-depth conversation with her later, when I could read and interpret her responses.

With little choice, I took large strides closer to the statue and the creatures that circled it in grim greed and need. As I moved closer to the statue, I heard the monotonous demand being repeated again, louder as I moved closer.

Give me an offering.

Give me an offering.

I moved as close to the statue as possible with its insistence echoing inside my head. Then I closed my eyes and concentrated on the wounds in my center, side, palms, and forehead. I pictured a gray cloud slowly and gently originating from those points and gaining substance a few inches in front of me.

Something unfurled and untwined from parts of my being, flesh being unstripped from bone, sinews being separated from nerves. I knew who the process had released before I opened my eyes.

Kevin stood before me, my eyes resting on his back, his shoulders set in a determined fashion. Then he moved forward with violent gestures. His hands would jerk outward in fists, and occasionally his legs would start forward with the foot turned sideways as though to kick. For a second, I thought he had understood my need and was responding to my intent. I thought he was trying to kill or capture one creature so I could give the required offering.

Something was wrong, though. His movements were unrelated to those of the creatures. My eyes filled with tears as I realized he was mimicking the movements he had made in his last fight, all those years ago. His last battle, when he had refuted and driven off those people unworthy of being called his friends.

I felt proud that he remembered that moment enough to want to relive it, but it would not get me what I needed. Remembering what Bea said about the connection between me and those I held, I raised my left hand

and concentrated on images of capture and violence. Kevin halted his movements and jumped upward before landing ramrod straight on his feet and moving robotically toward the creatures.

He was preternaturally strong now. Death and absorption into me had given him greater potency than he possessed in life. Kevin grabbed one creature as it ran by and jerked it toward him. The creature was slow with the backpack encumbering it, but still it turned and tried to defend itself by slashing at the gray form with hooked hands.

Kevin appeared unaffected by the attacks. He appeared invulnerable. The hands did not pass through Kevin's outline as I might have expected but bounced off his gray sides. Ignoring the creature, he applied his mighty strength to its back to tear the metal pack free.

It did not take long at all. A long, thin tear appeared, surging red with natural blood. Further force caused it to widen quickly, only the last few strands of metallic gold holding out for a few tortured seconds before it tore free. The creature screamed, a sound shocking because it was so human, and then collapsed to the ground, rocking from side to side in obvious extreme pain. Kevin stopped his assault and laid the rucksack behind its head.

I don't know what I expected to happen next. When intervention or cruel necessity had expelled the other Sideways People, I had never had to confront or interact with them afterwards. This was different. After Kevin had laid down the rucksack with the air of a man relinquishing his final burden, he turned his head and looked straight into my eyes.

It hurt. It did. I saw anguish and betrayal in the lines of his face and the twisting, trembling motion of his mouth. I tried to say something, but the words choked and silenced in my throat as I saw his lips move and form the outline of words. Kevin appeared unable to talk. Maybe the fact he had no breath in his body stopped that, but his lips clearly moved and formed words.

I loved you.

Over and over, while no actual noise was issued forth, his lips, with deliberate clarity, formed the same words in insistent accusation. I bowed my back and ducked my head to avoid the sight and the regret they showed, but always I would peer up, hoping there had been some mistake. Each time I did, I would only see his lips move and form the same accusation.

There was no avoiding it. I trembled and placed my hands over my eyes to block the vision. It didn't work. I ended up spreading my fingers and peeking through them, childlike, at Kevin. Still expecting to see his face twist into a display of forgiveness and love. It never did. But seeing that I had blocked him out of sight led him to cover his own face before sobbing into his hands and running past me, toward the light.

I waited for an age to pass. Mind roving over the same things. Remembering a knife and the screeching noise it made as it went in and struck bone. I kept crying and crying, trying to picture how I could make everything good again. No solution existed, and unlike previous occasions when the Sideways People departed, this time there was an undeniable rejection of me. *Me.* I could not even picture the two of us reuniting in heaven or take comfort in any of the standard platitudes.

As I stood there and wept, trying to think of ways I could appease Kevin and make all his sacrifices worthwhile, the statue kept making its same monotone and insistent demand.

Give me an offering.

Give me an offering.

And so, I moved downwards toward the metal golden rucksack that was placed so neatly behind the creature's head and which everyone, for now, had ignored.

I mentioned earlier; I don't think people understand their emotions or behavior. There is this defined clear division between Ego and Id, with one being the rational state of mind and thought, and the other being the rolling undercurrent of emotions and needs that flow and ebb underneath. Maybe for me, the two are separate to an unusually high extent. I am always surprised when I cry at odd moments for no apparent reason and can only presume something unknown is going on in my subconscious.

It is obvious I had endured a lot. That voice, releasing and losing Kevin and, even worse, his complete rejection of me coupled with the unhealing injuries and physical transformations, frayed my mental control. I had not realized the extent to which it had affected me, though, and it may explain what happened next.

I reached down and grabbed the rucksack only to feel my hand turn cold and pain spread upward through my veins. Shocked, I saw that the object had fused to my hand, replacing my fingers with cold gold-colored metal. I tried to shake it back and forth, to free and fling it away. It was heavy and burdensome, but I could not release it as it stuck to and became part of my hand. Tendrils of gold spread from where I had grabbed it and snaked like veins toward my elbow, as though to chain itself there for extra security.

I shook my hand to free it, while the creature that had carried it still lay on the floor, rolling backward and forward in agony, gibbering words and noises in a language that I did not understand nor want to comprehend. Around me, its fellow creatures carried on chasing each other and performing ongoing pointless surgery that sprayed red droplets through the air and caused screams and cutting noises. Throughout, the statue kept repeating its endless demands in that monotone. I snapped.

"Cunt! You fucking cunt." My voice squawked through a throat closed with the hatred and emotion trapped in my chest. I raised the heavy and infused with metal hand and bashed it down into the face of the laying creature. It screeched and rolled backward and forward, attempting to escape. Again and again, my heavy metal hand rained down on the creature.

The metallic skin of the creature crunched in, revealing red strips of flesh and broken bones. My hand raised up and rained down, a multitude of times. I saw white teeth and raised the metal hand to bash them in, hearing the crunch as teeth snapped and crushed, only to be replaced by flowing blood. Some of the blood clung to the backpack and, unnoticed, the furious force sprayed the statue with red droplets.

I carried on for a long time. The hatred and need to release all the anguish I had endured meant the hand kept on rising and falling, long after the creature stopped struggling. Even after the creature's head was bashed flat. It was exhaustion rather than regaining emotional control that forced me to stop.

I felt ill and nauseous. My stomach kept flipping and pushing to force non-existent food out through my mouth, but only bile rose to burn my throat. The anger and assault had caused adrenaline to flow through my body, and now it dissipated. I felt weak and sickened, and did not look at the broken remains of the creature I had murdered. Instead, I turned and looked at the statue which had driven me to this act. It had stopped the whispering that had plagued my ears but stood there impassive and silent. The creatures that had chased each other around it had also stopped. Everything was static, nothing moved.

I did not know what else remained to do. It was clear the statue was responsible for my pain, for my sickness and for making me do the terrible things I had just performed. I stepped forward and looked at it. The static but open mouth leered at me in triumph. Without stopping to think, I pulled back and swung the metal fused rucksack hand straight at its face.

With a muted clang, the rucksack stuck to its cruel visage, but my arm carried on, moving with a surprise of intense pain and the sudden feeling of being lighter. I looked at my right hand. My fingers were missing. As though my hand were perforated paper, a jagged flesh edge had appeared, and everything below the knuckle was torn away.

The blow also affected the statue. A patina of corrosion spread from where the blow landed, causing it to reduce and crumble as though made from cheap pot metal exposed to the elements for centuries. In silence, the metal creatures walked up and, in unified instinct, placed their hands on the decaying statue, causing the patina and corrosion to spread to them. They became absorbed within the statue; this did not cause the object to grow but accelerated its dissipation. It collapsed within itself in a spray of brown rust. Suddenly, there was nothing there. Just the barren ground and the pulverized remains of the one creature I had bludgeoned earlier.

I looked at my hand. After the initial pain settled into a dull throb, no blood fell from the wound but appeared in drips at the edge of the torn knuckles without ever spilling. I looked around, even now avoiding the sight of the crumpled creature whose head I had bashed in, and spotted something nearby.

It was a circle, about four feet wide, and within it sparks of red and brown light danced. I looked closer and saw the cause was whatever passed for light in this place, hitting fragments of rust and blood and refracting around the circle. I looked at Bea. She was at my side and kept alternatively looking at me and then at the circle. With a resigned shrug, I stepped in, and Bea followed.

Chapter Twenty-One

I had the sense of rushing. I felt like I was being crunched tight within myself, but also of being transparent and thinner. It seemed at one stage that the red and brown lights blurred through my body, then they danced in front of my eyes and merged into a hue of gray, blocking my vision. Throughout, I could not see Bea or feel her presence. The fury that had possessed me when I killed the creature still roiled and lurched within my stomach but was joined by other sickening base emotions.

I expected to land elsewhere, in a new place that had unique characteristics. It did not, therefore, surprise me when the gray in front of my eyes and the sense of traveling stopped and cleared. I found myself somewhere different, but it still had the same sense of wrongness. My feet were dragging me downward, further in.

The ground had the omnipresent slope downwards but was marshy and soft. There was a covering of green water within which swirls of brown mud floated. The overall sense was of wearying dinginess. No vibrancy or depth to the color. Everything just throbbed banality, except for the creatures that lived here. They were impossible to disregard and caused fear.

Across the surface of the water, things that were human with faces twisted in eye popping fury, flitted like water flies. When they saw each other, they invariably attacked in gouging fury, teeth snapping, arms and fists spinning and grappling. Their attacks would lead them to disappear beneath the surface of the water. The murky water would flow over them, thrash into white foam to show the marks of their struggle before healing over.

These creatures filled and roamed the land. They surrounded us in every direction as far as the eye could see. I was afraid for our safety. Unlike those previous lands, where the domestic creatures were so different to us, so obsessed with their own activities, that they had ignored and spared us major confrontation; here I was uncertain. These things were human and showed no mercy. Violence spread around us, and it felt like it would engulf us before long. I obeyed the instinct in my legs to move onward, hoping to find somewhere safer. I sank up to my knees and the water lapped and flowed around them in expanding circles.

I was going to continue, but the silence made me turn to Bea. She just stood there as though the water's surface had defeated her. I dragged my feet sideways toward her. Lifting them from the swallowing mud and pushing them down again was hard and tore at my knees. I forgot the nature of this land and turned to scour behind me to see any solid ground.

It was impossible. The land was so barren and dull that the piercing white light should not have existed, but it did. No natural sun could have filled my skull with such dull aching pain. Closing my eyes did no good. The light shone through, giving me headaches and unpleasant, incomprehensible afterimages that seemed to show hands raised in supplication and pleading. My stomach twisted again in revulsion. I turned my head downwards and with closed and covered eyes, blindly and carefully walked sideways to where Bea waited.

I reached her after what seemed an age. "What is it? We need to get moving."

Bea stayed silent but carried on looking at me. She had not sunk into the marshland but stayed above it as though her feet disdained to touch the ground. The top of my head rested level with her breasts. I had the absurd image of myself being a knight errant kneeling in service to a grand lady.

Then her hands moved and motioned that she could not walk on the ground. I looked at her questioningly, only to see her face become blank, with no answers revealed. I could not leave Bea behind. She was the only one who had bonded with me, the only one who would accompany me on this journey. I turned around, showing she should hold on to my back and I would carry her.

There was a brief sensation of movement, and in a collapsing moment, her weight shifted onto me. I gasped in pain, my back arching backward. Carrying Bea was monstrous. She was a boulder, and I was no beast capable of bearing it.

I don't know what happened. The water may have risen or the ground may have collapsed underneath me. The dank water submerged and surrounded me. It blocked out light and rushed into my mouth and nostrils, filling my lungs. These air sacks struggled and failed to expel the brackish liquid.

I received conclusive proof that the basic laws of biology did not apply anymore. The water could not drown me. My lungs and stomach, filled now, did not realize this and twisted and retched to clear themselves, only to fill again in a painful, endless cycle. Heaving and twisting, I scanned in desperation to find somewhere I could rise above the soil while being crushed under the weight of Bea.

My predicament would have given pleasure to another in that realm.

Mutated beyond measure, Michael stood in the room that he longed to own. Calm now. Mind frozen into cruel razor-edged logic by determination and need. They had beaten and driven him off. Michael had counted himself lucky to survive.

Normally, he would pace this room with quick, changing steps. Driven by irritation and fury. Now, however, he stood static and silent in the middle, thinking his way through the situation. The room felt responsive to his mood and seemed attuned to his thoughts.

The woman, he did not understand; her reasons for accompanying that Other were beyond him. The Other he could beat any day of the week, although he could not deny that twice now that cunt had defeated his released specters. He wanted to confront those weak fuckers again; his strength would be enhanced if he faced them in that fury circle. That was also a concern, though. That part of the land exhibited a powerful pull on him. If he lost his concentration, he might get trapped permanently.

He decided on another test. Something to test those two and understand their capabilities and see where they belonged. He swung his thoughts back to his past, to his deeds, considering one that, by his own high standards, could almost be deemed a failure.

Not a complete failure, he would admit. He had captured, tortured and killed the boy after all, but he hadn't quite smashed the spirit to the usual extent. At the end, after unbelievable cruelty and abuse, the boy tried to smile and reached out with trusting hands. Michael had drowned him out of sheer disgust.

However, this botched job might be what he needed. He reached inside himself and jerked the black formed revenant outward with rough thoughts and angry calls. The boy landed outside, trying to look around at his surroundings while seeing nothing. He was short, had round full cheeks, and a gentle smile that even now spread across his face—revealing his hope that this was some horrible misunderstanding that was now resolved, meaning he could return to Mummy and Daddy.

That would not happen. Michael hated looking at this failure, *hated it.* The boy should not behave like this. The boy should retch in fear and try to run away in absolute futility while Michael laughed. Angry, Michael commanded the boy to the Other. To see how they handled an innocent child. To discover what that Other could do.

I was underwater, trying to avoid falling flat on my face. The water was too murky to see through. I was panicking. The weight almost forced me over. I reached for the ground with my maimed hand and something snapped at it, making me glad the fingers had already gone. I concentrated and pushed my vision downwards.

On the floor, covered in the dingy soil and obscured by filthy water, were those who had fought and grabbed at each other on the surface. They were littered around, completely underwater, and many of them partially buried by boggy soil. Still, they fought and grabbed and bit at each other, and anyone else who was close enough. Each one had become, to varying degrees, decomposed by their environment and bore marks and injuries from their indiscriminate contest.

Flesh hung from them in decaying strips, gouged eyes stared around in hatred and fear, peeled lips snarled and parted to bite. I was standing on one, pinning it down. It tried to twist and reach for me, its skeletal form clothed in torn strips of sodden fabric and loose, bloated flesh. All around, others had seen me and were pulling themselves from their shallow watery graves to head toward me.

They would have overrun me. Their movements were sped by need and anger, but the need to punch and kick others nearby distracted them. I had limited choices. I was going to be torn apart by these fury-driven people or crushed underneath the extreme weight of Bea. As always, my only true salvation was my Sideways People.

On this occasion, I did not pause. Kevin had shown me the Sideways People could be virtually indestructible and would obey my need to behave in certain ways. I knew which Sideways Person I would call forth, but it took a moment to work out within myself how I would use him.

David. The gentlest person I have ever met. Everything about him spoke of meekness. His voice had been a whisper, his shoulders had hunched and rolled to present the smallest potential target. People used to ignore him or take advantage of his giving nature. I hadn't. I had just let him know I appreciated and understood his nature. At the end, at his very end, as my hands laced round his throat and I pressed, his eyes had been questioning and he had wrapped his arms around my shoulders in a brother's embrace. When the moment came to expel his last breath, he had smiled in an uncertain and almost embarrassed fashion.

His very nature would be an anathema to this place. I doubted this land had ever seen anyone like him. This release would differ from the others as well. David could not be allowed to be entirely independent or external. If I permitted this, the fury people around us might destroy him and attack me, anyway. Without his strength, I had little chance of carrying Bea's weight.

I called his name out within me, so soft that none but he would hear. He had been hiding in some strange corner of my soul, eyes sad and concerned. I motioned him toward me and then pictured him moving through my skin in a gray cloud and condensing into physical form outside. The process was slow, but I felt him obey my mental images to move through my skin and take physical form. I closed my eyes to shut out everything around me; the weight upon my shoulders, the fury people and the sensation of my lungs filled with water. Instead, I concentrated upon this precious soul I was expelling.

David moved out of me, but I stopped him with determined thoughts before his form became entirely distinct from mine. One additional gray leg came out of my hip; his dear face moved out of mine. My physical features were buried within the back of his head. David's partial expulsion conjoined us more intimately than any twins. His gray arms came out underneath mine. At this moment, I had three legs, four arms, and one merged, distended and distorted face.

That my face was buried in the back of his head meant that my nose was no longer breathing in the water. I twisted my lungs and felt the water expelled outward through his mouth. David did not appear to need to breathe water in, I felt able to breathe through him. I felt sweet relief as my lungs cleared. The additional leg meant I could carry Bea's weight and move forward.

I saw through his eyes. The water did not obscure his view; everything looked translucent and ineffectual through his eyes. He could see where the water was absent, where solid ground was, and the two looked only a little different to him. The fury people were insubstantial and caused no concern.

Merged heads meant I shared his thoughts and feelings. I loved David, and this aspect of his leaving caused me such pain. He was panicking and surging forward, trying to be free. The surrounding environment caused him no concern, but he wanted with undeniable desperation to be out of me and heading upward toward the light. He saw some bizarre safety and freedom there. He tried to force all of himself entirely separate from me. In need, I clenched my thoughts and held him where he was.

David redoubled his efforts to break out of me. His frenzied impetus to freedom caused the pair of us to surge forward. The water appeared to surge and split, pushed apart by our desperate movement. The fury people tried to attack us, to no avail. David was without peer in gentleness, but these assailants did not register as human. Every time one came close to us, the gray arms would turn to snap them like fragile twigs.

The power David exuded was incredible. He dragged me and Bea along with him as he surged forward. The entire environment tried to escape him and tore to avoid his flight. The fury people were nothing to him, and even they shrunk back in fear.

Throughout, David and I shared a merged skull and brain. I could read his thoughts. All that was there. An undeniable urge to end the connection between us and be free. I hated it. Utterly hated it. I almost wished I were floundering under the water, crushed by Bea's world-collapsing weight and on the verge of being torn apart. This time, it was me being rejected. David wanted to be out. It was no comfort to know the change in location must have confused him.

We traveled for an age. His gray leg blurring as it moved, my own legs struggling to keep up. As we moved, I pondered what I could see through his eyes. To David, this world appeared translucent and unnatural. I wondered if everything I had experienced was some horrific hallucination caused by my intense actions with Laura. Staring through David's eyes showed everything I saw but also displayed the environment as translucent fog incapable of stopping form or matter.

It was a comforting thought, and for a few moments, I allowed myself to believe the lie. But just as it was a Sideways Person who opened the door to this possibility, so it was the others that convinced me it couldn't be true. Cruel circumstances had sundered some from our mutual bliss. Our in-depth union had ended. The sheer pain of separation had been beyond my imagination. Some mundane hallucination could not be responsible. Could not have caused that much damage to my soul.

David appeared to have a set place as his intended destination. The water and the marshy soil had disappeared, and without warning, David stopped. We were atop a knoll, one that was boggy but firm. I wondered why David had halted his desperate flight. On the chase here, his overwhelming desire to be entirely separate had led to surging and determined movement. David still wanted independence and, more than anything, to be free from me. The sharing of brain matter revealed something had changed for him, though. I tried to move about more within his head, and all I could get was the general impression he had reached an instinctive end point.

Even now, even after this rejection, I tried hard to pull him back into me. I really did. Once there, he would understand I still wanted us to be together; that I would protect him forever. Even as I tried to pull his struggling form back inside, though, I realized something was already ruined. The milk soured by being spilled, once I had shown I would release him to answer my needs. I had betrayed the fundamental nature of our relationship. Realization led to immediate action.

With deliberate cruelty, I grabbed hold of his arms and heaved his gray form outward and to one side in the most brutal form of expulsion. I heard him sigh in agony before turning my eyes away, so I did not have to watch his reaction to my betrayal or see him scrabbling around abandoned in this strange land without my intimate protection.

I had forgotten it was David's strength that had largely been carrying Bea. Having ejected him, my strength was unequal to her burden. With sudden release, I collapsed under her crushing weight. A moment later, there was a sudden shift, the suggestion of movement, and the weight was gone. I could not turn to look at Bea in case I caught sight of David. I kept my eyes closed, placed my hands over my ears and waited a long while.

The other Sideways People left quickly after protecting or serving me. This time was no different. When I opened my eyes and uncovered my ears, I could not feel David's presence around me and knew he had gone. I turned to Bea, who had positioned herself down the hill from me. Her features were hidden and obscured beneath her hood, but I still got the impression she was looking to my side.

Staggering to feet that felt weary and torn, I walked toward Bea to demand she thank me for carrying her or at the very least acknowledge what I had achieved. She had made no motion or noise since dismounting from my back. The journey had cost me dearly. It is possible I would have had to summon David to deal with the fury people anyway, but it still did not seem fair that I alone should pay the burden of this journey. Bea made no move or acknowledgement but nodded to one side of me, her whole bearing screaming sadness and compassion.

I had not taken two steps toward her when a sound made me stop and look sideways. It was the sound of a soft sob. For a second, I feared it was David, and I steeled myself to turn and comfort him, but then I realized it was someone far younger. They had tried to stifle their cries out of shyness or fear; neither of which David would have felt toward me. I turned around and felt my heart wrench when I saw what was there.

It was a young boy, only just six. Surrounded by the black sheen that marked him as someone Michael had murdered. He stood just a few paces away, trying to shrink into himself. I slowly walked toward him, raising my hands to show I intended no harm. An ashen, shaky smile spread across my lips.

I had seen many victims of Michael and saw the inventive tortures he had visited upon them. All had been mutilated beyond belief. As I approached the boy, momentarily, I believed he had not suffered as much. It was a misbegotten hope—as I stepped closer; I saw the child had only empty sockets instead of eyes. For a second, my movement staggered in shock and tears formed a silver sheen in my eyes.

"I am going to kill you for this, Michael," I mumbled to no one in particular.

My steps had faltered, the smile had dropped, but I forced both back and closed the gap between the two of us.

"Hi there," I said in as friendly a fashion as possible. All of Michael's other victims had been hostile and attempted harm. This was very different. I sensed only innocence and a need for protection. Maybe in life the boy had lacked the capacity for harm or cruelty and, even after death and Michael's teachings, was still incapable of violence.

"Want to go home now," the murdered boy said in soft tones. The poor boy spoke so quietly and timidly. I missed it the first time and had to lean in to hear it the second time. I heard a rustle, and Bea kneeled next to me. Her hands reached out to the boy and engulfed him in a fierce embrace.

"We'll go," I said to the boy in tones that were as reassuring as possible. "I'll find you a way out." I reached out and ruffled his soft hair before gently peeling it away from the empty eye sockets. Bea turned to look at me, her expression unreadable. I gave into temptation and placed my arms around both of them.

I gained strength from the embrace and took stock of my surroundings. It was still boggy, dingy marshland, but the water had dissipated somehow. There was none to be seen except for small green ponds that would not reach the ankle. Bea seemed capable of walking around on this surface.

Slowly and reluctantly, I removed my arms from them both and caught a look of disappointment from Bea. It was almost as though she had enjoyed the embrace and taken equal strength from it; I itched to start it again. To bury my head between the two of them and drink in their smells and need. To be important and loved. But something caught my attention. The fury people had caught and surrounded us.

They appeared to have forgotten their animosity toward each other. Crouched and moving sinuously with fluid grace, they circled. They appeared both fascinated and repelled by the three of us. I wondered about this. David had been gentle, and completely unaffected by this part of the land. He had seen it as a barely noticeable mist. Any obstacles placed in his path had been easily overcome before he delivered us to a place without water and where the land was solid. Maybe the boy was the same. Maybe his purity and gentle nature meant the land responded to him differently.

That might be true, but the boy did not seem to realize his power here and remained locked in his tight embrace of Bea. All around us, in ever-increasing numbers, the fury people circled. This anomaly in their midst fascinated them, but I feared what would happen when their curiosity ended.

"We need to move." I turned and whispered urgently to Bea, "Where?"

"You lead us," she said in quiet response. This shocked me. Bea had stated that the journey was mine earlier, but she had always displayed knowledge of the land and guided me to the portals that transported us onwards. Now, despite the urgency of our need and the fact we had an innocent boy to protect, she was refusing to direct us to safety.

"I don't know where to go," I said, trying to keep my voice low to avoid attracting the fury people or scaring the young boy.

Bea's voice was calm and clear as she responded with, "You do. Your feet are compelled to—"

Go down. Go further in.

She was right. There was an imperative need in my joints that meant I had to progress downwards. Then Bea said, "Go where you belong."

I paused at this. Nowhere here seemed suitable. Perhaps there was somewhere within here I belonged, but I doubted it and just wanted to return home. There was nothing important or colorful here. No sensations. Only brief glimpses of emotions from Bea and need from this boy. That would not be enough. Bea needed to open another portal. We needed to go somewhere else.

I turned to the boy and kneeled next to him. "What's your name?" I asked, my voice gentle. He kept crying, his mouth throwing out gasps and defenseless noises. My eyes watered in response, and my bottom lip quivered with empathic sorrow. I reached out and separated the boy from Bea. Taking a breath, I placed him on my shoulders and felt his arms wrap around my forehead and legs around my neck.

I stared around at the fury people. They were keeping their distance. I tried to intimidate them wordlessly with my confident look, to make them think I was invincible. They had seen what one Sideways Person could do, and I had others within me who would do anything I needed.

I started walking at a slow pace. The boy weighed nothing at all but clung to me in need. For a second, I pictured myself as his father, carrying him to a picnic somewhere. The illusion did not last that long. More and more of the fury people kept gathering around, and I knew they would attack soon. Having seen the savagery that they practiced on each other; I knew they were more than capable of tearing the three of us apart.

I could not see behind me. It was uphill, and that dreadful white light would blind me, but I trusted either Bea would protect us from that direction or they were incapable of attacking us from there. Adrenaline flowed through my body, leaving me sick as I tried to fight its silent urge to run, trusting the illusion of fearlessness would serve me better than flight.

My feet itched with frustration and kept leading me downwards over the uneven swamp ground. At one point, unbidden by any conscious volition, they jerked to one side and took me down another path. I kept looking at the hate contorted faces of the fury people. Without intending to, I broke into a sudden run, partially in response to an evolutionary flight impulse and partially in response to the pervasive need in my legs. The fury people had been waiting for this sign of weakness. In a burst, they all started running toward me. Abandoning all pretense, I sprinted as fast as possible, hoping Bea could match my pace.

"Run!" the small boy fluted in fear as his arms tightened around my head, obscuring my vision. I needed no additional urging. As I stumbled ever-downward, I reached up with my one remaining good hand to steady him.

The other inhabitants converged from all sides toward us. As they ran, they still seemed to move on water; as their feet lifted, droplets splashed around them, and their movement seemed impeded and difficult. To me, the ground seemed solid and firm, allowing rapid movement. For a moment, I entertained the hope that I could outpace everyone and somehow find a haven for the three of us.

As I ran, I kept turning my head to either side to look at the fury people, to check whether any of them were getting closer. They had expressions of hatred and violence on their faces and moved with focused determination. I was outpacing them though; I ducked and dove around any object that blocked my path. One moment after I had turned to look to one side, I felt a bang and white light filled my eyes.

My feet had led me to a point where something had suddenly appeared, blocking my path, and stunned me. I turned to look at what had stopped my passage. It was impossible that I had not noticed it, or that it had burst unannounced from the ground in an instant.

It was a huge, ancient gray stone wall covered in moss and cracks. Something or someone had mortared together the individual blocks with a dark brown substance. Each block was huge and could not have been moved by normal human effort. Forgetting the desperation of my situation, I reached out with my maimed hand and touched the rough surface. I had to pull it away immediately while I gasped in pain. The surface was both hot, so that a brief touch burned, and sharp, causing the stumps of my fingers to bleed. The wall mocked me with the entirety of its presence. It filled the landscape with no obvious route around or over it.

I still had the sensation I needed to carry on downwards, and my feet itched to obey, but there was no path. Trapped, I turned and faced the fury people who surrounded me. I could barely see them. Looking at them meant looking upward toward the pale white light that burned down on me. I could only see the vaguest dark silhouettes of where they were but could feel the malevolence and violence in the air.

"You need to get moving," Bea whispered. "You don't belong here. They will tear you apart soon. The only thing that is stopping them is the boy and myself. I doubt that protection will last long."

Bea had appeared at my side. Again, she sheathed herself in yellow flame, and I think it was this that stopped the denizens from attacking us. "I can't get through that," I said to her, the speed with which the words spilled out showing my urgency.

"You have moved us to other places. You have opened other barriers," she responded.

"This is a great big fucking wall that has just appeared in front of me," I said back, trying to keep the anger out of my voice. "We have to move, and I don't know how. Just do it, just do whatever you are going to do and fucking open it."

"How did you do it previously? How did you open the other barriers?" Bea asked me quizzically. It felt like she was a patronizing teacher explaining basic material to a slow pupil, finding the whole process difficult and trying. I wanted to rail and shout to make her understand how dire our situation was but stopped myself. Bea understood this place better than I did, and if she did not feel in danger, then neither did I.

I stood there for a moment, carrying the child whose name I did not know, surrounded by creatures that snarled at me, path blocked by a massive wall that had not been there just a few moments before. It had never occurred to me how ludicrous the whole situation was.

I considered the previous aspects of this land that I had visited. "You opened the one barrier," I said. "So presumably that means that you could open another somehow—even if there is a stone wall in the way." I looked at her with hope, but she gave no response and remained impassive.

I paused for a second and carried on talking in the same calm, pondering voice. "In other places, the release of trapped souls has opened the barriers. Freeing the souls that Michael commands seems to be an act that allows the barriers to open." I had spoken without thinking, but an uncomfortable thought crossed my mind. I realized I was carrying one of Michael's souls on my shoulders. Not allowing myself to consider that, I rushed on and continued to speak. "The other barrier appeared to be opened by myself, losing my temper and crushing that inflicted animal."

Bea stayed silent. For a second, a bemused smile crossed her face. "Is that what you think opens barriers?" she asked. Silence answered her question. I did not understand what she was trying to say, and the boy on my shoulders was trying to crush my face and neck with panicked hands and feet.

"Well, if that has led to the barriers being opened, there is an obvious answer," Bea said, her voice turning stern and severe. I carried on looking at her in silence, pretending not to understand her suggestion.

"You have one of Michael's souls with you. The act of freeing it by killing it should give you some kind of passage." Bea stated in an even, expressionless tone.

I was stunned. I had always assumed that Bea was soft and compassionate. Earlier on, she embraced the boy as though dear to her. Now she suggested I murder him? My mouth gaped open in amazement. I thought we had been working together to keep the child safe. That was why I had run, carrying the child across my shoulders. I had hoped we could find somewhere safe and maybe form some kind of family that cared for each other. But now? I don't think the child heard us. Certainly, it said nothing. Although its arms and legs were still tight around my head and neck, the urgency of its grip did not change.

Bea must have understood some of what I was thinking. I could not hide my surprise. Her voice became gentle as she moved herself closer to me. "Do you honestly feel the boy could be safe here? Does the child belong anywhere in this land?"

I remained mute, trying to think of other answers and ways of getting what I needed to happen. All the while I was aware of the fury people surrounding us and could only see their blurred outlines. I marveled they had held back this long and did not expect our luck to last much longer. Uneasily, I considered the options for getting away from these creatures and through the next barrier.

A different idea occurred to me. One with costs assigned to it. It would hurt but might allow the unclaimed boy some measure of freedom and safety. One of my gentler Sideways People destroyed many of these creatures while carrying me and Bea underwater. Suppose I released two of my Sideways People to protect us all? Some inside had been blessed with an aptitude for violence. My relationships with them had been based on being the warrior sidekick, whose word was his bond. I could summon those forth and support them, fighting by their side in camaraderie and utter loyalty. Together, we would destroy these worthless enemies. They would appreciate the how and why of me calling them forth. They, for whom loyalty had been more than just a word, but a standard by which they lived their lives, would surely return inwards afterwards.

Excited, I closed my eyes and reached down into myself. I focused on those I had selected and screamed their names in need, expecting them to charge forth ruthlessly in my defense. Nothing happened. I called their names again and moved internally, urgently looking for them. I saw no Sideways People and had only the vaguest hint of their presence. Alarmed, I opened my eyes and looked for Bea. She stood by my side; her eyes were severe as she looked at me. She had pressed a firm hand against the wound in my midriff.

"Not here," she said. "Not them. That wouldn't be fair." I opened my mouth to shout. How dare she stand between me and those angels of my nature? Then something broke, and there was a sense of incredible movement, and a surge of pressing bodies buried me.

I staggered, trying to get back onto my knees. Something sent my head backward to smash into the stone wall behind me, and again, white flickering lights exploded across my vision. Blood trickled down, wet and red, from an unseen cut in the back of my head. Nausea started in the pit of my stomach and rose upward toward my mouth. Rough, vicious hands plucked the child from my shoulders. I threw out my good hand and grabbed hold of him before pulling him toward my chest in a determined embrace. My vision blurred and whirled as more and more hands reached for the child.

That would have been it. Again, Bea was my savior. Sheathed in golden flame she stepped directly in front of me, her blazing righteousness protecting me. Even looking up, I could see dismay and fear on the faces of the fury people. "Make your decision and decide where you and the child belong," Bea said, panting with effort. "Their urgency is too great to stop them for long."

I looked at the child. It was so small and trusting. Its eyeless face had turned toward me, and it had raised his head. Its small arms reached upward for an embrace.

"I don't like it here," its small voice said while crying. My vision swirled. Again tears dripped down the side of my mutilated nose. I reached out my hands.

Bea grabbed hold of my face and turned it so that I was looking into her eyes. They reminded me of someone else's, but everything was so blurry and difficult to focus on. Maybe if I hadn't been so concussed, I would have understood everything then—realized the truth.

"It's okay. It's a kindness. There is nowhere here for the child. It cannot be free. It has been trapped in cruelty for too long." Her voice was so gentle and filled with empathy that I nodded in agreement. I looked at the boy as it moved closer. Its face raised to look at me, arms reached out in trusting supplication. If it hadn't been for the black sheen that surrounded it, marking it forever as someone that Michael had already killed, I would never have been able to do what I did next.

My damaged hand shot out and grabbed hold of the child by its shoulder. I turned its surprised body around so I would not have to see its face. I placed my arm under its neck and lifted it up and tight against me to strangle it.

It was difficult, ungraceful. I lacked all skill and finesse. In other times and in a different world, my hands had skillfully reached for my intended targets, looking to make them one with me for now and forever. This was very different. My arm protested my intentions but remained true. I closed my eyes, so I did not see the sickening sight, but that did not block out the screams and cries, nor the feel of the small body against mine kicking and twisting in desperation.

I pressed the body roughly and inexpertly against my torso as tightly as possible, hoping to finish this painful and dark deed quickly. The boy lived still and kept living, no matter how tightly I pressed my forearm against his throat. I panicked. I turned myself and the boy toward the wall. All the time, his little legs were kicking as though to pump a swing backward and forward.

I, someone who had frozen people in set states so gently and lovingly previously, could only *try* to crush the boy's throat. Maybe it was the damaged hand that stopped my usual skills from surfacing. I had bent double from the force that was being pushed through the child's form onto my midriff. It is impossible to say how long this lasted, but it took me an age to realize my efforts were going to be unsuccessful.

I turned toward that infernal wall that blocked my path and rendered my current action so necessary. My eyes leaked tears in a never-ending stream. I moved closer to the stone, futilely maintaining the pressure my forearm was exerting all the time. Behind me I heard the fury people stampeding in motion but never coming closer. I dared not turn around to see them or Bea, knowing the white light would be there illuminating me in my infamy.

I bent my knees and crouched down. After taking a second to drag in my breath, I sprang forward toward the wall with the child held in front of me. With a loud clatter, we hit this thick inanimate surface as I attempted to crush the boy to a final true death against it.

The wall was hot and, despite having no obvious edges to it, cut deeply. Grown hooks and edges pierced through my cloth clothes into my shoulders and forearms. The wounds tore, pushed and crushed my flesh, but no blood leaked free. The child held in my grasp responded very differently and screamed high pitched wails of pain as it spurted shockingly bright red blood. I screamed in answer and pulled its small body back, only to throw it forward against the wall. Its blood spurted forth, and where it landed, the wall turned brown, and cracks spread in thin lines.

The child struggled in my arms and turned to face me. Its face twisted in pain and misery. Although it had a black sheen showing that it was a trapped soul, I could see the terrible gashes and tears in the face and flesh I had caused. Its mouth was twisted in a hurt grimace and let out sobbing noises; it had raised its arms across its chest to protect itself. I raised my knee high and kicked out the flat of my foot toward its unprotected face.

The back of its head collided backward against the wall, releasing further gushes of blood. I heard a crack and saw the back of its skull hang loose down the one side of its neck, crushed and torn free by the duality of the force of my kick and the peculiarly sharp tearing nature of the wall. Where the wall had received blood, the stones and mortar aged and looked centuries old. Cracks spread as though fed by the sacrifice and misery of the child.

I kicked the child's face again and again. It stopped being able to defend itself and my foot passed forward into its features and forced its head backward into the wall. It kept screaming until one forceful kick halted the appalling sound. With a sodden mulching noise, my foot crushed in the child's face and pushed straight through into the wall. The child stiffened and its small legs buckled while hands dropped to its side as though about to curtsey.

A last burst of blood from the back of the boy's head sprayed against the stone block behind it, further weakening it. My foot crashed into the same spot a millisecond later, and great chunks of rock and slab burst free. The child dissolved into the soil while the crack spread upward and sideways on the wall, spewing forth bits of sharp stone.

With a sudden burst of trapped air, a clear channel through which I could fit appeared in the wall. It appeared almost perfectly shaped to grant me access. It was the same height as me and widened sideways at the exact spot where my shoulders would pass through. Bea pushed on my shoulder from behind, and her voice whispered in my ear, "Time to move on."

I stepped into the crack and, indeed, moved on.

Chapter Twenty-Two

Walking through the wall took me somewhere different. In just a few steps, I felt I had traveled many miles. Even though I only walked through a crack about a meter long, the air got warmer and more stale. After taking my last step through, I noticed the slope had gone. The ground was now perfectly level. My feet still felt compelled to go in a set direction, but this was no longer downwards; instead, it seemed to compel me to follow a narrow dirt path that had sprung up beside me. I looked at the passageway to see if any creatures followed me.

The wall was not there. It had disappeared as impossibly as it had appeared. The land was unbroken by this shape, and I had the sense of incredible space going on for infinity, smearing into smudges on the horizon. I could look behind me. The white light had gone.

No sun was in sight. There was a light somewhere illuminating the world, but I could not see it, and the air felt hot and thin. Beneath me, the ground was dry, gray and hard. It didn't appear to have soil or edges but was a solid bumpy gray that stretched onwards. It was raining without clouds in a sky that was reddish-brown. Great droplets fell from this sky and hit hard upon me. They felt acidic and burned where they landed. I saw one fall on my undamaged hand. It splashed hugely across my fingers, smoldered, and released smoke into the air. The pain was like spilling boiling water onto an unprepared section of flesh. It was better when the rain landed on clothed areas. The pain was much less then, although still noticeable. I tried to hunch and pull my skin under the cloth to protect myself.

I turned to Bea. She stood near me, stance impassive and her face set but serene. I felt raw over what I had done to the boy. My stomach felt tight. With a sense of shame, I realized I hadn't even asked the boy his name, where his parents were or anything personal. One moment I had been considering making some kind of surrogate family with him, the next he was utterly and irrevocably gone, with no trace remaining.

"What happened to him?" I said to Bea. My voice felt constricted and unnatural.

Bea's face was calm and unaffected. "What does it matter to you?" She responded with quiet curiosity.

"I bashed his head in on your suggestion and then he just disappeared." My voice came out dead and sullen. The unshed tears constricted and changed the pattern of my speech.

"You bashed his head in to answer your own need," said Bea before raising her hand to forestall my objection. "It's okay. Have you not realized yet? People get what they deserve and go where they belong. The child did not belong here and went somewhere else."

Bea then looked at me. "You should be relieved. Those you carry will get what they deserve. That is important to you, isn't it?" Bea's response stopped my complaints, the understanding making me feel much better.

It was true, and the idea of natural and true justice cheered me immensely. If everyone got what they deserved, then soon my Sideways People would be where they needed to be, enriched through being unified with me. As always, when I thought about my Sideways People, my thoughts turned to Laura and the precious moments we had shared. That wondrous achievement of perfection we had reached in the forest where we consummated our love.

Thoughts of Laura always aroused strange emotions in me. I felt so proud of our shared experience. That she understood *the what* and *why* of my offering and took part in it so willingly. It also aroused other, less positive emotions. I felt sorrow that I had not experienced her thoughts and emotions. Since we had merged, I had had no chance to explore her and had only the vaguest sense of her presence. This felt like a betrayal or spurning of her precious gift. Certainly, I felt intense guilt. Bea's admonishment that things worked out for the best gave me hope. Soon I would return to where I should be, where I could savor Laura and her presence inside of me.

Re-invigorated then, I stretched out tall, only to hunch myself smaller again within my clothes when a droplet of burning rain landed across the back of my neck.

"Shall we get going then?" I said in cheerful tones to Bea. For just a split second, Bea appeared to smile, and her arms moved upward, as though to grasp me in her embrace. I moved forward eagerly to accept the clasp, but then her hands dropped back down to her sides. The rain that fell on and burned me didn't land near her.

With my ruined hand, I motioned to the path by my side and followed it. It wound ever onwards in great looping circles. The ground was hard and pressed upon my feet, bruising the soles. Everything appeared tinged with fire and heat. The sky had a red patina; the rain burned, and the air scalded lungs as it was forced inwards with great gasps. But the smell was worse.

As we traveled further and further along the path, the smell grew stronger and stronger. When we first arrived here, I thought the air smelled stagnant, but as we moved further on and deeper in, I realized it now had a smell of burning. It was like cooked and charred flesh.

Time, as always, was uncertain and impossible to track. I do not know how long we walked, or the distance traveled. Everything was indeterminate. But on our journey, we passed mounds that jutted up from the ground. They were tapered: thinner at the bottom, but they spread outward at shoulder height before going thinner again and finally coming to a square edge at the top.

The mounds glowed cherry red with an extreme heat I could feel from a distance. Passing closer to them, I saw the mounds split in two around the edges. Each had a stone door, with a slight space on one side that enabled sight inwards. They looked like red-hot stone coffins with the lid opened just enough to peer inside.

I moved closer to one of these objects and with a jolt realized the impression of them being stone coffins was accurate. Within the one I was closest to, a man resided. Flames licked the internal stone walls, and the man struggled against the fire with a mouth opened wide in a voiceless scream. His wide eyes darted around in search of an exit. The obvious route through the partially opened door appeared to be unnoticed.

I looked at him. He seemed an average man dressed in very average clothes. He gave an overall impression of gray, and most of his garments were that bland color. Nothing at all stood out about him. This land had not distorted or changed him, except it had imprisoned him within this searing stone prison.

I looked at Bea quizzically, hoping she would provide an explanation. She looked at me and raised her shoulders in an indifferent shrug. I carried on looking at her, hoping for more information, before moving to another of the stone sarcophagi.

It was the same story for each of the stone coffins I visited. In each, a nondescript person was trapped. All of them screaming in silence and, with absolute desperation, trying to find their way out. Sometimes I would call to them and motion them to come out through the open doors. None of them could see or hear me, and they would continue clawing at molten sides in uninterrupted, futile desperation. With each, I would unsuccessfully try to communicate with the inhabitant before quitting and moving on to another.

I tried many tombs with no success, but in the last I saw someone I recognized. Someone I had thought of recently, a failure, and someone who had been unworthy of my love and effort. He was dead and had died a long time ago. Not dead in the sense of transformation and merging, but dead in terms of rotting flesh disposed of at an impersonal convenient dump site.

It was John. Someone who I had believed could have been a Sideways Person but who just did not have the refinement of spirit to appreciate what I was offering him. I felt torn. In some ways, the sight of him dismayed me, and I wanted to get away—to pretend I had never seen this failure. But it was the only familiar face I had seen since arriving here, and I wanted answers. I needed to understand what had gone wrong between us, to get an accurate picture of why it had failed. All abandoned lovers need to understand why things soured before they can achieve proper closure.

I looked round at Bea and motioned toward the coffin. She remained motionless and showed no understanding of my needs. I had hoped she would open the hot coffin for me, as I did not want to burn myself. Bea could be, and on this occasion was, impossible to read or understand. I pulled my shirt down over my damaged and fingerless hand and reached toward the relevant coffin door. It was cool to the touch and swung open with the merest contact. With the same damaged hand, I grabbed hold of John and pulled him out of his prison.

John blinked in the light. His flesh and clothes gave off clouds of black smoke that smelled of rotten eggs. Nothing had been burned or destroyed, though. The fire caused agony but never consumed him or his clothes. Suddenly, the hot rain fell down hard upon him. After the first impact, he flinched and collapsed to the floor, trying to curl into a tiny tight ball to present the smallest possible target to the hostile environment. I kneeled down next to him and patted him on the shoulder, making hushing noises whilst remembering the softness I had felt toward him.

Although the rain hurt, through my efforts, John was free from his appalling confinement, and he recovered rapidly. It was not long until his head distended itself from his hunched body and he turned to look at me.

"I knew you would come here. I knew we would meet again," he said. John's voice was just as I remembered it, and he spoke in unsurprised, clipped and even tones. For a second, I looked at him with such tenderness, at the eyes framed with wrinkles he had tried so hard to hide with makeup, and the receding hairline he had tried to cover over. A surge of compassion waved over me. I reached out my good hand and gently stroked his cheek. "Did you know I would come and save you? Did you pray for us to meet again?"

John looked surprised, but the surprise suddenly turned to anger and open hostility. He moved onto his haunches and stood. I also rose and stood opposite him, surprised by the negative mood that had erupted without warning between us.

John moved toward me with such clear, violent intent, I raised my hands to keep him at bay. "What?" he yelled. "Don't tell me you still believe your own fucking shit."

The anger caught me off guard. "I only tried to give you what you needed," I said, trying to justify myself. "The fault is not mine. You lacked something. Why else are you here?" I don't think I meant it as a serious question. I said it more to defend myself from the accusations, but I noticed Bea had moved to stand beside me.

"Tell him," she whispered, in a voice that hinted of commandment.

John stopped and looked like he wanted to say something cruel. Then he restrained himself and shot Bea a venomous look. When he spoke, the words were dragged from a great depth.

"When I was alive, you know, before I met you, I did not appreciate the world. I did not see the beauty surrounding me. I did not appreciate the friends I had. Nature was a closed book, and I did not contemplate the spiritual aspects of life. My chief concern was prestige, with being seen as important. I wanted to be impressive, admired. That was my central goal. I closed myself off to what the poets would call "abstruser musings"—in life, I did not even read poetry. My god, my primary commandment was material things and the respect of strangers." He spoke in a voice constricted with resentment while looking at me through narrowed eyes.

He stopped talking. I nodded. It made sense; it was why we had failed. A touch of anger rose within me as I remembered the pain of his rejection. I said nothing in response, but my hostility grew.

John looked at me before continuing in an even monotone, "I was never in love. It never occurred to me that I should ever try. Sometimes I would convince myself I was. Like when I was with you. You were everything I wanted. I was so proud when people saw us together. But I didn't feel love toward you. You were younger, had a good job and were handsome. I thought people would respect me more because I was with you. I loved the illusion we projected, that of a good-looking successful couple. Nothing else mattered."

The grim anger that had been building within me increased and solidified as I realized how he had used me. I remembered what Bea had said about everyone getting what they deserved. John had been surrounded by beauty, love and opportunities for the ethereal, but had closed himself to them. Now he had no opportunities to understand and appreciate them and was literally locked in a world of pain.

I got to my feet. John remained hunched on the floor, and I stood over him as I passed judgment. "If you had allowed yourself to love, understood the greater depth in the world and people around you, then even now you would be safe. I would carry you within and you would have everything that I am, and I would not let you be here," I intoned.

John's face distorted, his lips grimaced in anger, and his hands raised as though to strike. "I wouldn't want to be in you, you fucking twat," he spat back with wide eyes and lips drawn broadly back in a snarl. "You still don't see what the fuck you are, do you?"

I had tried to be steady in passing judgment on John, but now my patience frayed. Acting on dark instincts that whispered within my blood, I raised my ruined, fingerless hand and twisted it counter-clockwise in the air. The acid rain that had stopped during our conversation now fell on him in great torrents. John yelped as it ran over his flesh, leaving trails of smoke rising from him, and he collapsed again in a heap on the ground.

I felt satisfaction. I was righteous in my judgment, and even the very environment would bend to my will to support me as I passed sentence upon him. "Are you ready?" I asked as I stood over his collapsed form. John looked at me in confusion.

"We all get what we deserve here," I said, and reached down to pick him up by the scruff of his neck.

John felt as light as a feather, and I could control him with ease. I wrapped my arms around him in a tighter and truer embrace than we had ever shared when we were lovers and pushed him backward toward his stone coffin. John realized my intentions and struggled and punched without impact or success. "You can't do this to me," he said in panic. "Why do you get to do this?"

"We all get what we deserve," I repeated as my legs and arms forced him backward toward the cell from which I had freed him. "You deserve this," he said, not in anger but in desperation, almost as though he was trying to bargain with me.

We had reached the coffin, and John had his back toward it and was only a pace away from being imprisoned again. The door sprung open, and I could see the flames licking and rising throughout its interior walls. The heat was extraordinary. John's hands were twisting and trying to punch my shoulders in desperate futility.

I reached up and pulled his hair so his head tilted backward and moved my eyes close to his so he could see my expression, the lack of compassion I felt toward him; I, the man who had once offered to share his soul.

"If I deserved this, I would be stuck here. But I am not. I would have given you everything. I would have spared you this, John. Think on that." In a final sad salute to all we could have been to each other, I kissed him gently on his lips before pushing him backward into the stone coffin.

John started screaming indistinguishable words, trying to express excruciating pain as the flames licked around him. His eyes crunched closed, trying to deny the reality of what was happening, and his hands swung desperately, trying to brush away the fire that would never finish consuming him. I watched for a while and realized the few moments of freedom he had enjoyed had led to the flames hurting him more. Satisfied, I closed the coffin door and walked away.

Chapter Twenty-Three

Bea watched me as I walked away from the coffin. One edge of her lips twisted upward. I will never understand what that expression conveyed. Contempt, and anger certainly, but also something that suggested a smile or at least acknowledgement of potential righteousness. I hoped she remembered everyone got what they deserved, that I had justification for imprisoning John again.

I paused and looked again at Bea, considering her. She felt attached or bound to me for unknown reasons. At our first meeting, she had been waiting for me and seemed clear about my path. Whereas the journey had amended and mutilated me, Bea had just seemed to gain in power and confidence. She was my guide. Bea knew where I was going, had the power to get me there and, at certain points, had given clear indications she cared about me. But I also felt manipulated and detected scorn. She had, on occasion, forced me to eject those cherished within me into an external and independent form.

I wondered why she accompanied me, and even as I did so, I felt the familiar twinge in my feet as they demanded I go in a set direction. It was possible that Bea suffered a similar compulsion to accompany me, and the thought made me sad. I wanted Bea to travel with me because she wanted to, not because of some unknown force. As I walked toward her, I saw the silent intensity of her gaze. It reminded me of Laura and the way I always had her undivided attention.

"We need to talk soon. I want to understand things better. This is a place where the dead live," I said as I approached her. My tone was friendly. I still felt pleased that I finally understood why John and I had been unsuccessful in our relationship, but meeting someone I knew was deceased gave me cause for concern.

I understand the world was much more than simple laws of physics and biology. On the rare occasions where someone had discovered the physical remains of one of my Sideways People after their final transformation, the discoverer would describe the discovered as "dead". I would almost laugh when I read or heard this. The lack of understanding it showed was phenomenal. My Sideways People were not dead but exalted and eternal. Those considered dead could still impact and be part of the living, could still be felt and experienced. Still, I needed a greater understanding of this place and what was happening.

Bea nodded and waited for me next to the path I already knew I would take. My feet itched to follow this broad rocky route that appeared to lead down a steep slope. The path comprised sharp fragments of stone that stood on top of hard ground. Even though I wore shoes, I could feel the edges of the stones cutting through and bruising my soles. I gritted my teeth and, feeling my momentary good humor vanish, continued down the path with Bea following me. As we moved, the rain continued splashing around. Sometimes it landed on my flesh, leading me to jump upward in sudden pain.

As we kept on our journey downward, I felt the environment change. There was a sense of either darkness or blackness surrounding us. Before, I could determine no source of light, but now, faintly in the reddish dark sky, I glimpsed faint pinpricks of stars. As we moved onwards, the smell of cooking, rotten flesh grew stronger but mixed with the stench of decay and staleness. By the time we reached the end of that interminable slope, the smell was so strong it made me lightheaded, and my legs trembled carrying my weight.

By the slope's end, there was a clearing where more stone coffins rose from the ground. Weakly, I stood there, swaying from side-to-side. I could not get enough air into my lungs. It was too thick with smells and stenches. It was physically impossible to breathe this air soup. My sight blurred. I reached out to grab Bea to steady myself and felt surprised at how cool and solid her arm was.

Bea turned and briefly held me. I took that moment to gather strength from her familiar smell and the serenity of her presence. "We will wait over there until you get used to the smell," Bea said, her voice suggesting concern and compassion. "Once you get your breath back, we can talk." Bea led me to a sheltered enclave behind one of the burning coffins. I collapsed to the ground.

"Tell me about this place," I said. My trembling voice, revealing how ill and lost I felt.

"What do you want to know?" Her whole demeanor remained calm, unaffected by the stench and the atmosphere. The rain never fell near or affected her. Her form was as perfectly shaped as the first time I met her.

"Everything," was my bleak response. Bea nodded as though expecting that answer. She spent a few moments considering her answer. Then spoke in a clear and concise manner, as though deciding to fully assume the role of teacher.

"This is a place of natural justice. People go where they belong. What happens to them is what they deserve," Bea said. "Before breaching that stone wall, the people we met, and they were people, all of them. Their crimes and relative punishments were mild. They were just guilty of being weak or ignorant."

I said nothing about that. To me, if weakness was their only crime, then the punishment seemed disproportionate. Bea continued, "Before the wall, the land was segmented according to the exact nature of the crime committed by the people stuck within that area. Between each segment, there were unseen walls—Michael called them barriers. You could only cross these barriers by either weakening them through freeing people that did not belong in that segment or by belonging in some manner to the next segment to which you wished to travel."

Bea looked at me. I nodded and realized that was why I found traveling through different segments so difficult. I did not belong in any; had committed no crime that needed punishing in such a manner. Something, however, was disturbing me. My mind kept bouncing back to university, trying to remember something I had once read that felt familiar or pertinent.

"How do I get out?" I asked.

Bea gave me a long look, paused and said, "The center contains the only way out. Your feet are leading you there." I nodded slowly and thoughtfully. Glad that unknown forces had realized my presence here was wrong and set my feet to follow a guaranteed path to freedom.

Bea watched in silence as I continued nodding. After a while she spoke again. "After the wall, the crimes and punishments are greater. The last segment contained people who offended against spirituality and the human condition. They knew that life is much more than can be tangibly seen, but didn't explore this further. They betrayed themselves of living a fuller, richer life."

Bea paused before going on. "There are only a few segments left. Three in total, each split by different crimes. The center is the last segment. These last few segments are reserved for those who committed the very worst crimes and betrayals against themselves, others and nature. The punishments are correspondingly more severe. Barriers between these last segments are more obvious but more difficult to cross. We may need help. We have almost reached the next barrier."

I nodded to myself. I felt stronger and better for the information. Freedom lay in front of me, and I was being guided toward it. Hope changed everything around me; the air felt thinner, and I found myself able to draw enough into my lungs to steady myself. Above me, the thin pinpricks of light seemed to shine just a touch more brightly. A map, if only I knew how to read it, that would guide me back home.

Chapter Twenty-Four

Elsewhere, my opponent was feeling less optimistic.

Michael stood at the room's center, lost in concentration and thought. His thoughts were rigidly fixed on that woman and the Other. Air ran through the squalid room and brushed through his cells. He felt his form change in response to each of these fetid breaths. Everything was a failure and caused him pain. That Other and the woman had beaten him, and his nemesis moved ever closer.

Michael was not the type to pity himself. His thoughts focused on causing pain and re-establishing his control and mastery of the situation and environment. He was well aware of the endured losses, of the damage done to him. But more than anything, he knew he wanted to strike back. Knew he wanted to hurt them more than they had ever thought possible.

His shoulders still held three heads. The outer two now slumped forward, eyes closed, as though dead. Only the central head showed any life, eyelids partially shut, with thin slits of yellow pupils revealed. As the air moved through his form, his shape changed in response to the bestial nature of his thoughts. He became hairier. The central head sprouted horns and took on a bovine aspect. Michael deeply felt the pain his morphing and moving cells caused but could not prevent it.

It was not just his physical shape he could no longer control. Michael had sensed and monitored the Others without their knowledge, had selected those shades within himself and sent them where he wanted them to go, had moved from one place to another at will.

Things were different now. Dark shadows, the shades of those he had so brutally destroyed, swept and brushed past him. Sometimes these black shapes would contort into human features that screamed in rage. Other times the shadows would grow hands that tore at him with sharpened fingers. Michael felt blood trickling down his torso and rocked backward and forward in fury. Those two fuckers had caused this insult and all this pain, by sweet fucking heaven they would fucking scream when he fucked them up. He was the biggest motherfucker there ever was. The thoughts appeared to influence the shadows that whispered around him, and they coalesced into a solid ball that covered his entire broken body. With a sudden blink, he moved elsewhere.

Bea and I did not rest long. My lungs had accustomed themselves to the air, and their expansion and contraction satisfied some physical need. In the clearing after we had finished talking, the land had twisted itself and a path had sprung up next to us. Covered in rocks and sharp jagged stones, it led downwards past rocky cliff sides.

The path was narrow and steep, hard to traverse. It was only wide enough to travel down in single file. I led the way downwards, scrabbling eagerly along the path, hoping to get home without further delay. I paused only to look behind me to ensure Bea could keep pace. Sometimes I would offer an unnecessary steadying hand and encouraging smile.

Bea did not need my help. She appeared to glide over the rough surface and sharp obstacles as though her feet were not touching the ground. With a silent shake of her head, she would reject offers of help. Every time I looked round, I saw and felt her eyes upon me. Her bearing suggested sorrow.

We continued downwards. I stumbled over the rocks. Sometimes I would cut myself on their sharp edges, and small flecks of blood could be seen on exposed skin. My clothes would tear normally. My skin was different still. The flesh would push open in response to sharp edges, and blood would accumulate at the surface in slashes of red, but dripping or healing did not occur. These wounds and those I had suffered earlier tormented me terribly. My determined strides turned into stumbling steps.

My feet still obeyed the compulsion to head downward and follow a path only they knew. The rest of me wilted and sagged. I concentrated my thoughts on achieving the exit at the center, and of finally being free from this place and the distressing transformations and pains.

Maybe it was the lack of attention, or the damage my flesh was taking, or in response to some yet unperceived danger, but I suddenly felt a suffocating, stabbing pain at the top of my midriff. Like the most extreme indigestion, but with extra tearing pain. I gasped for breath.

I looked at the source of such agony. The origin point was the wound that ran down the center of my chest. With surprise and horror, I saw two gray and insubstantial fingers poking out through the wound. They moved from side-to-side as though to further open my form.

It was a Sideways Person trying to escape. I didn't know why. Maybe it was out of confusion and uncertainty, or a desire to help and protect me, but even as I watched, the fingers grew longer and I saw the tips of other fingers appearing. I reached down, roughly grabbed hold of the digits in my hands, and pushed them back inside. My hands disappeared briefly inside my chest and reappeared, covered in a red patina when pulled free.

Bea moved next to me, placed her hands around my shoulders and helped me lie down sideways across the path. Hands moved around in my insides, pushing at the edges of my wounds. I closed my eyes in misery and concentrated on holding them all in.

"Release them, let them push out," said Bea, her voice both urgent and softened with concern. I looked with eyes that would have streamed water had something as natural and wholesome as tears been permitted.

"It's not releasing them. Please understand that. It would be a terrible expulsion. If I release them, then I am betraying them and all we were together. I would belong here if I could willingly do that. They are me and I am them." I tried to convince her of the sincerity of my need and emotion, my voice faltering as it tried to express something beyond importance.

Bea moved her face closer so that I could see her expression. "Are you so very sure?" she asked, with her lips next to my ear. I nodded, and the movement of my head brought me back again into contact with the edge of a rock, causing the skin to split and hair to tear free.

Screams and bellows interrupted the moment. It took me a while to realize I was not making them. Bea moved to the side and looked downwards over the edge. I shook myself and flopped toward her, body too abused to respond fully to my mental commands.

A look over the edge brought a smile to my face, although one tinged with fear. Below us, by about six meters, Michael paced backward and forward with his suffering both obvious and extreme. Something had changed his form to shapes more damaged than fearful. Where once I had seen three heads, two now drooped, abandoned from his shoulders like dead meat. The remaining head was a merging of a man's and bull's skull with little strips of flesh covering it. His voice bellowed out in fury and pain. His body was even more muscular than previously, but rivulets of blood streamed down him. All around him the dark shadows, the vengeful shades of those he had murdered, circled and danced, taking turns to close in and shout at him or swipe at his body with spectral and sharpened hands.

Michael's voice was yelling out in fury, a curious mixture of the bass lowing of a cow and the throaty, graveled voice of a man. "You're fucking mine, you fucking cunts. You ain't fucking escaping, you fuckers, don't even fucking try," he screamed at the righteous ghosts before appearing to get confused and swaying his remaining head slowly from side-to-side. "Where the fuck are they? Where the fucking hell are they? The fucking center is mine. That's it: those fucking cunts end here, whatever the fuck they do."

Michael stood next to the rock face and did not notice that above him was a path on which two people were watching him. He was flapping around him with his hands, trying to swat away the dark shadows as though they were troublesome flies. His feet capered randomly a few steps in every direction and pawed at the ground.

I moved away from the edge of the path, keeping myself as low as possible to remain hidden. Bea moved away with me, also keeping low. She gazed at me. "You need to release another of those inside you," she said. With unwavering determination, I vigorously shook my head in absolute denial before she said, "We won't be able to get past him otherwise."

My head slumped backward in disappointment and sorrow. The back of my skull hit the sharp edge of a rock, but I ignored the physical pain. I searched for the words that would enable me to explain to Bea how wrong that would be. To summon forth some kind of plea for her to intercede and move us past this obstacle without me needing to force another sundering.

Fortunately, I did not need to betray another of my Sideways People, nor did Bea need to confront Michael on my behalf. Michael's feet had been forcing him backward and forward in a hopping prance movement. Now and then, this movement would move him next to the rock wall that supported our path. The one time he moved closer, his hand clenched into a fist that he flung against the surface of the rock in anger.

We felt the force of the blow; it shook the foundations of everything and jolted the entire world we were on. It jerked us around in response. Around us there was a groan as rocks split. In alarm, I moved back to where I could watch the monster. Below us, oblivious to the effect his punch had, Michael moved around and swatted at his abused dead while mouthing threats of violence and mindless obscenities. Eventually, his fury could not be contained or satiated by mindless hits and swipes. He gained some level of control over his feet and moved himself to face the rock wall from a distance of a few meters.

Michael bent himself double from the waist and his feet pawed at the floor, like he was a bull about to charge with murderous intent at a mocking matador. It was only when he bent over that I saw two cruel ivory horns had sprouted out from above his temples. Michael pawed his feet at the ground, as though building his fury to the point it had to be spent. Suddenly, he uncoiled and charged at the wall, hitting his horns against it with stunning force.

The force of the blow threw me and Bea into the air. The whole rock path shook and split. Splinters of rock jumped in the air. There were breaking and snapping noises. A crack spread along the path, looking like a crooked grin, laughing with creaks and broken earth noises. There was a sense of tilting backward and being surrounded by flying pebbles, jagged edges while falling and then being buried underneath them into darkness.

Chapter Twenty-Five

I lay in darkness. Sharp edges pressed down. I could feel a thousand cuts across my skin and body. The fall had forced my head sideways and my body sloped downwards. My arms had spread away from my body.

My first impression was that the weight that crushed me was unmovable. The stones pinned me statically where I was. But with determined effort and sharp pushing motions, the debris that had landed around me moved and flowed away like a sharp black wave. Moving my arms and legs in circular motions created more space. Encouraged by this unexpected freedom, I kept moving my limbs around, getting more space until I could sit upright and move my waist above the level of stone.

My first sight was of Bea seated on a rock. As always, she looked dispassionate and unperturbed, as though knowing I would appear at that exact second. I gave her an irked look and further examined my hands and arms. Thousands of minor cuts and nicks caused a faint spiderweb of red to spread across my palms and fingers.

"What happened to Michael?" I asked. As though summoned, a sudden shower of rocks exploded upward, and Michael's deformed heads and twisted torso appeared. I should have run in fear, but he looked so pathetic. Two useless heads dangled in front of him. His charge into the rock face had pushed his horns backward into his skull, causing blood to leak over his bovine face. His befuddled head shook. I sat there, not moving, before his eyes cleared and focused on me.

"You cunt. You absolute fucking cunt," he lolled at me from cow-like lips. His voice was weary and despairing. He was trying to free himself from the rockslide but with little energy or success. I looked closer at him and realized he was almost crying. "The fucking center is mine—I earned it," he continued in a voice that sounded earnest but had little vigor.

With a sudden effortless burst, I freed myself from the broken shale. With slow deliberateness, I moved toward Michael, scanning my surroundings to find a heavy enough rock or boulder. I saw one on my route, picked it up with both hands and carried on toward him.

"Fuck off. Just fuck off, you fucking coward. You wouldn't fucking dare. I am fucking greater than you," said Michael, trying to project a macho voice that was belied by the fear in his eyes. I moved closer and let him see the sneer spread across my thinning lips. For a sweet moment, I savored the power, knowing justification existed for whatever I did. Michael had done everything I could think of and much worse to many others.

For a brief second, I realized I was the absolute center of his world, that my actions were as important to him as anyone's ever would be. Maybe this was Michael's version of Sideways People—the inversion and exact opposite of my own, based on fear and pain rather than love and need.

I don't know what would have happened if I had reached him. I wish to Christ I had. Just before I moved within crushing distance, my feet locked to the spot, twisted around and walked in a different direction. I had no choice but to follow them. Bea moved next to me, all while maintaining her air of serenity and lack of surprise. Her hand reached out and stroked my arm. "Time to go further in," she said.

The compulsion in my feet continued and made me move away in an unflagging stride. Michael appeared to be trapped under the rubble and stones and, with the swift, never tiring pace set by my feet, disappeared out of sight in moments.

"What is happening to him?" I asked Bea.

She looked at me in surprise. "The same as everyone else here. His cruel passions and sins are being used against him to create his worst nightmares. He didn't enjoy seeing you standing over him while being at your mercy."

I nodded, smiled and, for a second, relished the memory of sneering in his face. "He also keeps changing forms, and the latest one did not appear to be successful," I said.

Bea nodded and kept walking. "He gave in to animal urges many years ago. In here, restrictions on form are looser, and he is changing into different creatures."

I looked at her before saying, "How do you know so much about everything?" I think I meant it almost as a flirtatious, empty piece of praise, but Bea took it as a serious question.

She paused for thought, pursed her lips, and said, "I don't belong here, and I used to watch things and people to understand what was happening. It is possible that me not belonging here means I see things differently. My watching people to gain understanding means here I understand what happens to them."

I nodded and asked the most important question on my mind. "Those that were inside him, those he trapped, are freeing themselves?" I was specifically asking about how the souls were escaping, seeking to understand why my own seemed to release themselves by mistake from my form.

Bea answered a different question from the one that I was asking. "You saw what Michael did to them. You understand how he broke them. When he first captured them, they were different people. After he had finished with them, they had changed beyond all recognition *because* of him. His victory was complete and his importance to them, for all it is unwanted, was undeniable. It meant they became part of him and bonded. They had to accompany him when he came here. That bond and containment is ending. Michael is becoming unrecognizable and different from what he was when he trapped them. Those contained within him do not belong here. Everyone goes where they deserve to go. It is important the trapped souls are freed as quickly as possible. Their suffering is abominable. But their release is guaranteed anyway, providing Michael continues to change, abandoning himself and his hold on them."

This almost prompted the obvious follow-up question. I wanted to ask how I could solidify my form so that those inside would be safe and homed there forever. The question hung unasked in my mouth, though. I worried Bea may feel jealous of the bond I shared with these other people. She might feel excluded, think there was not enough space or love left for new and important relationships. So, I remained quiet but kept stealing sideways glances at Bea, hoping she would guess my unasked question and answer it anyway.

We carried on walking. My feet still felt compelled to travel in a set direction across the barren landscape. In the distance, a long way away, some mirage appeared; shimmering shapes that shifted back and forth, noises like screams and cries reached me in snatches, along with a faint underlying smell of copper. My feet were, without deviation, heading toward it.

You remember distance is different in this place? That time was unusual? I seemed to have forgone sleep since the first section of this odd realm; it never occurred again, even though the trek continued past the exhaustion of my feet and body. My journey and changes had dulled other natural responses. I could not shed tears nor bleed or heal, As I moved toward the flickering vision, shooting stabs of pain spread from my compelled feet as without change of stride or pace, without my will or volition, they continued at speed to their chosen direction. This pain spread upward through my legs to my thighs before continuing to my left side, as though I had suffered a stroke. The wound in my midriff felt like it was slowly tearing open, like stitching was coming undone. My shoulders ached as though they carried the weight of the world.

I do not know whether I traveled days or minutes that seemed like centuries, but getting to the promised mirage tore and exhausted me. My lungs twisted and gasped to fill themselves. Everything blurred and was hard to see. Maybe I passed out and my feet kept on walking because, in a sudden flash, the distant spectacle appeared a few meters straight in front of me. My feet stopped as though waiting for my command to move again.

It was a huge red river spreading across the entire landscape. The red water rushed first in one direction before abruptly stopping and charging in great spumes of red froth in the other. The smell of copper was all pervasive, and I retched emptily again. The far river side was barely visible, and the landscape there appeared much darker, making it difficult to distinguish anything.

Within the river itself teemed every type of human and creature and potential joining of the two that evolution and creation could conceive. There were horses joined as men plowing through the water; spiders and frogs with the arms and faces of screaming women swam submerged under the surface, trying with agonized desperation to break free. Bears trapped and merged with children roared and barked in pain. More traditional human forms were visible in other places. One man in ancient papal robes stood almost as though floating on the surface of the water with his feet from the ankles downwards submerged, chanting feverishly with eyes scrunched tight. Near me, submerged under the surface, a tall man flopped backward and forward, around and around, with his mouth shutting and opening, pleading for mercy in a voice no one could hear.

The water gave off incredible and inexplicable heat. Some creatures within or on the lake struck in furious violence around them, while others remained absorbed in their own world of misery.

It was as though the compulsion in my feet had been waiting for me to understand the barrier before demanding I cross. Without warning, my right foot shot forward as though to take a step into this fiery, blood-colored water. The only possible evasion was to throw myself bodily backward, causing me to land on my back a short distance from the water's edge. Without pause, I lifted my feet away from the floor only to feel, to my horror, my knees fold and place my feet flat on the ground. Once these treacherous limbs had sufficient purchase, they pulled me toward the river, even though I was still on my back.

It was urgent, my need. Utterly. Otherwise, I would not have done what I did. I clawed my hand and shoved it hard inside my midriff wound, reaching for the Sideways Person whose fingers had escaped my body. I pulled the gray form outward and with a mental shout gave orders while struggling to upright myself so I could, at least, see what was going to happen next.

Adrenaline and fear enabled me to regain my feet and stand. I looked over the red river to see which of the Sideways People I had ejected. The violence and urgency of expulsion prevented me from registering through an examination of my soul and feelings, and I needed to confirm the identity of loss through vision.

It was Kim. One of my earliest (I think, although memory fades, that I met her straight after Kevin), we had worked for the same organization. She had been quiet in the office and conscientious in her work ethic. Everyone else took advantage of her virtuosity. They had given her their work to complete and sent her out to get coffee and doughnuts whenever they fancied a treat, as though she was some kind of slave.

I never took advantage of her and made sure she knew I appreciated her hard work. One night, after everyone had given her extra work, I noticed she was close to tears. I stayed late and helped her complete everything. It was dark when we finished, and she had bobbed thanks and shyly asked if I wanted a quick celebratory drink. I had seen the gratitude and thanks in her eyes, so I moved my hands to her neck. The next day I told everyone she had quit in disgust, and they should feel ashamed (to their credit, some appeared upset by the news).

Now she stood, sheathed in gray, on the surface of the boiling red water surrounded by dreadful perversions of nature, uncertain how to obey my mental shout of, *"Save me!"* I urgently cast my eyes on the surface of the water and saw what I needed. I looked back at Kim and forced the command into her mind. Her eyes widened. She turned around and sped off to retrieve the identified target.

It was a merging of a gigantic horse with a decrepit old man. A wizened old face with a saggy, loose-skinned torso, drooping old man's breasts joined into a magnificent charger's body. Four horse's legs submerged under the surface and appeared to propel the horse as though it were a duck. The main trunk of its body was broad, and its back was above the surface of the water. Standing on it would allow me safe passage while still moving me in the intended direction.

Kim reached down and grabbed this man-beast thing. Her fingers twisted around into its mouth; she dragged it speedily toward me as though landing a fish by a hook. I had reached the surface of the water, and my next step would have placed me inside the red river, but Kim, in response to my thoughts, had turned it around so that my feet landed on its flesh enabling me to stand on its back.

Its back was broad and spacious, and I remained upright. With little physical effort, Kim pulled the creature with blurring speed in the direction my legs compelled me to travel. Once I was moving in the right direction, the compulsion to stride faded. For the moment. With an explosive release of pent-up breath, I turned to look for Bea.

Bea was walking—floating might be more appropriate—on the surface of the water. Her legs moved and the water surface distorted into cylindrical ripples, as though disturbed by her physical form. Her feet, however, never appeared to touch the water. Everyone and everything moved to the side to avoid touching or impeding her. She shone bright white. For a split second, I realized how beautiful and unique to everyone else Bea was.

I surveyed the other creatures and people in the water as we sped past. They screamed in hatred. My steed stepped and trampled over some of them, pushing others to one side. Others moved to intercept us with natural weapons and violent claws. Each time, Kim increased the speed at which she dragged the creature, and we would shoot past.

Near the end of the crossing, another creature, an immense man with a grinning and screaming buffoon mouth and ape lips and arms, reached into the water and threw great droplets of the red fluid at me. I danced to one side on the centaur's back to evade it, but my right foot slipped into the water.

The pain was beyond any comprehension and explanation. There was burning. The flames moved up my leg and past the knees, searing and cauterizing the flesh. Bones twisted, broke, and contorted into new shapes. The existing connections between these white sticks broke and fused to reform new connections at different and unexpected angles. Sinews and tendons broke to melt into flexible shapes that operated under unprecedented separate stresses and pressure. My mouth opened and I screamed in high-pitched childish protest. I would have fallen backward into the devastating water except Bea, with extreme foresight, had moved herself into a position to catch and steady me upright on the mount's back.

Looking downwards at the submerged leg, I realized I had suffered another unnatural alteration. The foot on that leg twisted in the wrong direction, the toes now pointed behind me. This reversal carried on upward. The shin was also opposite the normal place with this reverse contortion, meaning the kneecap was on the back. The thigh and down to the knee remained the correct and natural way around.

I sank and kneeled on my normal knee, stretching the other leg out in front of me. It was painful and aching. Flexing it backward and forward showed it could now bend both ways as though made of stiff rubber. I was unsure whether I could walk on it. Once I reassured myself that I was secure on my transport, I closed my eyes and pressed my despairing hands over the shut lids to block out everything.

I may well have stayed like that indefinitely. The world was safer and less intimidating while enclosed in self-chosen darkness. Only a sudden itch in my feet, a twitching shift in them as though to stand again, forced open my eyes.

The river still ran red around us. The heat was still extraordinary. Everything was tinged red, but a few feet in front was the other river side. The shoreline itself was rocky and dark. The light suddenly ended at the edge of the river, cut down into a sudden line of impenetrability. I looked at Kim. Like Bea, she was walking on the surface of the water. Her arm reached behind her to drag the mount to where I would dismount.

Kim dragged the creature to the dark bank. As we got closer, I stood on my good foot, the one I knew I could trust, and hopped to the ground. Even before landing, I turned my head to catch a last look at Kim. She had already started to half turn, and I glimpsed her resigned, sad face before I landed.

My landing hurt. Cold shot up through my shoes, cramping my muscles. The world lost light and color; all memories of touch and warmth and friendship disappeared. Hands reached out to the icy, thin soil that covered rock riddled terrain to steady myself. I realized I was crying without control or any possibility of stopping. There was no hope, no point, and everyone had abandoned me. I curled into the fetal position on the floor and drew myself into myself.

It was my Sideways People that saved me again. If not for them, I may well have laid down and spent eternity wrapped in the world's misery within that benighted place. One of them moved inside and seeped through one of my numb wounds, causing me to rouse myself and start getting to my feet.

I was not alone; that was demonstrably false, and I had significance.

In response to my mounting will and focus, my feet again expressed a compulsion to go in a set direction. I moved my hands across my face and felt the tears smear. I looked back for Bea, expecting to see her serenely standing nearby, unaffected by despair and depression.

She was prostrate on the floor, tears flooding down her pale and leached face, dry silent sobs heaving her shoulders, running through her entire body. A growth of emotion splintered in my chest as I realized, for the first time in so long, someone needed me. Forgetting mutated legs, damaged form and the soul drenching despair that surrounded us, I threw myself at Bea and embraced her tightly.

I pulled her to my chest and cradled her close, lifting her head to press it against me so she could cry into my embrace. She clutched hard as I made hushing noises and stroked her hair. I drank in her need, the salvation I provided, and could see the depth of emotion flowing out from between us in golden bands. I realized here, wherever we were at that moment, Bea was susceptible and in danger. With that, I dragged her upward onto her feet as she made small despairing noises of complaint.

It was dark, difficult to see where I was going. Wane pinpricks of white light hovered in the air, but did not support navigation or accurate sight. I had to obey my feet and the direction they dictated. With my reversed leg, I could only walk at a stumble. Sometimes the knee would buckle, and I would fall forward or backward, depending on which way it bent. The joint was only sporadically capable of strength or locking, and it could give way in any direction. My movement was still easier than Bea's, though. All her strength had disappeared, and she seemed unable to move on her own. I half carried and half dragged her along our route.

I heard and glimpsed other things moving in the surrounding darkness. Sometimes the forms were of small humans, naked, pale, eyes blank, running fleetingly across the dark land with no care for accident or collision. Other shapes included dogs or other creatures that ran on four legs, growling with feral abandon. Maybe chasing or escaping from each other. I bore them little mind, my attention focused on Bea and her needs and sudden vulnerability. She said nothing, and her eyes were vacant, revealing none of her thoughts or humanity.

In darkness, we wandered into a nasty, half-dead forest. I don't know where or when this happened, only noticing it when thin white branches impeded our movement. Around us, small scratchy bushes scattered and clung to dwarfed, bleached trees that gave off a faint white light that only highlighted the darkness.

Within the forest's darkness, the other lost things moved. I heard them crashing around in the night. Sometimes close by. One young lady with shining black eyes flew past in silence, her flight ensnaring her in one thorn bush strewn in her path. I had not seen or heard the hound thing chasing her, but it suddenly appeared snarling and drooling. It surged after the lady, and to escape, she ran without restraint through the grasping thorn bushes. The sharp needles grabbed hold and punctured her skin, tearing shreds of flesh from her face. Two savage, cruel creepers whipped across her eyes. As she tried escaping in desperate haste, the jellied goo tore free from their sockets and hung like trophies from the prickled vines.

The girl was trapped, hanging in unaccepted surrender from the thorn bush, arms and legs held immobile. She struggled to free herself with shaking gestures. With each shuddering movement, the thorns and strands tore deeper, dark blood leaked downwards in thick rivulets. The chasing hound jumped upward and disappeared into the darkness. The girl kept on struggling, tearing more and more flesh off her limbs until bones became visible. Her last violent struggles caused twigs and vines to break with dead snapping noises while a wide swathe of flesh tore free from her neck. This last violation of flesh was enough. She faded from view.

The world filled with whispering, sad voices. Too low and quiet to distinguish individual words, but the tone of sorrow and despair was unmistakable. Curious, I reached out and snapped a brittle twig from a tree near me. Blood leaked from the broken edge, and again I heard that soft murmuring of regretful words spoken on the cusp of hearing.

I had shrunk against the trees at the hound's approach and stayed silent as I listened to the surrounding sounds. I wanted to move out of this whispering, depressing place with its darkness and looming dead trees. Determined to make Bea safe and restore her to previous glory. My eyes searched the darkest shadows, trying to identify any creatures that could be there. Satisfied at last that there was no one and nothing around us, I reached behind me to grasp Bea's hand to lead her to safety.

My hand touched cold, unyielding flesh. I tried to jerk Bea toward me, but she did not move. Turning round, I looked at her in shock. Her face was static, her eyes distant, everything else locked rigid. I looked down at her unmoving body. Everything was motionless and emitted a pale white light. Like me, Bea was undergoing a transformation. Her legs and feet had changed. Now they splayed away from her body to root and disappeared into the soil.

I knew what was happening. This must be where Bea belonged, and she was transforming to match her sins. I refused to let this happen. Whatever crimes or flaws Bea had (and I had seen precious little evidence of any) they paled beside the help she had given me, the need we had felt for each other. She was the only person I could relate to in this place. No one else had come close.

"Is this where you belong?" I asked Bea as I cupped her face. She did not answer. When I glanced down, the flesh around her feet had taken on the appearance of old dead wood. With urgent desperation, I moved my maimed hand backward and slapped her face hard three times.

A slight shift in features and a focus of eyes showed the return of some sentience. "Is this where you belong?" I asked Bea again, and she nodded in terrified response. Acting on instinct, I went inside to identify a Sideways Person I could call forth to defend us before I realized they would be of no use; the threat was not external.

"I don't believe it is your sin," I said as I cupped her face and moved closer so she could see the sincerity and conviction in my eyes. "There has been a mistake." I paused before saying the words that flowed into my head. "I am with you." The words echoed inside, awakened old feelings, and I said to Bea the only thing I could think of, "Let the crime and punishment be mine."

I do not know why I spoke or what I thought the consequences would be, but Bea nodded, and her hand jerked to touch my shoulder. Something physical passed between us during the connection. Something of silver and rot combined, something that stimulated and revolted me.

Bea's will and personality seemed to return, and she started awake. For a second, her hands moved as though to embrace me, before she regained control of herself, and composed her face to its usual expression. I glanced down at her legs and saw they had returned to normal; they were flesh, and the feet were just feet, not roots.

The thing that transferred from Bea to me, though, solidified and lengthened in my arm. It grew like some obscene, lengthy cancer, but then it moved down and around my body. Its passage was painful, but bearable. There was a feeling of tearing flesh, though nothing serious.

Then the growth appeared to change in direction. I felt its passage and sensed skin and flesh opening before, with a sudden burst, a silver shaft of tree wood grew and sprouted from the wound in my front. I watched with dwindling surprise as it grew from me. My legs felt heavy and immobile and wanted to remain attached to the ground.

This transmutation was not mine. It originated in Bea. My personality or actions had not driven me here. The creeping changes could not take real hold within my being. For all I had accepted responsibility, this was not my sin or flaw. I may have begun the change into something that suited this environment, but my head remained clear and found the will to resist the process. Looking down at the silver branch growing out of my midriff, I reached with a determined hand, and with a twist, snapped the growth.

It shattered into splinters in my hand. The destruction stopped the process of adaptation. My feet could move, and I was no longer locked in immobility. I looked around at Bea, expecting her to comment and lead me onwards, but her face held embarrassment and almost appeared to blush in the moonlight. Then I heard it, the sad voice softly speaking, but this time I could make out the quiet words.

"I loved him so much, think I still do. Knew what he was but accepted it. It did not seem important compared to our feelings, how close and deep our relationship was. I was the center of his world, the absolute center. No one else noticed or felt the way he did about me. I wanted to return this favor. To make him the absolute center of my world. So, I fulfilled his desire regardless of the cost to me. Convinced him of how important he was."

The words trailed off into silence. I looked at Bea in surprise. The words came from the fragment of branch I had destroyed with my hands. Bea looked so abashed and embarrassed, I realized the words were hers somehow; that they revealed her truth and why she was here. I wanted to show her I appreciated the emotions expressed by the act of destruction, that she need not feel embarrassed with me, that we were kindred spirits, and I appreciated her depth and refinement of feeling.

Moving closer to her, I placed my arms around her shoulders and placed the softest of kisses on her forehead. She sank her head into my shoulder, and wet tears trickled down my neck. I turned my head down and kissed the moisture away from her eyes.

"Let's go," I whispered and took her by the hand. Bea agreed with a barely noticeable nod, and we moved on.

We journeyed a while and still heard other creatures and people crashing through the darkened forest in abandoned plight. Sometimes they or we would snap twigs or break branches, and the breakage filled the world with mournful sighs and rueful voices.

Our movement did not appear to get us out of the forest. We were lost and moved in circles. The darkness appeared to leach all vitality and give nothing in return. I sat down and drew Bea with me.

"We need to leave," I said. "Normally, my feet lead us to where we need to go. I still feel a compulsion to go somewhere, but it is undirected." Bea looked at me, and then her hand reached up and stroked my face.

"There is a link between both of us now and this forest. In some ways, we both belong here. It will be harder to leave."

I nodded and pondered the best way to navigate us from this place. "Your feet will still want to take you where you belong. Particularly the one that was damaged by being dropped in the lake. That water baptized it to purpose. Concentrate on it and it should move us on. Take us deeper in."

I looked down at the distorted leg and concentrated on movement, on getting to the next barrier. I expected the compulsion to lead in a defined direction. That is not what happened. As I watched, the leg and foot drooped and elongated as though it were not flesh and bone but impossibly stretchy rubber.

This moving, expanding leg formed and folded before bending itself underneath me. I could feel unnatural muscles that felt like a mix of jelly, water, and ice tighten and bunch. I grabbed hold of Bea, sensing something was about to happen. The leg tightened and sprung forward like a pole vault and, with a blur and sense of blackness and height, we moved on.

Chapter Twenty-Six

The propulsion had moved us somewhere new. The ground was pure rock, and the sky red. Flakes and embers of fire drifted lazily down but burned on contact. I yelped and started as one landed on my face and appeared to burst across my features. My leg had lost its extreme length and tightening elasticity (it was still backward) but now felt weaker, and I had to drag it behind me whilst being careful to put little weight on it.

The flakes appeared drawn toward my sideways nose. As we walked onwards, they landed in greater numbers on the ridges of it. I turned my head downwards to provide greater protection, but this provided scant safety. The flakes still drifted to it as moths to a flame. Raising my hand to check the damage caused my palm to come away black after touching bone.

I don't know how the rest of me fared with the embers. Repulsion of the changes forced on my form, and fear of the damage stopped me from scrutinizing myself closely. Bea continued by my side, seeming to have regained her previous intransigence. Nothing touched her, and she glided onwards with feet that appeared to not touch the ground.

"What was the forest for? Where are we? What sins belonged there and here?" I asked to distract myself.

Bea turned to look at me. "What does it matter? Why do you want to know? This is not for you. This isn't a freak show. No one is here for your amusement. They are receiving intended justice."

"I just want to understand this place. It will help me understand you," I replied, trying to catch her eye. Bea avoided my gaze and struggled with the answer.

"The forest was for those who committed violence against themselves. They had rejected their bodies and so it gives them alternative forms they cannot damage but which others can hurt." Bea paused, and with defiance, looked at me, expecting further questions about why that place almost trapped her. I did not ask, savoring the possibility she would share without being prompted. Bea continued, "This place is for those violent against the entire world, violent at a fundamental level that transcends natural laws."

Bea had declined to share more about the forest, despite having an obvious opportunity to do so. To hide my disappointment, I scanned around. I had to raise my hands to my eyes, partially to stop the lights obscuring my vision and partially to block flakes from landing on my nose.

I had seen no one prior to Bea speaking, but now, as though summoned by her words, I saw them all around me. There were men and women in abundance. Some sat on the ground, others strode back and forth, reaching down with hands bent into shovel shapes to scratch the stone surface as though to dig holes in it. Wherever they sat or touched, the stone would burst into flames and scorch them. The fire had blackened every one of them, covering each in charred, blackened flesh. It was hard to tell gender. Flesh had either been burned off or melted like wax to dribble and form in sexless shapes.

Some forms, presumably those trapped here longest, were little more than blackened skeletons with a few clinging globs of flesh remaining. Now I saw them, other senses registered distressing news. My ears heard their screams of pain and desperation, my nose sniffed their flesh cooking.

I reeled back in dismay, the sheer horror of this place finally seeping in. Those trapped here noticed us and realized we were different. The ground around me and Bea did not erupt with flames, and we were burned the least. Maybe they thought we offered salvation. I saw some trying to stand and make their way toward us. One man had been sitting for so long that as he stood, a black soot covered leg that lacked all flesh dangled behind him. Another lady was missing part of her face, showing her skull underneath, and a bone hand hung unresponsive from a blackened wrist.

Soon a great horde of them drifted toward me and Bea, shambling and stumbling in that broken and unhealing way, the air heaving with their cries and that stench forever forcing its way into my stomach.

My own twisted and mutated form repulsed me, and seeing them reminded me of how I must look. I had a twisted sideways nose, a leg on backward, a shirt that became part of my flesh, cuts and marks that just did not bleed or heal. I knew I looked no better and hated them for this reminder.

My contorted and exhausted limbs staggered away. It was not fast. I could feel them around me, could hear their screams, their stench invading my pores. The final straw was when something dry and rough brushed across my face, and I realized with stomach turning nausea that it was burned flesh.

The Sideways People jumped around, shifting inside me. It was tempting. It would have been easy to release one to destroy everything around me. I couldn't, though. Overwhelmed by shame, I realized how effortlessly I was expelling them, these people who had given me everything. These whom I loved more than the world could understand. I had not even mourned Kim or given her more than a passing glance after I ejected her from the safety of her eternal home.

My thoughts scrambled from one idea to another. I remembered John, and how I had controlled the environment to release justice and burning. Acting on instinct and driven by a need to drive away these disgusting half-human things that so distressed me, I raised my maimed right hand and twirled it cylindrically around my head.

I felt the heat, the fury of motion. I smelled the burning flesh. Opening my eyes, I saw the lazy drift of flame flakes had turned into a torrent, expanding ever outward in circles around me and Bea. The creatures were running away from us, their blackened forms moving as fast as injuries and destruction allowed.

The fire-rain was faster. It chased after and exploded upon them. Some creatures ignored the pain and kept running, chased by the burning flakes, while others collapsed to the ground. The fire engulfed those on the ground. I dropped my hands to my side, clenched them into fists, and then raised them up again. Fire raged from the ground, reaching the heights of mountains.

In exultation, I unclenched my hands and raised them high in the air, screaming with uncontrolled laughter as I did so. *Look at me, look at my control!* The thought rang throughout my mind. Everything else was silent. There were no screams, no motion. My will had cleansed the world.

I limped and staggered toward the nearest remnants. Only a shriveled skeleton remained. The heat had stripped all the flesh away, and it had landed around the bones in concentric circles of ash. I bent over to look at the twisted remains with curious interest when I noticed slight movements. The fingers twitched, the wrist moved spasmodically up and down. As I watched, small red flames sprang forth from the ground around the skeleton and continued the process of torture.

I looked up and scanned the horizon. As far as eyesight permitted, those whose eternal destiny was to remain here were scattered around in cylindrical patterns of black flesh and destitute bones. The flames, previously obedient to my will and quietened after responding to my desires, now appeared to be rising in strength and were springing around the living remains.

A tiny flake of fire swirled downwards and burst into startling pain against my nose. I jumped and then clenched my jaw in determination before moving my maimed hand forward in a pushing motion. The fire-rain swirled before responding to my desires. Flakes would descend and drift toward me but hit an invisible barrier and move in a new direction.

I turned to Bea with a triumphant smile, lips parted wide. She seemed appalled; her face twisted in sickness. "You have power over this place," she said, her tone strict with severe judgment.

"I know. Everything bends to my will; every element does what I want it to here." I tried to keep the gloating satisfaction out of my voice.

Bea's mouth elongated and thinned before asking, "Why do you think that is?" Her tone was judgmental. I paused, uncertain as to the cause of this sudden hostility.

Shrugging my shoulders, I responded, "Maybe it is because this is meant to happen to them," and showed the burned bones surrounding us. "Everyone gets what they deserve here," I reminded her. Bea moved backward away, as though in horror, as though my very presence was unbearable.

After a few steps, she shook herself as though to wake from a bad dream and hissed, "I cannot control the fire here. It avoids me. If it was right that they be burned, then I could do it. But I can't. Just you."

I finally understood what was happening. Bea thought my additional special powers exalted me above and beyond her in some fashion—that I might not need her anymore. "You are still special. This place has changed me in costly ways." I highlighted my misshapen form with my undamaged hand. "You are unaffected. I would swap places." Bea seemed angry and opened her mouth as though to shout something, before she stopped and drew her lips closed into a tight line. Only her eyes still showed unguessable emotions.

"Let's get moving," Bea said, her voice even. "I presume your feet are still leading you toward where you need to go."

I nodded, wishing I knew how to make things better.

We carried on in the direction that my feet led us. Every time we passed one of the burned but still living skeletons, Bea would view it, looking on even as the flames sprang back to life and consumed them. Each time she looked at one, her features would become more severe. Occasionally, she would shoot hostile looks at me and carry on staring, even if she noticed me looking. Each time that happened, I would pretend I had not noticed.

This uncomfortable silence continued as the distance passed. I looked for the barrier or some kind of shape that would move me from one segment in this land to another, but for ages I saw nothing. Only after an awkward eternity did something appear. Visible in the distance was a gigantic horizontal strip of black. I moved toward it.

It was an enormous crater, surrounded by a thin lip. The visible darkness echoed from its depths and roared upward. Its dark depth was unfathomable, and there was an undeniable sense of distance and enormity.

I waited at the lip of this crater. The passage downwards was unknowable but gave an impression of vastness. Still, my feet were compelled to head into it, to plunge downwards. For the moment, I could control the need, but I was afraid they would eventually force me downwards, that they would force my death.

I would steal glances at Bea when I thought she might not notice. Bea was ignoring me and seemed unconcerned about my fear, but also appeared to have regained her calmness. She kept looking around as though expecting someone.

I felt it then—the atmosphere tightening, as though in the presence of hot tin. My vision took on a blackish tinge, and I smelled attar and rot. It surprised no one when Michael appeared in a condensation of black, not five paces from me.

Michael smiled lasciviously when he saw me and, with deliberate menace, slowly hunched his way forward. The only thing that caused him to pause was the fact that I was smiling, unafraid, and had raised my maimed hand to shoulder height. I was ready to summon the fury of this land upon him, to raise the fire and light from the very ground to obliterate him.

His various transformations and our contests had damaged Michael. He was more laughable than fearsome now. His form was no longer muscular and equipped to cause pain but was rather flabby and rubbery. His legs appeared barely able to hold his weight. Two heads hung downwards and were decaying. The live head hung low and slumped below his shoulders, limbs were now misshapen and unsuitable for any discernible purpose. I knew with my control and lordship over this land and its elements, Michael stood no chance against me.

Maybe it was the confidence I was exuding, or because he wished to study me, but Michael paused in his advance. We stayed motionless, standing as though equals on level ground, facing each other in utter silence before I spoke in a slow and deliberate tone.

"Michael," I spoke as I passed judgment, "I have seen you and what you have done, you fucking psychopath. You are a monster. The cruelest of the cruel. Vicious and murderous. You belong to every punishment this land can give you." I was going to carry on, to pass my sentence upon him, then raise my hand to bring forth destructive flames, but Michael spoke.

Initially, when I had spoken, he had looked confused, but then his expression changed to one of pleasure. He interrupted me by shrugging his distorted shoulders and nodding his head whilst grunting out, "I am what I am." Michael moved forward toward me, violence his clear intent.

I shook my head in weary despair and raised my hand in a twirling motion, concentrating on bringing cleansing fire and purifying rain to scourge Michael and bring about his long overdue punishment. Nothing happened. I panicked and twirled my hand again. The flames refused my will. In desperation, I looked toward Bea, a scream for help pushing through my throat. It died as I saw the satisfied expression on her face, one that almost suggested enjoyment in my dire situation. She stepped a couple of paces back, as though to give us more room.

I scanned around to see if I could find an escape route. Behind me, the dark pit loomed, as inescapable as fate. My feet still pulled toward it, but I could not see any ladder or safe route down, only sheer sides and drop were visible through the crushing darkness. I looked back at Michael, opening my mouth to bargain.

Michael had stopped a mere step away from me. His bovine-mutated face twisted into an expression of mock pity and concern. "Did you think that would work on me? I am the master of this land. I belong in the center; you are nothing compared to me."

He would have said more, re-affirmed his own pathetic notions of superiority, except I leaned forward and jabbed my good fist straight into his eye. I tried to follow up by slamming my knee into his chest, but the reversed leg crumbled underneath the sudden shift in weight, and I fell against him. His arms, all four of them, looped round me and crushed inwards. I responded by bringing my good hand round to dig my fingers into his eyes while pulling my face away from his snarling features.

We stayed locked in the bitter stalemate embrace for a moment, and then I twisted my face downwards to his chest and bit. The flesh tore away rottenly and slid down my throat, vile stagnant juices following, spreading nausea downwards through my body. Michael screamed in fury. I saw his face snarling in determination as his legs bunched, propelling us into darkness and descent. The pit swallowed us.

We fell in absolute darkness, locked close in each other's arms. I could see nothing, nothing at all. The black swallowed everything. I was just aware of him, his unnatural touch, and I swung my hands and fists in determined combat, feeling his blows and the rakes of his nails and teeth across my protesting flesh. We plummeted downwards, fighting with all our might, unconcerned with what would happen when the fall ended.

Chapter Twenty-Seven

The fall ended. I know that. I sometimes wonder what happened. We went somewhere else, somewhere darker, where little was visible, where hard, sharp stones with jagged edges covered the entire ground.

It felt like I had escaped my physical body and was looking at everything from outside. The impact of hitting unforgiving ground after such a descent had torn my body into separate pieces. My skull scalped off and bashed in, teeth and eyes impossibly hidden beneath red mess smeared across unforgiving stones. Scraps and remnants of my spinal cord hung from the base of my broken torso but ended abruptly after a few inches. One leg, the bad one, lay a few meters away, twisted and bleeding, separated entirely. Around me, gray clouds floated as though trying to reconnect the disparate parts together.

It was dark. Even the limited dim light had a black tinge. By this half-light, I saw Michael had landed close by, his form crushed and sunk into the ground. One of his arms reached out to me as though he had discovered friendship in his last moments and wished to hold my hand. Spreading around him in an ever-increasing circle was a pitch-black tarry substance. In this pool, the faces and shapes of tortured bodies would appear and disappear. Gradually, these temporary phantoms took more permanent forms, creating shapes for themselves out of the black surface.

These shapes showed me once again what Michael was capable of and how he gained his pleasures. The forms lacked limbs, had scars and welts covering their entirety, with skin peeled back to reveal blackened pulsing organs. I took satisfaction in having stopped Michael, that I had spared the world his actions. I smiled sadly at what remained of my body and prepared to pass over to where I belonged; certain I was dead or dying.

That was not true. A white bar reached down and grabbed hold of my wrist. For a second, I could swear my physical form was separate from consciousness, but I looked and saw Bea staring at me. She pulled at my wrist, and I stood. I looked around at the fallen bodies, but Bea grabbed the sides of my face with both hands, stopping me. "We must go," she said, dragging me onwards in the direction my feet wanted to head.

"I don't understand," I said. "I was falling. So far and so deep. I could not have survived." Bea kept going. She had dropped her hands from my face and reached behind her to grab hold of my wrists, pulling me with ever-increasing speed forward. She never turned round, but I heard her voice clearly as she spoke. "You cannot die here. You only go where you belong. Your feet are still leading you onwards. I know."

Bea was right. My feet were still heading on a pre-destined path, taking large strides of their own volition. No mental control on my part was possible. They carried me ever onwards. "What about Michael?" I spoke. "He looked dead."

Bea moved onwards while saying. "People always finish where they belong. This isn't where he belongs. He will carry on."

I was disappointed and concerned. "I saw those trapped within him becoming free."

Bea carried on moving. "Michael is disintegrating. He cannot keep them trapped. He is concentrating on beating you, and his body is mutating too much. At last, they are free."

I smiled and nodded at Bea's back. "They are free," I repeated and sighed. "I am so glad. So very glad." Modestly, I tried not to reflect it had been me that freed them but felt deep satisfaction at doing the right thing. Bea carried on walking in the same direction with the same brisk pace but released my wrists and dropped back so she strode by my side rather than in front.

"That's the reason we need to hurry. They are free. For so long, Michael trapped them in anger and pain. They have become lost to themselves and know neither kindness nor restraint. They will destroy everyone they come across until they either remember themselves and their humanity or end up where they are meant to be."

I remembered the distorted and broken forms that had taken shape and understood the haste. Doubts and concerns still needed to be expressed, though. I wanted to ask Bea about the anger she had shown me earlier. When she had stepped away from me and Michael in anticipation of conflict, it had felt like betrayal. I wanted to know what Bea felt toward me; she had always been here by my side, leading and helping me onwards. After all this time, I did not know what she wanted or how to become what she needed.

We continued, lost in uncomfortable and thoughtful silence. I checked behind to see if Michael or his released were close. They had disappeared, but I could see a rising black fog on the distant horizon, moving in seemingly violent agitation and crawling toward us. Bea did not appear concerned, even when distant sounds of screaming and destruction reached us.

"Where is this place?" I asked Bea, "I can't see anyone."

"This is for the worst. Those with the intelligence and awareness to know their actions were wrong but did it anyway. People who caused great harm to others and the society around them. You will see other people here. They are up ahead. They are kept in separate valleys." I looked and saw the stone shale ground rose in several places, creating valleys that looked like pockets. They were in a line, and my feet headed on a path that would take me into the first. These pockets, presumably, holding those that belonged here.

"Michael must belong here then," I asked. "He caused incredible pain to others around him. Deliberately. Takes pride knowing that no one else has ever caused that amount of pain to that many people. He had a choice in this. Knew what he was doing was wrong."

Bea nodded. "There is one more segment after this. One last one where the very worst go, those who have utterly betrayed or violated fundamental, sacred laws. That is where Michael, for whatever reason, aspires to belong. It also contains the only escape. Your feet are leading you there. There will be a last barrier to cross. A physical obstacle you will have to overcome."

I nodded and moved forward. The shale was jagged and sharp, and as I moved forward, the edges pressed crisscrossing cuts into my soles or sharping their way through the cloth covering my legs. The wounds hurt but did not bleed, nor did they stop me from heading toward the first stone pocket in my haste. Here, I saw the first set of people receiving ordained justice, dictated by their crimes and the nature of this area of land.

Stepping up the slight slant to the first ridge, I acted on impulse and reached to grab hold of Bea's hand. I squeezed it tight and looked at her. I wanted to be close; wanted her to know I appreciated her help, that I understood her wisdom. She looked startled to begin with, and then, in a compelling, charming fashion, dropped her head downwards in awkward embarrassment. I moved forward to embrace her and place my lips on hers. Her hand moved, and she placed a gentle palm on the wound in my chest.

"Not here. Not now. That time has gone," she whispered to me. I smiled, nodding at her, thinking she had already revealed her needs and that soon she would be mine regardless of what she tried to protest.

We crossed over the top rim of the hill and looked down at those contained within this pocket. There was a great horde of naked, broken-looking people following each other barefoot. Each person was blindfolded with faded black hoods and appeared to have horse bits drilled bloodily through their jaw. Each had reins hanging from the bits. All reins were held by someone else, and each held someone else's reins. They each dragged or were being dragged in a direction by another stranger in near complete silence.

They were all walking and bumping into each other, tearing their bare feet to a sticky mess on the ground underneath them. Blood dripped onto the ground from their torn jaws. They struggled at the bottom of the valley, locked close together in an opening far too small for that multitude. I wanted to talk to Bea. To question and understand what was happening here, but she shook her head and carried on walking around the slope above the heads of those trapped here.

"We must keep moving," she said. "Those released from Michael are getting closer; we do not have time to watch other people's punishment. We must be away before they catch us." The sounds of tearing and screeching destruction from behind prompted me to move faster.

My feet both helped and hindered this process. The overriding compulsion meant they moved faster, but they also felt heavy and almost glued to the ground. When I looked down, they appeared to be stretching like rubber, deformed by these two paradoxical needs. When lifted free of the ground, they reverted and snapped back to their normal length.

In some ways, it surprised me that none of the trapped people had escaped. The sides were not steep. But they were blind and locked into their current mode of behavior; they could not break free. I paused briefly to consider them on my journey across the rim. I wondered what they had done to make this their chosen punishment; something about leading others into destruction or pain was my guess, although I was uncertain why they wore blindfolds. Conversations with Bea had revealed deliberate knowledge and choice caused the worst punishments, so maybe in life they had acted with perfect understanding and vision. Maybe the symbolism was too obscure to be understood.

My musings about their fate changed nothing. We still had to move fast, driven by need and fear of those following us. We crossed as speedily as possible, entering the next valley as fast as we could. As we moved, we heard Michael's freed army of tormented souls coming ever closer.

The next valley was amusing in its own way, but also nearly had serious consequences for me. The basin of the valley was an enormous liquid pool of shit. Within its foul depths, indistinct, ever-changing forms flapped back and forth, attempting to surface. Only the lips were distinct and gave any impression of real physical presence. When these lips reached near the surface, they would part as though to scream, and instead great buckets and streams of stinking feces would shoot upward.

The first time I saw this, I opened my mouth to snort laughter; instead of chortles of mirth, mounds of shit spewed forth from my shocked orifice, and kept spewing, landing on the shale stones before the ejected brown slid and rolled stickily into the existing pool. I had a moment of detached calmness where I realized I no longer breathed and was grateful for that, before the pain of continual vomiting distracted me. My feet threatened to force me into the pool, and I looked downwards in horror at my reflection. I saw my form had faded and become less substantial. Where the shit had landed on top of me, I could see solid lumps of it sticking, reflected more clearly than whichever part of me it had landed on.

I was near the edge of the foul pool when Bea grabbed hold of me. She struggled for a second, trying to pull me upward before moving herself to stand next to me. Tilting me sideways, she picked me up; I stretched my arms around her shoulders in a tight embrace and rested my head on her bosom. I opened my lips to thank her, but only shit spewed forth to splatter against her robes. It clung there and shone in brown globs before sliding downwards. When the brown chunks fell off Bea, they left no trace or streaks. Bea was clothed as she had always been and appeared unaffected by the experience. Certainly, she showed no revulsion at my unusual vomit.

Bea moved with speed and strength toward the edge of this valley. I tried to keep my eyes shut, as I didn't want to see this place or think about why it exerted such a hold on me. As Bea moved with me cradled in her arms, I kept vomiting that foul substance all over myself and the surrounding area.

It stopped the moment Bea stepped over the edge of the valley. I choked out the last soft morsel from my mouth and spat out free brown fragments. While I purged myself, Bea turned around to see whether those following us were still there, whether they had dissipated or passed into the distance. For the first time in a long time, I saw her face tighten with concern. She shifted my weight and placed me down. Unfortunately, most of my weight landed on my mutated leg and it bent unnaturally, sending me sprawling to the ground. My arms spread to prevent my face from smashing into the hard surface and pushed into the soft leavings expelled from my mouth. I rolled around, trying to get myself upright.

Whereas fecal matter had left Bea unstained, all of my clothes and body had been soiled. Smears of shit tattooed me.

"We need to move much faster," Bea said, looking down at me. "They are gaining and growing in ferocity. They are in so much pain. Everything that made them people, individuals—Michael has stripped, ground away in anguish and torture."

I nodded and stood. Tried to think how best to thank Bea for granting me salvation but could not think of an adequate way to express my gratitude at being saved from drowning for eternity in a pool of shit.

Instead, I accepted her urgency as my own and followed her across the land into the next valley.

"How many of these valleys are here?" I asked. "How many parts of this 'segment' are there before we move onto the next place?"

Bea stared at me. With a flash of irritation, she asked, "How should I know?"

Her response caused me to pause. I simply expected Bea to always understand the nature of this place, just as I knew she would always be by my side.

We moved on through the remaining valleys. I witnessed people sliced in two, dividing themselves, being reformed and sliced again, others transformed into animals before transforming again into different ones, people buried while cruel monsters forced them deeper and deeper into the ground. The sights were both extraordinary and terrifying. The misery of those enclosed and trapped did not end but grew ever greater as time passed.

As we moved, the sounds of Michael's damned grew closer. It forced us to rush past pockets of punishment onto the next one without discussion. In one of the last valleys, I turned to see how close they were to us, whether they had mutated into other forms or dissipated as their rage passed.

They were ever closer. A great wave of solid black forms hurtling through space. Distorted and destroyed people who still bore the wounds and implements of their torture. Chains and razors replaced fingers and arms. It was not only their mutilations that affected them, but the nature of their hatred and need for revenge. Some had taken the forms of dreadful creatures of vengeance with extra fanged teeth or claws.

Wherever they passed, they destroyed everything. All people, creatures, even the land itself, was desecrated beyond comprehension. Even through the darkened light, they surrounded themselves with a permanent aura of devastation. I saw them pass through the first pockets and heard the screams rise higher and louder. Punished souls who thought their torment and anguish could not be worse, discovered they had been so very wrong. As I watched, I saw chunks of flesh thrown upward through the darkened air, horse bits and reins flew in abundance.

The act of destruction did not slow these wretched creatures in their escape from Michael. If anything, the opportunity to release their venom and anguish increased their urgent speed and puissance. Soon, the very earth we stood on cracked and distorted under their weight. Splits spread from where they stood and reached toward us. I looked down one such split to see it didn't show deeper down rock but revealed the stuff and substance of this land was shifting eternal blackness—utterly enchanting and fascinating. I found myself rooted to the spot, looking at this darkness, trying to understand it. The understrata was both seductive in its all-encompassing velvet blanketing blackness and terrifying in its vastness and nature.

The ground buckled and shook under the force of destruction performed upon it. I wondered how Michael had trapped so many people and removed all traces of humanity. Bea only interrupted my reverie by grabbing hold of my wrist and pulling me to the center.

We moved as fast as the shaking ground and my backward leg would allow. Crossing over the pockets as fast as possible, knowing as we passed that their destruction would follow in our wake. I wondered what would happen after Michael's shades moved through this area. Previous experience showed that nothing here could be destroyed or permanently removed from its chosen punishment. If that was the case, then would the existing denizens continue with their allocated tasks even when torn into tiny, tortured chunks, or would some ending mercy be shown?

We crossed the side of the last pocket, where everyone appeared to be afflicted with different diseases that rotted and deformed them. These diseases appeared to transfer from one to the other and affected them heart, mind, body, and soul. Their wails of pain were undeniable, but still likely to pale compared to what was coming toward them. To our dismay, but lack of surprise, we saw the shades enter the same valley immediately behind us.

The cracks in the earth spread out in greater size and power. I was standing on one such crack and almost toppled over downwards into the swallowing darkness, but Bea grabbed me and pulled me to safety. We hurried over the lip of the last pocket, my eyes fixed on vast horizons, looking for a way to escape.

As I passed over this last rim, I was forced to pause in astonishment. This place had shown me amazement and things I could not comprehend. This topped everything. After the last valley, there was a great vastness of level shale rock that rested calmly within the dark light, its size dwarfing everything seen so far and swallowing sound. For a second, I forgot everything behind me and contemplated what lay ahead in silent awe.

It was not the vastness, nor the silence, that invoked such a response. In the far distance, so huge it was still clearly visible, was something that resembled a gigantic Venus flytrap plant. It had a fat body that appeared rooted into the ground. Three heads shot upward on thick, black vines. One head was red, another pure black, and the last a diseased yellow. Each head had its mouth split open to reveal rows of serrated teeth. These heads darted around the body, slamming into the ground in undeniable hunger and desperate predation, trying to chew and eat the very substance of the earth that supported it.

The creature appeared to sense our presence. One head hooked around and traveled across leagues, miles, and unmeasurable distances to consume us. It almost reached us, but its central body could not move, forcing it to stop just short. It made no noise, but as the mouth opened to reveal darkness compounded with teeth, I got the impression it would scream in hatred if it could.

"We must get past," Bea said calmly, but I sensed a hint of sadness in her voice. I snorted in derision and raised my eyebrows in mock surprise.

"Well. That should be easy. Let's just walk past that thing, calling 'Good Afternoon' as we go," I said. Bea carried on staring at me.

"We need to get past the last barrier before the results of Michael's deeds catch up with us. That thing before us is pure, undiminished appetite. The things behind us learned cruelty and rage from Michael."

I looked at the crashing heads, saw the hugeness of them, saw the vast leagues they covered, saw how quickly they could dart down with the speed of a striking serpent. I thought back to the previous barriers mentioned by Michael so long ago. This was the first one that was a living creature, and the very last one I would have to cross.

"How do I get past it?" I asked Bea.

She looked across and showed she knew everything by saying, "You have always adapted yourself to become whatever someone else wants. In this place, any constraints upon you are removed. Your form can change according to need or desire. It has started already. The environment exerted a pull on you, and your nose and leg changed as demanded. Become what it wants, offer what it needs, and maybe we will get past. Otherwise, everything is going to become unpleasant here, and we cannot pass forward." Bea seemed to understate the severity of the situation deliberately, to give me a choice of how I should respond.

I realized Bea must also be in danger. Without giving myself time to think about what I was going to do, I stood and walked toward the creature, examining it while trying to understand what it wanted and needed most in the world. Its appearance was of a being of pure hunger and destruction. Nothing more. Nothing less. One of a kind. Nothing like it anywhere else.

As I walked, I mused upon this. I considered a creature like this would share the most common elemental desire; to see and have another like it, an equal it could contend with to see its own worth and virtue reflected. I did not doubt that its idea of virtue and worth would differ from mine.

As I moved toward it, my form expanded and stretched to meet its needs. My legs covered massive distances with just a few quick strides and planted themselves closer to it, pushing down through the shale and barren ground to seek nourishment from the velvety darkness and hunger that lay beneath. My midriff swelled outward, and my neck split into three. There was a second of confusion when the world split into multiples as I developed new, gigantic heads. For a second, three unique sights swooped around me, but then I saw a similar head straight in front of mine and jerked forward with eager teeth to consume. Dry, loose skin tore into my mouth, and I swallowed in starvation. I tasted attar and venom. The original creature responded eagerly in kind. Grateful at last for the opportunity to vent its rage and fulfill its hunger on an equal that could survive its onslaught and respond with equal savagery.

Around and around each other, our heads swayed, jerking and darting to bite and crush. I felt the pain and screamed with it, but it paled into insignificance when compared to the need to strike back, to kill and destroy the thing in front of me. The darkness spread from rooted legs, savage delight in might and destruction. Other dark needs also took seed within my form, and I continued to swell and grow stronger with the need to be even more destructive than I was. The original creature mirrored this need and swelled even further to put itself in a position where it could crush me even more completely.

We fought equally against each other for an unknown age. Then Michael's shades, those he had murdered and broken the spirits of so completely that they had forgotten humanity and concepts of gentleness, swarmed around and attacked. Their hatred and needs made them strong and cruel. But we were world enders. I barely felt their presence as they stung, slashed and bit. I focused my attention on the original creature and kept biting, trying to get through a neck so I could tear a head off. Whenever one set of eyes saw a black shade in front of it, the mouth would snap forward to crunch it into pieces, before spitting out dismembered hunks at the ground. I tasted their pain, their sorrow and need to be free, but it mattered not. All that mattered was destroying the massive creature.

I saw it grow bigger, to give itself an advantage over me. I reached out through my form toward the darkness that ran under the rocks and swallowed it in vast greed. Once again, my size expanded and mutated to shadow even this massive landscape. This was one growth too far. I could no longer hold the Sideways People within me anymore. The massive adaptation of my flesh forced open a door and pushed them through. They fell from me like gray sycamore seeds and drifted downwards. Where they landed, they seemed to merge with remnants of black, before fading away. The darkness in this part of the land seemed to ease.

None of that mattered to me, not in the slightest. As each of the Sideways People left, it tore parts of my soul. I lost my ability to have emotions, to love or to feel a partnership with another. I became like an animal; a pure focus of hate and hunger—except for one thing. At the very end, as the last of the Sideways People fell from me, a dim flickering piece of my original self noticed one had not departed. The one that eclipsed all others and gave entire meaning to my life, the one I loved more than anyone and who had loved me with equal passion. She had not left because she had never been inside.

Even in my new form, a form that could tear heavens and destroy the earth through sheer force, I felt such agonizing despair. Each of my heads reached toward the sky and then jerked downwards with undeniable ferocity upon the heads of my opponent.

One last time, I tasted its flesh and felt corruption flow down my throat. This time, it tasted of the darkness it had soaked and swallowed during our contest to make itself grow bigger. It tasted of bloodlust, of hatred, of devouring desire, of joy in deception and denial. Everything bad about humanity was in the taste, and I pushed my teeth further down in hunger and violence. With a sudden snap, it was over. The creature crashed dead to the floor before disappearing, as though something so significant could never have existed.

When it departed, the need to match it and to answer its desires disappeared. I shrank back to my normal size, became human again. As I did, some of my humanity returned, and tears flowed unrestricted down my face. Only some parts were restored. With the departure of my Sideways People, great swaths of my soul had also departed. The pieces that make a person human were no longer present. The ability to romanticize had disappeared; the feelings and emotions had gone. Maybe I saw things more clearly, but that was no blessing. All this enhanced clear vision could see was shit and ruin and decay, turning and rotting into more shit and ruin and decay.

I hugged my newly returned arms around myself. With a slight detachment, I noticed my form had restored to normal. My wounds and changes had all healed. My nose pointed down, my fingers were restored, and my leg was the right way around. It did not matter; it did not ease my pain.

I knew where I was; think I had always known. I knew I deserved it. Worse, I knew who Bea was. I knew I was going to the center, and I knew it was not to be given a way out. I knew everything, and everything was bitter.

228

Chapter Twenty-Eight

Bea approached and kneeled beside me. I had not considered what would happen to Bea if Michael's shades had caught up with us. While transformed, I had not noticed or considered her needs. I think I presumed she would be inviolate, but that was not the case. Bea's clothes had been torn from her in several places, exposing breasts and midriff. I shuddered at the thought of what they had done. Chunks of flesh had been ripped free, digits mangled, hair snatched from the scalp with skin peeled back from the head. Blood covered every part of her. My heart wept to see the damage they had done to my beloved.

As I watched, Bea's hurts healed themselves, flesh torn from her back and discarded in the distance dragged itself along the ground behind her before climbing itself up the back of her legs and slowly attaching itself again. This healing process was not perfect. The wounds did not merge back with exacting precision; they got stitched back slightly off. The marks and welts were visible in the bumps and indents of her rebuilt flesh. I wanted to speak to her, but all I could manage were tears that blurred and obscured my vision. When my mouth opened to form words, only sorrowful spit sprayed forth. Snot streamed from my straightened nose.

Bea did not appear to notice the physical wounds so cruelly inflicted upon her, but her eyes bled tears while her mouth quivered from a straight line. "You never asked what my punishment was," she said in a quiet voice that screamed misery. "It was to take you to the center and understand what you were and know you deserved it, while still feeling such love toward you. To understand what I did and how I betrayed myself. Everything is clear now."

I trembled and my mind raced to find the right thing to say, to justify myself, to make everything better. "I love you," I said in an uncertain voice. Bea nodded and her tears carried on falling. She took deep steadying breaths. She reached out and placed a comforting hand on my shoulder.

"It is time. The path is open now. You need to move on. Go further in, go deeper, go to the center."

I rocked myself backward and forward for a second, then my trembling lips forced out the words. "Please. Not me. Someone else. Please, not this."

Bea softly, with tears streaming down her face, proved she loved me still by saying, "I am with you." And with that, the compulsion in my feet grew irresistible, and they forced me to stand and carry on with my journey.

As I stood, I looked around, hoping to see my Sideways People, even just one, someone to whom I could look to for answers or some kind of justification for my life. None remained. How I wished at least one had stayed for some kind of farewell. The all-pervasive dark gloom had lightened, and I knew this was in response to Michael's souls being freed from their torment. I wondered whether my Sideways People had helped them somehow, merged with them to open a door to sweeter places.

I looked in the direction that my feet were taking me. There was little distance left. Ahead, a great curtain of darkness bisected the land in front of me, cutting down into the earth. Beyond the dark curtain, I had an impression of cold and ice, and unending complete darkness.

Crossing this curtain was a simple matter. My feet charged forward in determined flight, carrying the rest of my protesting body. Once I reached it, my body stepped in and across from dusk gloom to nighttime dark.

I plunged and fell forward, losing my balance. The ground suddenly sloped steeply down and was composed of deep green ice. My torso twisted backward and landed hard on this unforgiving surface, stunning me into pain and silence. My feet never stopped taking greater and greater strides toward the very center, surefooted on even this most treacherous surface.

Flowing backward and forward over everything was this foul, sickening stench wind. First, it would push me away and then suck in to drag me closer. It was as if a giant that forcefully exhaled halitosis and inhaled despair resided at the very center.

I could not get myself upright, and my feet dragged the rest of my body downwards toward the end goal. As I was forced forward, I twisted myself around to find something I could grab hold of. I noticed the ice was a frozen ocean with solid waves and swells rippling the surface. It was impossible to grab hold of these swells; the momentum set by my feet and the smoothness of the ice prevented me from either slowing my movement or allowing me to push myself upright.

I tried to break my speed by clawing my hands and pushing my fingers and nails into the ice surface, hoping to slow myself. Something tore horribly at one of my hands, and I looked at the moving ice surface to see what it was. I never saw what hurt my hand, but I saw something that pained me far more.

Beneath the cold and dark surface of the ice, my Sideways People lay posed in the moments after I had finished with them. I could see their cold, stiff, pale forms in ways I had not noticed before. Their final wounds were proudly on show, and each was unmistakably dead. Necks were twisted to the side with strangulation marks on show, eyes were bloodshot, a bleeding knife wound was clearly displayed. One lady had the cherry red complexion of carbon monoxide poisoning. The only thing each had in common was the stiff flesh displayed no personality, aroused no gentle memories, and all caused me pain. There were others contained under the frozen waves as well, less easy to justify, those that I did not like to think about, let alone discuss. Not even with you.

This horror show continued as I slid across the frozen ocean. I would finish viewing one corpse, only to be dragged onto the next. My adult life displayed in a series of broken flesh tableaus.

"Michael is at the center," Bea said. She was not warning me, just telling me. I already knew he would be there. He couldn't belong anywhere else. He wanted to own it. I looked at Bea and realized she was not walking on the surface of the ice but floated ethereally above it. I could not find the right words but kept staring at her. She noticed me looking and, in an act of kindness, reached down and pulled my arm to enable me to at least stand upright.

I was grateful for this mercy. It allowed me to look around, away from the revealing ice, and downwards at the center. I saw what was there, or at least I saw one angle of it. It was a broken-down cottage; one window covered by a broken, sagging wooden shutter. Something had constructed the cottage from moss-covered dirty, uneven stones. Out of the top of it, a huge, jagged chimney stretched upward out of sight. I could only see the cottage because of the wan yellow light that leaked out of the shuttered window.

My feet increased their pace toward this, my intended last destination. My strides grew even longer, stretching my legs ever further, and the feet stamped down into the ice to ensure I got there. In forlorn hope, I looked around for an escape, or at least something I could cling onto, but there was nothing.

There was no choice but to wait while my feet got me there. Close by, I noticed the cottage appeared to sink deep into the ice, and from the great chimney, yellow moss spread downwards like snot. The whole impression was one of ruination and decrepitude. The compulsion in my feet finally ended. For the first time in however long, I was where I belonged.

I walked around the side of the cottage. I saw Bea in front of me. She had her eyes closed as though she could not bear to watch; between the shuttered lids, tears fell. Bea was standing next to the door, which sprung open as I approached, untouched by any hand. From the door's outline, yellow light spilled. I stood for a few moments, contemplating my life and Bea before, in resignation, I went inside to meet Michael alone. The door slammed shut behind me.

Chapter Twenty-Nine

The inside of the broken cottage looked like the outside. The walls comprised vast blocks that were lumped on top of each other. They were green with mold and splattered with blood. The floor had the same stones. In the corner, a ragged fireplace was lit and burned, pushing black smoke up the chimney. The fetid air pushed up and down the chimney. This poisoned breath flowed through my entire form, tingeing each cell with sickness. At the center of the room, waiting for my arrival, was Michael.

Michael's degenerative transformations had continued. Most of his recent changes suggested sickness and rotting. His skin had turned gray and diseased, covering a huge rubbery gut that stuck out in front of him. Four arms windmilled uncontrollably from his sides, and his elongated legs sagged underneath him as though made from weak rubber.

Michael gaped at me in dismay when he first saw me enter the room. Only then did I consider how my shape and body had returned to a normal and healthy-looking form, and Michael must have perceived it. My body was in proportion, and I had only the faintest scrapes from where my feet had dragged me across the ice. I smiled awkwardly at Michael.

"You," Michael said, voice coming out slurred and broken through his amended face. "Get out. This place is mine. The center. I was the worst. The absolute *worst*. I killed more than you ever could. You could never imagine what I did to them. I broke and destroyed them so completely that they became part of me."

The misshapen mouth distorted his voice too much to understand the underlying emotion. There was a definite element of anger but also pleading.

"I did not choose to come here. You can have it. I don't want to be here. Take it. I have been forced here. I want to leave." To emphasize the point, I tried to turn toward the door. My feet remained fixed in place, preventing my exit.

"Fuck off. *Fuck off, fuck off, fuck off*!" Michael screamed at the top of his voice, losing all emotional control. He paced backward and forward, screaming the same obscenities at me, before anger overcame his fear or restraint and he jumped at me with fury.

We wrestled ineffectually with each other, falling over onto the floor in each other's arms. Michael's form was too butter-soft to bring much force to bear. He tried to rake his nails across my face, but they were brittle and broke before they caused much damage. I tried to punch him with my hands, but they just sank into the flab, causing no pain.

There was, however, one determining difference between the two of us. Michael still had his fury, his anger, and envy. Michael punched and fought as though trying to utterly destroy me.

I had nothing. I was hollow. No desire, no one to fight for or protect. My life had been a lie. I did not want to lose. I did not want the pain I knew Michael intended to cause me, but no spark or urgency underpinned my struggles. Slowly, and in farcical fashion, Michael started to win. A punch across my face left swirls of white light.

Michael grabbed hold of my flailing arms and pulled me upward. He knew he had won, could do what he wanted. I would be his last and most terrifying victim. His mouth opened wide in a vicious smile, and his fiery breath pressed damp on my face.

"Look at the wall," he slurred and lolled at me, nodding his head in one direction. Obediently, I turned to look. Chains, razors, manacles, hooks of every conceivable shape and purpose hung there upon a wall that had been bare before. "This room is going to help me. I am going to make you scream my name. *Endlessly*. You will not die. You will not escape. I am the worst, the cruelest and most evil fucker ever dreamed of, and you are mine. You are nothing compared to me. I am going to fucking prove it."

It was the look of relish, of dreamful lust and sadism, that broke me. "Laura. Please. If you love me, if you ever loved me. Help me!" I screamed as loudly as my lungs allowed, screaming again and again until my voice became hoarse and came from me in croaks.

Michael became furious and moved one arm across my face in a vicious punch. My head jerked sideways. Michael dragged me across the floor toward the wall, his body taut with purpose and pleasure. My feet skittered on the floor, trying to find a purchase that would allow me to run.

There was a sudden screeching sound. Unknown, unexpected. A normal noise of wood twisting and scraping against stone. We turned to look at the door and saw the top bulge inwards. The bottom stuck unmoving against the stone floor.

In the gap freed open by the bulge, two delicate white hands pushed through and twisted. Something was wrong, as I watched blood blossomed on the surface of the satin skin and dripped onto the floor. There was a sudden pop, and the door burst open, banging loudly against the wall behind it.

Bea, or rather, Laura, stood there. Her eyes, which in life had been filled with dreams, were pinched tight in concentration and anguish; they fixed first on me before focusing on Michael. She strode squarely across the floor toward him, no deviation or pause in her stride. It was immediately clear something was wrong, that Laura was not meant to be a factor in this last confrontation and had to pay a terrible price for her presence.

Between the door and the place on the floor where I and Michael fought was a mere three paces, but with each step Laura appeared to disintegrate. Michael's shades had hurt and sliced her apart, with flesh reforming imperfectly. Now, as she moved inside that terrible room, her healing unstitched. Parts of Laura's body fell from her, like ice melting from a warming roof. I could see decaying bones.

With each step, more flesh fell and landed in a steaming, boneless heap on the floor. By the time Laura reached us, there was hardly anything left, just an arm and her mouth and those beautiful eyes fixed on Michael. I wish that, right at the very end, she had shifted her gaze onto me, but the severity of her need prohibited that. The mouth moved to say the primary truth of her whole being.

"I am with you."

And then the arm reached and tore Michael's remaining live head from his shoulders. Even as it splattered free, Michael's look changed to astonishment, and Laura disintegrated into red sludge, purple whorls, and desiccated bone that splashed onto the floor.

"No!" I screamed and ran in a pathetic circle around the revolting bits, trying to think of a way to undo the damage my cowardly screaming had caused. I never noticed the shadow flowing free from Michael and pooling like black tar in the corner, nor did I notice the blood that had pumped free from his neck had become suspended in the air near the fireplace. I wish I noticed both quicker.

Cunt, free. Cunt beaten. Will be back. Will teach. Will cause pain. Kill. Murder. Slash. Bite. Kill, kill, kill. Mutilate. Tear. Beat. Bite. Slash. Cut. Needle. Fight. Stab. Burn. Bite. Kill. Get revenge, revenge, revenge. Will teach... Will teach. Revenge... Make that cunt scream.

The black tar formed into a metal hooked shape, perfectly designed for cruelty and force. This started in the corner, hidden in darkness. I collapsed on my knees in the mess and sludge that had been my dearest love. Distracted, I handled slender bones and floating bits of flesh, trying to link them back together into life.

I rocked back onto my haunches at my last failure of reconstruction. With tears streaming, I raised my eyes to the fireplace, trying to keep my gaze fixed away from what I was kneeling in. I saw it then. Michael's blood hung suspended in a glistening black cloud, moving gently toward the fireplace. It danced invitingly in the air, moving in response to the breaths that shook through the chimney.

I remembered then. The portal that had led me here. I had breathed in white vapor released during Laura's first sacrifice. It had transported me here somehow. This black cloud looked like the exact inversion of that wholesome release. Torn from cruelty and evil, rather than given during an act of loving sacrifice. However, maybe it would give me a path out of here, back to where I belonged.

I pushed down the palms of my hands, ignoring the squelching stickiness that bubbled past my fingers. Raising myself to my knees, I ascended onto aching, freed feet and took slow footsteps toward the black mist. The few steps took all I had. Everything hurt.

I stopped in front of the suspended particles and considered them for a while. They were fascinating, appearing to float in the air. I had nothing to lose and leaned forward to breathe them in.

Cunt. Cunt! Getting free. Getting free. Will destroy, will beat, will tear, will tear. Not getting away. Never getting away. Never ever, ever getting away.

The dark shape, Michael's grim shade, burst from the shadows in the corner, lunging toward me. Things that resembled arms but repurposed for cruelty reached and tore into me, tore me instantaneously into two. Not physically, but psychically?

I had two sets of eyes. I saw a gray form of myself staring at me in terror and pain as Michael reached through its midriff and started tearing. But I also saw through eyes that detached and spiraled toward the floor, another version of me breathing in the noxious black cloud, transforming into dark smoke and being drawn out the chimney.

The one of me that escaped through the chimney woke in the woods where it had all begun. Home at last, but far from free. I was still in two places and feeling two sets of anguish. I was there in the cottage with Michael, hate fucking me in every conceivable way, being torn into pieces again, and again, and again. Eyes, torn, castrated, hands forced all the way down throat, reaching toward stomach, rape. Everything.

Make him scream. Make him scream. Make him acknowledge me as his master.

What the fuck is happening? What—

Tear him, bite him, rip him, break him. Scream. Scream. Scream!

The other part of me was in the forest, staring at Laura's broken and stiff body. Saw how ugly and graceless everything looked. Laura's eyes open, sightlessly staring, tinged red through the manner of her murder. The smell of ammonia where her bladder had released itself in her last moment stung in my lungs.

I closed my eyes, pressed my trembling palms over my ears, and ran screeching back to my car, attempting to deny the two realities that trapped me.

PostScript

So, here we are then. I wish I could understand the wooden look on your face.

Disbelief? Contempt? Concern? I can't read expressions anymore, can't understand what they mean or how people feel. I wander around, going from coffee shops to bus stops, sitting and waiting for people to notice me. Often, they do, and I tell my tale to explain myself and block out what is happening to me. I'm the mariner forced to repeat my rhyme. I've told this story to endless versions of you.

Or at least one aspect of me endlessly talks of my fall. The other aspect is still stuck in hell, in that cottage with Michael's specter exercising every hatred and venom that his considerable imagination can envisage upon my screaming, undying spirit.

I know I was in Hell. I have thought about it often to understand what is being done to me. Michael's punishment is obvious. The deadliest of all the seven sins is Pride, and Michael embodies that. He felt he was the worst, that no one that had ever walked the earth could match him. Believe me, even as we talk, I can confirm no one can equal Michael in terms of pure sadism. His cruelty and capacity to inflict pain are unparalleled. For Michael, the punishment was to feel that I had beaten him in some manner; that the center wanted me as its ruler and viewed me as more than his equal. Believe me, the fury this causes has added to both his inventiveness and natural sadism.

What of my punishment and what I did to deserve it? At university, I read Inferno, which describes how the innermost circle of hell is reserved for those who committed the worst betrayals. That describes me. It is irrefutable, I can't deny it. I am the Judas that Judas would spit upon. I betrayed love itself, betrayed the people who loved me and the people whom I loved. My cherished Sideways People. I released them to save myself, rendering all we had been together meaningless and fake. I suppose that means I deserve the punishment I am receiving.

Part of me is stuck in hell. Locked in a room with the destroyed remains of my truest love, while the cruelest, evilest bastard ever spat forth by a human cunt uses every trick he can think of to cause me torment. The other part of me is forever wandering around alone and isolated, unable to build bonds despite being surrounded by people. I am Tantalus, forever immersed in water and desperately thirsty, but unable to drink.

My eyes may reveal some of this. Sometimes when people mutter their excuses and turn away to leave, they catch my gaze. When this happens, their faces go bloodless, presumably in fear. Maybe when you leave, making fake excuses and polite comments, you will also look into my eyes. Maybe you will be different, maybe your face will twist in empathy and understanding.

I wish I had met you before all this happened. We could have been something special.

ACKNOWLEDGEMENTS

To protect their privacy I won't be listing specific names—they know who they are. I want to thank the family members who pushed me to not give up on writing the kind of story I wanted the most, the beta readers who put up with my hovering, the editors dealing with someone who'd never taken a formal writing class, and the friends who cheered me on. I also want to thank a certain Enby H, who was the first to give this story a chance, along with Graveside Press.